KRISTOPHER JEROME

THE GODS AND MEN CYCLE

BEFORE THE BREAKING

PRELUDES TO THE BROKEN PACT

Cover art by Cristina Tanase

Maps by Ralarismaps

Cover design by Miblart.

First Edition, April 2024

Hardcover ISBN 978-1-951138-16-5

Paperback ISBN 978-1-951138-17-2

Dark Tidings Press LLC

PO Box 593

Albany, OR 97321

darktidingspress.com

CONTENTS

ALSO FROM DARK TIDINGS PRESS

THE GODS AND MEN CYCLE

By Kristopher Jerome

The Broken Pact Trilogy:

- Wrath of the Fallen
- Cries of the Forsaken
- Tears of the Godless

The Nightbreaker

White Wings from Grey Ash

Before the Breaking:

- A Bandit's Balance
- A Voice from the Darkness
- In the Shadow of Light
- The Sons of Lighthammer
- The Bard's Demons
- Disciples of the First Cycle
- Ten of Seatown
- The Last Gift of Kane Darksend
- The Grey God's Edict
- The Blood-Soaked Sacrament

Artorus
The Rim of Paradise
Lioss
The Grey Temple
Rinwaiche
Eligan
Dyeth
Seatown
Kliwen
Amel
Strega
Illux
Ostarth
Firan
Ryun
The Great Chasm
Marna
The Nameless Sea
The High God's Tears
Godsend

The Grey God's Shrine
Ayyslid
The High God's Throne
The Basin
Infernaak

INTRODUCTION

What a long, strange trip it's been.

I first wrote and released *A Bandit's Balance* back in 2017, nearly a year after the first Gods and Men Cycle book, *Wrath of the Fallen* was released. *A Bandit's Balance* was originally meant to be a free ebook given out to subscribers of my newsletter. Of course, I didn't want to write a story just for an out-of-setting purpose, so I chose to write about one of my favorite characters to flesh out his backstory and do a little world-building in the process. I didn't realize that nearly seven years later I would be publishing a collection of ten pieces of short fiction set in this world. My, how this book has changed during its development.

Originally, when I came up with the idea for a collected edition titled *Before the Breaking*, the story makeup was going to be quite different. The two novellas *The Nightbreaker* and *White Wings from Grey Ash* were going to be included, for instance. I struggled with whether or not it made sense to include a story that took place one thousand years before the others, as much as I felt that *The Nightbreaker* was really a prequel to the second novel of the Broken Pact trilogy, *Cries of the Forsaken*. Eventually, *The Nightbreaker* was cut, and instead, it was going to get bundled with another collection set during the appropriate time period. Then I decided it needed to be released on its own, and I didn't want *White Wings* to be treated differently, so it ended up getting its own physical release as well!

Once I had finally settled on the ten stories that would be included, I needed to determine what order to place them in the book. I'm a huge canon/chronology nerd with fantasy settings, so published order didn't make sense to my brain (even though I didn't write them chronologically, I wrote them as inspiration struck). This posed the Star Wars dilemma of whether or not reading them in chronological order created a lesser experience for the reader than published order did. Spoiler alert: I decided that it didn't. Flipping through this book you will see the dates in which the stories take place under their first (and sometimes subsequent) chapter headings. These stories start by overlapping with *White Wings* and the forthcoming novels *Breaksword* and *Whispers of a Red God* and then continue right up until *Wrath of the Fallen*.

As I mentioned earlier, I didn't want any of these stories to feel like "fluff". That meant walking a fine line between making the stories matter to the characters and the reader, while also not wanting to penalize those who only read the novels. If you stick to just the larger works in this series, you'll get the story, but unless you look in the nooks and crannies and follow along with the short fiction, you won't get the *whole* story. Every short story and novelette in here expands on either a character's motivation, a piece of lore for the world, or in some cases sets up a story or threat to come in the future. I like them all for one reason or another, and I don't think any could be cut out without damaging the whole.

Finally, I wanted to take a moment to address some of the content in these shorts. More than one deals with themes of sexual violence. I didn't do this lightly (though I've grown a lot as a person and a writer, and I would write the scene in *A Bandit's Balance* much differently now). None of the sexual violence is portrayed directly on the page, for a variety of reasons, but the different ways that people react to it is often the focus. While I am very fortunate to have never been abused myself, several close family members of mine, including my wife, have been, and as such, I don't think these instances should be included in a story unless there is a purpose beyond "raising the stakes". Hopefully, I was successful.

Anyway, that's enough words from me keeping you from reading more words from me.

-Kristopher Jerome

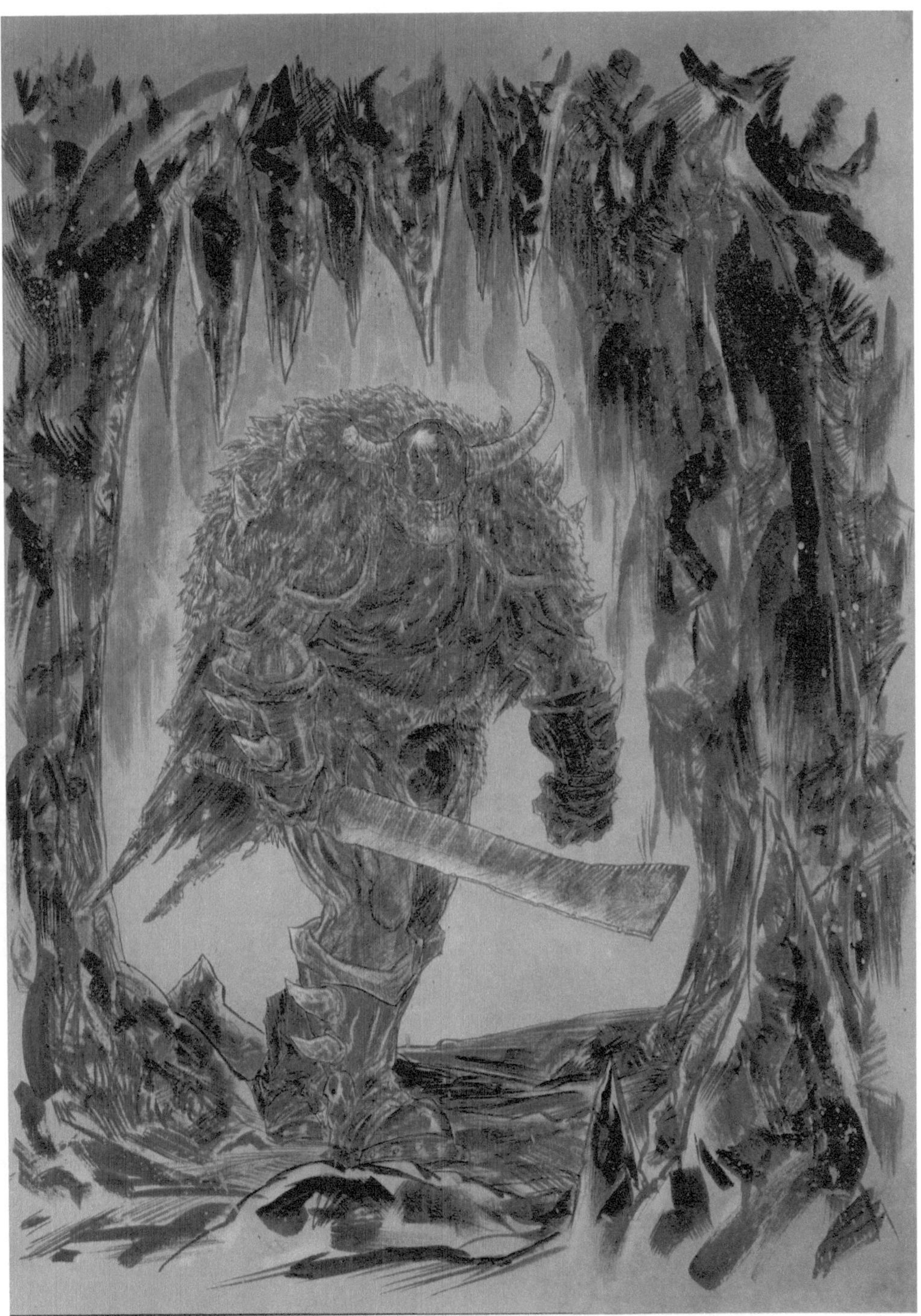

BEFORE THE BREAKING

A VOICE FROM
THE DARKNESS

A VOICE FROM THE DARKNESS

1034 AP

The Herald's wing snapped with a stomach-churning crack. He squealed in pain like a human child would have. It was disgusting. He was ashamed of himself—but he was also afraid, and the fear was winning. The Seraph Jerrok could kill him in this moment, and what would remain of the Darkness then? Would the gods even make a new Herald, or would they continue to sulk in Infernaak, waiting for the end of the world?

The field below was filled with Paladins and Demons, Humans and Accursed. It was a pitched battle the likes of which hadn't been seen in nearly a generation. Perhaps, for the first time since the Purge of Illux, it was not the armies of Darkness that had started this. Jerrok had come out from behind his walls to do what the Seraphs before him could not: wipe out their hated enemy once and for all—the Grey God be damned. In this moment, it seemed that he would succeed.

Gods, help me! Save your servant!

The Herald tore at Jerrok with his free claw, trying to break loose of the iron grip that the Seraph had on him. At the same time, he swung at the Seraph with the black staff that he held in his other hand. Nightbreaker sung as it passed through the wooden shaft, sending a shower of ebony shards below. Jerrok had killed the last Herald in single combat, and it looked like he would kill this one too.

Acting purely on instinct, the Herald stabbed Jerrok through the wing with the broken staff, following it up with a gout of black flame that sent the Seraph spinning away. The creature turned and fled downward as quickly as its injured wing would allow. It was then that the Armies of Light broke through the line of Demons and Accursed, sending them into a rout.

He ignored that. He ignored the feelings of shame for his cowardice that washed over him. He ignored the disappointment that he felt in his mind emanating from his gods. They would not speak to him, but they would make their displeasure known. Now, survival was all that he could hope for, so he would fly down to the earth and flee like all the rest.

Running Demons looked up at him balefully through horned helms. They despised him for his cowardice, for his weakness. He lashed out with bursts of energy that he couldn't afford to expend, destroying any figure that dared to accuse him with its gaze. Looking over his shoulder, he saw that Jerrok had returned to the ground. Gods willing, the man would stay there.

The Herald saw a tight cluster of rocky hills in the distance. This would be his salvation. There he could hide from friend and foe alike...

A blast of flame struck him from below, sending him spinning into the tide of fleeing creatures under him, where he was swallowed up in a cloud of smoke and dust.

"I'LL BREAK your other finger if you don't stop crying," the older boy said.

His chipped teeth seemed like daggers when he scowled. His lumpy face had turned scarlet, his fist balled up—ready to strike again. The younger boy cried, cradling his broken finger close to his body. It was raining...or was that blood from his nose dripping onto his legs?

"Please," he whimpered. "Please stop. I won't come down your street again. I promise."

The older boy lifted his fist even higher before he struck.

"You won't come back again, or I'll kill you. You get it? Now stop crying."

Another finger snapped.

TWO DEMONS GRIPPED him by the wings, twisting them in unnatural directions. His already-broken wing couldn't take much more of this. He was weak, and they were punishing him for it. They should have used their wicked blades to hack him to pieces and be done with it, but instead, they were choosing cruelty over prudence, as was their nature. They couldn't help themselves. Even so, he would make them regret that. Even cowards had the instinct to survive at all costs.

Treacherous dogs.

The Herald shook them loose and rolled onto his back, wrenching his broken and twisted wings from the grip of his attackers. He knocked them both back with a burst of flame—possibly his last. His energy was waning. His injuries were too severe to heal himself now, not while he was fighting for his life.

Even Divine Blood could dry up.

He pushed himself to his feet and tried to join the flood of mindless Accursed, shambling along just slightly faster than the corpse-warriors. He knew that the Demons wouldn't be down for long, and if he so much as turned to look for them, he would be overtaken.

Ahead, another Demon turned to look over its shoulder. The eyeless visage locked onto the Herald. It was over for him. His weakness had finally been his undoing. His gods had forsaken him, just as they had forsaken every other Herald since the formation of the Pact. The Herald dropped to a crouch and howled like a beast. The shambling Accursed parted around him. The Demon sprang through the air, sword drawn.

. . .

THE BOY FOLLOWED his father as they walked to the market. The spring air was cool, even if the scattered golden rays of sunlight that crept over the walls of Illux brought warmth. The boy's father clutched tightly at a coin purse that was strapped to his belt. The few stolen copper coins inside clinked faintly. The slums of Illux were no place to keep your valuables where they could be easily taken—a fact that his father knew all too well.

The boy's father wasn't a bad man. He tried his best to do honest work, sometimes as a smith's apprentice, sometimes as a carpenter, or even as a member of the City Watch. Sadly, he was never able to hold onto work for long due to his various ailments. His eyesight had been poor since birth, a defect from the gods, and as a result, he had lost half of his left hand in an accident when he was barely a man. Even so, he tried to provide for his son as much as he was able. His son never starved, even if it meant that he needed to steal. The gods would forgive him for that, he reasoned.

The muddy crossroads where the makeshift market had sprung up between the sagging and dilapidated buildings was filled with throngs of people. More than the boy had seen in this part of the slums before. They pressed against the stalls, barking out orders and haggling over crops brought in from the farms outside the city.

The boy stopped at the edge of the market where a dark shape caught his eye. Something was hiding under an overturned basket; just shielded enough that none of the passing adults could see it. Once he reached the basket, the boy crouched down and lifted it, finding a dog lying on its side. The dog was breathing, but given the way its skin was pulled taut over its ribs he guessed that it wouldn't make it another few days.

By the time the boy's father returned to find him, he had the dog up and licking his broken fingers.

THE DEMON FLEW DIRECTLY over the top of the Herald, landing with a thud behind him. He spun around, anticipating a sudden attack that he would be defenseless to stop. Instead, he saw that the Demon was engaged with two of its compatriots, deadlocked in a struggle to prevent them from advancing on the Herald.

"Go!" it hissed. "Some of us are still loyal!"

The Herald nodded and stumbled off. He had never truly felt gratitude before. Accursed were mindless servants, only doing what they were told or reacting out of fear of pain. Demons, on the other hand, were filled with a cold and calculating intellect, and as such, a Demon could rarely be cajoled into doing something that it did not want to do. Why then would this one choose to help such a weakling? It mattered not. All that mattered was survival.

Curse you for forsaking me. Curse you all.

His condemnation was met with further silence. None of the Gods of Darkness, it seemed, would even dignify him with a response. As the fleeing army surged around him, the Herald continued to drag himself up toward the rocky outcropping. Soon, he was lost in the twisting defiles of the rise, clawing his way ever onward to the salvation above. After what seemed like hours, he made it to the mouth of the cave, a cut in the rock that resembled the eye socket of a skull.

The Herald looked back at the field of battle one final time, seeing that the route of his forces was complete. Jerrok's army had stopped chasing the retreat for the time being, and regrouped to the west. The Herald collapsed into the cave, enveloped by Darkness.

"This way, son," his father said. "If you want to keep that dog he'll hurry up too. We have no time to waste!"

The boy motioned for his new dog to follow as the three of them quickly darted down an alley that led out of the inner city and back toward their home in the slums. The boy and his father both carried an armful of bread and fruit taken from the nicer shops closer to the Grand Cathedral. His father's coin purse had remained empty since the day the boy had found the dog, but still, they needed to eat. They had nearly been caught in the act by a group of Paladin recruits on their way to the sparring grounds. The pair had only just escaped due to quick thinking by the boy and a distraction caused by the dog. His father had been proud of him then.

They rounded a corner and found themselves on a familiar street. The boy felt his stomach churn. He nearly dropped the stolen goods from his sweaty palms once he realized where they were—the street that the older boy who had broken his fingers had laid claim to. He slowed his step, casting a wary glance around for any sign of his tormentor. Though he was walking ahead, the boy's father somehow noticed the change in his son. He stopped and turned back to look at the boy.

"What is it, son?" the man asked.

"It's nothing, father."

"Then we mustn't slow."

When they were halfway down the street, he saw the older boy. The bully was crouched in the doorway of a rundown house, poking at some unseen object with a stick. The two boys' eyes met for a brief moment, then the older boy was gone, ducking through an alley onto another street. The boy's dog licked at his leg reassuringly as he let out a sigh of relief.

How long it had been since he had found the cave, he was unsure. Normally, the darkness of such a space would be comforting for one such as him, but for the first time since he had been made into this *thing* that he was, he felt true fear from it. It was very possible that just outside, an entire battalion of Paladins was preparing to enter and destroy him. It was also possible that the Seraph Jerrok had taken it upon himself to end the Herald's miserable existence. He even imagined that those traitorous Demons that he had evaded had come to punish his cowardice, no doubt at the behest of the very gods that had forsaken him.

He pulled himself upright again, leaning against one of the rough-hewn walls of the cave. Slowly, he began to probe the injuries along his body. His wings were certainly broken, and would need to be reset before he could use his healing magic on them. His ribs had also been fractured, and his breathing was labored. The Herald swore aloud as his fingers brushed over his side, his voice echoing deeper into the chamber. He hadn't felt this alone since his life as a mortal, a life that he only remembered in bits and pieces.

A life filled with pain.

"Where are you now?" he cried. "What kind of gods are you?"

Even the pinpoint of light from the mouth of the cave fluttered and died.

THE DOOR to their home wasn't very sturdy. It had been kicked in a time or two, and never was quite right since. When it was kicked open this time, the hinges gave way along with the feeble lock, sending shards of rotten wood and masonry into the room. The dog started barking and growling until the boy clamped his hands around its snout. He knew what happened to small creatures that made too much noise when the powerful were near.

Three members of the City Watch swarmed into the room, each with swords and axes drawn as if they expected to find an army waiting for them, rather than a crippled man and his young son. Following behind the members of the Watch was another man, armored in their garb yet somehow apart, and beside him stood the bully from a few streets over. The man standing beside the bully carried himself as if he were above everyone else in the room.

"What have we done?" the boy's father asked, though he already knew.

"Were these them, son?" The man at the back asked the older boy.

"Yes, father, these is the ones I saw with more food than they could afford. Just look at 'em!" The older boy belted. "Thieves!"

The man motioned to his subordinates, and they grabbed the boy's father and dragged him from the house. The crippled man didn't argue. He knew that there was no point. Once he was outside on the street, the boy could hear him faintly pleading as they carried him away.

"What of my boy? What will happen to him? Please, show mercy. It isn't his fault."

The City Watch Commander looked over the boy and then turned back to his son.

"You did good, Enoc. I will be sure to let your mother have a few more coppers this month that she may choose to spend on you. You let me know if you see this boy skulking around again, and he will join his father." He turned back to the boy. "This home is yours no longer. It will be given to the shop owners from whom you and your father stole. Get out."

THE HERALD AWOKE SOMETIME LATER, feeling a small amount of his strength returning. There was still light emanating from the mouth of the cave, so it couldn't have been more than a few hours since he lost consciousness. The creature pushed himself up on shaky feet and stumbled toward the light. Once outside in the blinding radiance, he propped himself up against a large boulder and gazed out over what had been the field of battle.

The dead and dying were still strewn about, but there was no sign of the fighting forces. Carrion birds had started to descend, a sight which once brought him great joy but now filled him with dread. His forces had been completely routed. If he ever had a chance of gathering the Demons together after such a loss, he had ruined it by fleeing from Jerrok. They would never rally behind a coward.

You are no coward.

The distant voice cut through his mind like a ragged blade. It was strange and familiar to him all at once.

"I am a coward," he whispered. "And so are you. All of you."

The others are, yes. But I have not forsaken you.

Just then, the Herald saw a shape making its way up the rocky defiles toward him. From this distance, he could still make out that it was a great brute of a Paladin astride a white horse, and in his hand was a lance.

"You have forsaken me."

. . .

THE BOY CRIED for the first few days, but finally, his tears had all dried up. He knew that he would never see his father again. While it was certainly possible that he would only receive a short imprisonment and then be back on the streets, how would he find his son in a city so large? Would he even look for him? It was also possible that he was to be banished; thrown out of the gates of the city, and commanded never to return. What then? How would the boy even know? No one cared. Not the Paladins or the priests. The Gods of Light had forsaken him. He had no one and nothing except his dog.

The dog whimpered and licked the boy's mangled fingers. He scratched the dog behind the ears. They were squatting behind some crates and stacks of rotten potatoes in an alley near where his home had been. At first, he had considered trying to find his way to the inner city to petition the Seraph, but deep down, he knew that would get him nothing but his own possible banishment. No one cared for the people of the slums.

He tried one of the potatoes again. Just like the last time, he nearly vomited. It was more green than brown; so soft that it squished between his fingers as he tried to force it down. The boy cried again, leaning his head back against the wall of the building behind him. He hoped, just for a moment, that he would die in his sleep that night—if he got any sleep at all. While his eyes were closed, he imagined killing the boy Enoc and his wicked father. The thoughts made him feel worse than he before. Suddenly, he could feel his dog stand up as a low growl rumbled deep in its chest.

His eyes snapped open and he saw a cat licking its paws in the street beyond the alley. The boy's hand went to steady his dog, but a moment too late. The dog bolted after the cat, snarling and snapping as it chased the other animal around the corner. The boy jumped to his feet and chased after, crying and screaming at the same time.

I can't lose you, too! Please come back.

The dog and cat barreled down the street, ducking under carts and running between the small crowds that were going about their day.

The boy could barely keep up, his tears streaking back across his face as he ran, almost blindly, after his dog. Then the two animals rounded another corner and rushed down the street. The boy stopped in his tracks and nearly collapsed.

He had been warned never to return to this street again. He knew that Enoc would be waiting for him.

Do not give up hope. Defeat him, and the path to vengeance shall open before you.

The Herald tried to ignore the godly voice that echoed through his mind. He didn't need this latecomer's advice, nor its sympathy. This Paladin that came up the rise had come to kill him, and he would most likely succeed. All the Herald could hope for was either the salvation of a quick death or the knowledge that he had mortally wounded his adversary, casting them both into the oblivion of the beyond. There was no hope of his survival.

The hulking Paladin brute continued up the rise, moving with a deliberate pace that made it seem as if he couldn't be stopped. He was a force of nature made flesh, come to punish the wicked and weak little thing that cowered in the mouth of the cave.

The man's horse was weighed down by sparkling silver plate that cast blinding reflections of the sun in all directions. The Paladin was olive-skinned with black hair held back behind his head with a blue ribbon. As he got closer, the Herald could more clearly make out the white lance that the man gripped. Its surface was altogether unmarred; no doubt it was freshly enameled with the same substance that encased the armor of the Paladin. The gold and blue filigrees that adorned the thing made its identity obvious: the Lance of Retribution.

The Lance of Retribution was a storied weapon that the people of Illux had assigned nearly as much reverence to as the blade Night-breaker, though it was far younger of an object. The Lance had been used by the Seraph Arendt to kill his predecessor when he led his rebellion for the future of Illux. Since then, it had been used by Arendt and Jerrok to each slay a Herald, the most recent of which being only a hundred years ago. Rumors swirled around the Lance, with many believing it to be a holy object that guaranteed the vanquishing of evil, if only it were to find its mark.

Ignore the Lance. It is nothing more than metal and wood. You hold the blood of the gods. My blood.

"Leave me alone!" The Herald shouted. "Let me die in peace!"

It was then that the Paladin drew near, rearing his horse and preparing it for an uphill charge. No doubt he had mistaken that the Herald's outburst as was directed at him.

"I will not leave you, beast," the warrior said, each word cold and measured. "For I am Kane of House Darksend, and I have been sent by the Seraph Jerrok to wipe your stain from this world. No doubt you recognize the Lance of Retribution? As it has killed your forebears, so it shall kill you."

"Do you forget your own history, Paladin? It has killed Seraphs as well. It is more fickle than you think," the Herald said, trying to put on false confidence. "Are you ready to meet your High God, Kane Darksend?"

The Lance began to glow faintly blue as magic from the Paladin's hand raced down its length. The Herald stepped back into the mouth of the cave, crouching down as his own faltering magic sprang to life. He felt small and broken then, a frail frame hidden under loose red robes. The shattered memories of his mortal life returned to him again, and he knew that he had felt like this before.

Pain. I can cause you pain at least.

The Paladin spurred his horse and charged. Magic from the Lance shot out, meeting the red flames that erupted from the black claws of the Herald. The horse seemed to scream as it barreled forward with its rider, the glowing Lance aimed for the Herald's heart. Then the Herald's strength failed, as did his magic. The blue light from the Lance of Retribution sent him flying backward into the wall, where he landed with a wet crunch.

Just as quickly, he felt the sharp pain of the Lance driving through his shoulder and pinning him to the wall. The dying Herald lashed out madly, trying to find purchase with his claws somewhere. He couldn't reach its rider, but he could reach the horse. He found a gap in its armor near the throat. Tearing as much flesh as he could, the Herald shouted at the top of his lungs. The animal shuddered and screamed again, throwing Kane from his saddle.

THE BOY STOOD at the mouth of the street, trying not to let it consume him, for this street was no mere dirt road, but a beast that was hungry and waiting for him. Enoc had told him that if he came back here he would kill him, and the boy believed it. He couldn't see the older boy, but that did nothing to dispel the fear that had overtaken him. He didn't see what had become of his dog and the cat it had been chasing either, though he could still hear the dog barking.

Just like that, the barking stopped. No one else walking by seemed to notice any change, but the boy knew what that had to mean. Tears began to fall freely again. His father was gone, and now his dog was gone too. All because of him. All because he was a coward. There was nothing worse than a coward. Even Demons and Accursed were better than cowards. He wiped away his tears and started down the street, warily glancing to his left and right, looking for any possible sign of the boy Enoc.

When he was about halfway down the street, the boy turned and saw exactly what he had feared. Enoc was crouched in an alley, beating the boy's dog with a great stick. He nearly turned and ran. What could he do? The older boy's father was a commander in the City Watch. There was no hurting someone like that, even if he had the strength to do so.

I'm sorry, pup. I'm so sorry.

Then he heard it. The loud crack that accompanied every blow against the ribs of his dog. He heard the whimpers as it clung to life, no doubt wondering to itself what it had done to deserve such punishment. He clenched his fists and sprinted down the alley, all fear disappearing. Enoc heard the footfalls and looked up, just as the boy jumped onto him.

"Leave my dog alone!" he shouted.

Enoc was knocked from his feet, his stick dropping to the ground next to the dog. The boy sunk his teeth into his tormentor, ripping a piece of juicy flesh from the older boy's shoulder. He punched him again and again, bringing his misshapen hand down on Enoc's face over and over. Blood ran down the boy's chin, and he could feel the bits of flesh that still stuck between his teeth. Enoc didn't once fight back. The boy's attack had been too unexpected, too ferocious.

After another minute of pummeling Enoc, the boy rolled off of him, his blood no longer boiling as it had been. The rage left him, and he felt hollow. Moments later, he vomited the rotten potatoes onto the ground. He wiped his mouth and looked down at the bloody and broken face of the older boy. Enoc would never look the same. He whimpered softly, just like the dog did, pressing his hand over the wound on his shoulder.

The boy then went to his dog, cradling the poor beast in his arms. Its breathing was ragged, but he could see the relief in its eyes when it noticed him. Weakly, its tongue lolled out to lick his fingers.

"You're gonna be alright," the boy lied. "We will see my father again, and you will be alright."

The dog sighed and was no more. The boy lay there, crying freely again as he held the corpse of his last friend. No one came to see what had happened. No one cared about the fight between the two street children and a dog. No one cared but the boy.

Enoc started to whimper louder.

"Please," he pleaded weakly. "I need my father."

The boy wanted to be a good man like his father had been, but look at what had happened to him. He stood and grabbed the stick off the ground, turning back toward Enoc.

"I need my father, too."

THE PALADIN STOOD, drawing his sword, and approached the Herald. The Creature of Darkness was still pinned to the wall, his life-force slowly ebbing away. There was something comforting about the thought of death in that moment. Perhaps he would finally find peace in oblivion, away from the weakness of mortals and gods alike.

Will you trust me?

There was the voice again, speaking to him from the darkness of the cave, the darkness of his mind. He tried to shut it out, but it wouldn't go away. He wasn't sure why, but suddenly he found himself clinging to it like a lifeline.

I can save you if you trust in me. I will show you the path. We will purge the Light, all of it. Starting with this one.

The Paladin had started to glow again, his magic springing to life. The deep shadows on his face gave him the visage of a skull. He stepped forward, raising his sword above his head.

Show me.

"I am Kane Darksend, and I am your undoing!"

Suddenly, the Herald felt a warmth spread through his body, the power of his Divine Blood being reinforced by the energy of his god. Kane's sword plunged and the Herald caught it, his claws covered with a black energy that drained the rest of the light from the cave, plunging them both into true darkness.

"I have a name too, Paladin," he said, confidence returning to his voice. "It's the one name that I can remember from my mortal life. I don't even remember my own name from that life, but I remember this. My name is Enoc. Let me show you why I chose this name for myself."

Using the surge of newfound strength, the Herald ripped himself from the wall, sending the Lance clattering to the darkened floor. He gripped the sword tightly, its blade cutting deeply into the flesh of his hands. Yanking with all of his might, he removed the sword from Kane's grip and tossed it aside. The faint light returned to the cave just as the Herald grabbed the Paladin by the neck with one hand and tore his sword arm from its socket with the other, sending a fountain of blood gushing onto the floor. He licked his lips as he pinned the dying warrior to the wall.

Good. Do you trust me now?

I am yours.

Then finish him and I will show you the way to cleanse the Mortal Plane. You don't need Vardic or Rhenaris. You only need me.

A shiver of anticipation ran down the Herald's spine. The Fallen One was his savior. The onetime God of Light was the one who would show him the way. Of course. That was the way that it had to happen. He had followed the Light once, too.

"My blood consecrates this ground," the Paladin choked out. "This Lance that pierced you foretells of your undoing. Soon you will die, and all of your ilk shall follow. Mark my words, Enoc the Herald. I have killed you."

Feeling the last bit of his renewed strength failing, the Herald snapped Kane's neck and dropped him to the ground. Casting one last look toward the Lance of Retribution, the Herald stumbled from the mouth of the cave into the light beyond. One day soon, when he had recovered fully, he would return and seal this place so that the anointed weapon would never be raised against him again, but for now, he would leave it with the corpse of the Paladin.

What shall we do now, master?

Find the last loyal Demons. I have a plan for them. The others will bow to you in time.

The Herald allowed himself a small smile as he made his way down to the battlefield below.

A BANDIT'S BALANCE

I.

1041 AP

The winds whipped through the tall grasses that the men and woman hid in, bringing with it the scent of horse. Those at his back were getting restless, just as they always did when the wait for an ambush was this long. Over the birdcalls and the gentle murmur of the breeze, he could distantly hear the sounds of idle chatter and the rolling clatter of wooden wheels on the poorly maintained road. His eyes closed, Teo sat motionless as he listened and waited. He knew that it wouldn't be long now before they came, it wouldn't be long before he could eat something other than roots again.

Behind him the faint rustle of armor and leather gradually grew louder. This would be the first real blood that they had spilled in weeks. It had been a longer gap between ambushes than it had been in some time. Paladins from Illux had finally begun to track them, forcing the bandits to space out their raids on the shipments of goods to the city. One mistake would result in the lot of them getting killed. Teo had no desire to face the noose or the block any time soon.

Jin reached out and stroked his inner thigh from behind. Teo inhaled slowly, trying to keep his desire in check. She often toyed with him like this before combat, clouding his mind in what was most likely some half-assed attempt at getting him killed so that she could take his place as the second in command to Drex. It would have been harder for him to ignore if they didn't regularly engage in certain nocturnal activities when the mood struck them both.

Damn you, woman.

He slipped his dirk from his side and bounced gently on the balls of his feet. Jin unclasped her small axe and moved fully beside him, casting him a sideways smirk. It was like she had read his thoughts, as it seemed that she often did. No doubt she fancied herself smarter than him, and on most days Teo was likely to agree with her. He looked her over for a moment, wondering to himself how this woman had bested him in so many ways over their time together. There was no question that he was the better fighter, but she had more guile, and could lead the most suspicious enemy into a trap. She kept her blonde hair short so that it stayed out of her dazzling green eyes. The woman was so beautiful and dangerous that she might have been an avatar of the dark goddess Rhenaris herself.

Finally, it emerged from between the hills on the small roadway beneath them: a small cadre of farmers and villagers carting a load of supplies for the City of Light. Teo sighed. There weren't as many as he had hoped for. Drex wouldn't be happy. Teo had been the one to choose this route, promising that this would be a large enough bounty to make up for the forced drought of the past few weeks. It appeared that he had been wrong.

The city couldn't survive without these routine shipments from the villages, nor could the various bandits that prowled the country-side. The larger groups would sometimes have a Paladin or two to guard the villagers as they made the multi-day trek. Those hulking brutes were men and women that had been empowered by the Gods of Light with divine energies that gave them superhuman strength and access to magical abilities. Although he regretted that this meant there was less food, Teo was relieved that none such enemies walked below him now. This smaller shipment was mostly unguarded except for a few loosely-armed simpletons. None of the heavy-hitters were on the trail today.

Just a little farther.

Even with the smaller size of this shipment the bandits were outnumbered by the villagers by at least two to one, possibly the best odds they had seen in months. What made these raids so successful was the small number that Teo brought with him. The larger operations attracted too much attention from the city and its holy warriors, attention that had finally fallen on them now that Drex had begun taking in so many new members.

The cart passed directly below now, almost to the position that would spell their doom. The winds seemed to die down then, the hills holding their breath along with the bandits. Teo raised a hand and two men with bows materialized at his and Jin's side. Arrows flew through the stillness, striking one of the armed men at the head of the group, along with the horse pulling the cart. Blood splattered those beside the man and beast before they even knew what happened. The screams of the men and women below were drowned out by the painful sounds of the dying horse.

Teo lifted his dirk and shouted a wordless battle cry, running down the hillside and into his prey below. The nearest man sat atop another horse, swinging the animal about as he drew his aged blade. He was lightly armored with chainmail that looked as if it were a generation old and had belonged to a man too fat to make actual use of it. Teo jumped into the air, knocking the farmer to the ground. He pulled his dirk across the man's unprotected throat, just deep enough for him to choke on his own blood. Teo rolled off of him, preparing to move on to his next victim.

His back gave with an audible snap as he collapsed to the ground.

The sharp pain in his back seemed to overtake all other sensations of what was going on around him. After a few moments he realized that it had been the horse of the man whom he had just ended that had kicked him as it bucked and twisted wildly, an arrow buried deep in its neck. It seemed that his archers either did not care what they hit or were more out of practice than he had assumed.

We could have used that horse.

Gritting his teeth, the bandit pushed himself to his feet and buried his dirk in the horse's neck just below its head, holding on tightly as the beast thrashed and shuddered before collapsing under its own weight. Around him he noticed that the others seemed to be faring better, thriving on the chaos of the unprepared farmers. Jin had her axe buried in the face of some screaming woman who had sought refuge in the cart. As the axe was pulled free it splattered some of the foodstuffs with brains and blood. Jin quickly kicked the woman off of the cart and began sifting through its contents. Teo looked at the corpse of the dead woman for a few moments, for some reason reminded of his long dead mother.

A sharp cry spun him about. Ahead, he could see a man running away from the chaos, making his way in the vague direction of Illux. It would have been a futile attempt even if the city wasn't still some days' journey away. Even so, they couldn't let this coward escape in case he stumbled across some other group, who would then be alerted to their presence. If Demons or Accursed happened to be prowling along this same road, they would surely follow the bandits just the same as any Paladins.

Teo scanned the area looking for the final horse that he had seen from the hilltop. The frightened beast was on the other side of the fighting, trying desperately to lose its dead rider, whose corpse still somehow dumbly clutched at the reigns. This one had been a woman, bettered armored than the male rider had been, yet an arrow still found its way into her left eye.

The bandit rushed past several surviving villagers who fled from his approach, sure that he was bringing death to them. When he finally reached the bucking horse, he grabbed the desperate animal's reigns and pulled tightly, willing it to stop its frenzied panic. When the jostling of the corpse-laden steed slowed, he was able to grip the dead woman and dislodge her. Once he had replaced the other rider, Teo was leaning forward in the saddle, bearing down on the fleeing villager at break-neck speed. Within moments, he had ridden him down, the cries of man and horse mingling as hooves crushed the coward into the dirt.

Turning about, Teo rode back toward the cart, surveying the

carnage that he and his ilk had caused. Bodies lay strewn about in all directions, some of which desperately clung to life, moaning or crying out. These villagers were quickly silenced by the blades of the other bandits who had begun picking over the bodies for anything valuable. Money would be taken. Jewels and other valuables could be sold in the seedier parts of Illux and Seatown, providing them with the income they needed to buy more weapons and supplies needed to survive in the wilderness for another couple of months.

Overhead, birds had already begun to circle, drawn to the smell of death quicker even than Teo thought possible. They would need to move quickly lest those same birds serve to draw enemies to them.

Teo rode alongside the cart, addressing Jin. "What did we get?" His voice was gravel, rarely used and always coarse.

"Less than usual," she replied matter-of-factly. "Some salted beef, a few chickens, grain mostly. Not enough for us to eat as good as we have been wanting. Drex will be pissed."

Teo ran his fingers through his horse's mane a moment before responding.

"We can eat the other two horses. No need to waste the meat."

Behind him a woman began to scream. There was no need for him to see what was happening. It was what always happened after the bloodlust had worn off and women were around. Jin was only spared such atrocities because she was tougher than most of the men that she rode with. Dickless Jack was living proof of what happened when a man tried to have his way with her uninvited. After that incident, no one ever tried to touch her uninvited again.

Teo dismounted and hitched his horse to the cart, the animal nervously nickering at the sight of its dead companion still harnessed and rapidly attracting flies. Jin hopped down and grabbed Teo by the arm, leading him back to the tall grasses like a giddy child. The thrill of battle had the same effect on her as it did on the men, even with the sounds of another woman being defiled just behind them. He himself had begun to feel the desires that he had put away on the hilltop resurface with a ferocity that he had almost forgotten had existed.

They reached a secluded area, behind a fallen tree obstructed by grass and brush and quickly undressed, leaving all weapons comfortably out of reach. There was no trust between them, even when they shared one body.

Once they had finished, nearly at the same time, and the men had tired of their plaything below, Jin executed the woman. The bandits gathered up all of their spoils into the cart, now hitched to the single living horse. Quickly they left the road behind, the crows and vultures already laying claim to what little was left. It would be another hour before they reached the clearing where they had stashed their horses that morning. Once all of them were mounted again it would take another half day's ride to reach the camp where they had left Drex and the others. Teo gritted his teeth at the thought of their return that night.

It would not be a happy homecoming. It rarely was.

THE SUN HAD SET about an hour before they rode into camp; a clearing in the center of a small wood at the base of the mountains, nestled between the foothills. They had stayed in this place for the last few months, all of them deciding that they'd had enough of hoofing it through the hills every few nights to avoid detection. All of them and Drex, that is. After all, nothing was decided without his approval. The bandit captain fancied himself a king at times, and none so far had seen fit to challenge him. When the suggestion to find a more permanent location to settle had arisen, Quake had suggested that they move even further into the Rim. He claimed that he could find a place that even the Paladins would be afraid to go. Quake was a religious fool, though. His was a higher cause.

Fucking idiots. Both of them.

The sentries nodded in greeting as Teo and his band rode through the trees, following after them to see what spoils they brought. Teo couldn't see them clearly in the darkness, but he figured that by the way the left one limped he was most likely Dickless Jack. His injury prevented him from raiding with the others, a fact that Jin never let the man forget.

Ahead of them in the clearing was a random assortment of tents; some were of the nicer variety purchased in Illux, while some were the result of animal skins haphazardly stitched together. Throughout the camp was the reek of the latrine pits dug farther into the trees. A sign that they had been here too long. In the center of it all was a large campfire and carved wooden chair that loosely resembled paintings of the High God's Throne. Upon the chair sat a figure with flowing black hair and a salted beard.

Teo and his party circled the around the throne and campfire, dismounting as they did so. Teo moved to open the back of the wagon, but found that Jin beat him to it, spilling what little they had gathered onto the ground. Remaining in the back of the wagon were the grains and butchered meat of the horses, already beginning to stink and attract a swarm of flies. The lounging man stood from the throne and began to run one of his hands through the small pile of coins and jewels on the ground, the other hand tightening on the horn of ale that it held.

"Is this really all of it?" he spat.

"Yes," Teo responded.

The ale was in Teo's face before he had time to react. The insulted bandit quickly dropped his hand to the hilt of his dirk. Another set of fingers tightened over his own and prevented him from drawing the blade free. He saw that it was Jin who stopped him from settling the score. Or from making a fool of himself.

What is she playing at?

"The group was smaller than we had been lead to believe," she said.

Drex seemed to ignore her. He walked along the side of the cart, examining what little food was within. With a click of his tongue and a sharp motion Dickless Jack and one of the Jakobs began unloading the horsemeat and preparing it for the fire. It was clear that if they didn't eat it tonight there was no way that it would keep.

After the food had been seen to, Drex returned to face Teo and Jin, his hands resting upon the blades at his sides. Teo studied the man, looking for any weaknesses that he would be able to exploit. Drex was covered in black furs and leathers, forgoing the steel chainmail that many of the others favored. He preferred style over substance, a flaw that Teo could make use of. The older man leaned to his left, keeping some weight off of his right leg, which had been wounded by a Paladin some years back when Teo had first joined with him. If Teo could move quickly enough, the two swords that Drex expertly wielded wouldn't matter.

"You were the one who promised us that this would be our biggest haul in ages. What do you have to say for your failure?" Drex asked slowly.

"My contact in Amel mislead me. I will deal with his failure the next time we pass through."

Drex grunted and turned, walking back to sit upon his throne. The only reason he refused to push the matter and punish Teo was that he truly had become a coward in his old age. Once he had ruled through fear, meting out harsh punishments to those who failed him, quelling dissent with his superior swordsmanship. But now? Now he was old, and weak, and afraid. Perhaps now would be the time to challenge him, regardless of the insult he had just splashed upon Teo's face.

"You are weak, old man!" Jin shouted at Teo's left, approaching Drex with her axe drawn.

Damn her!

It seemed that she had again read his mind, and it was too late for him to do a damn thing about it. She continued her approach around the fire, but for some reason the old bastard didn't seemed worried. In fact, he barely even seemed to take notice.

"I challenge—" She was cut off by a hand that clamped over her mouth. It was the hand of Dickless Jack. Two others grabbed her arms and prevented her from using her axe on the man. She struggled and even bit down on the hand that held her mouth, but it was to no avail. Dickless Jack pulled back on her hair with his other hand to try and stop her savage assault on his fingers. Teo quickly drew his own weapon.

"What is this?" he shouted. "She has the right to challenge. None of you are to get involved!"

It angered him that she had been the one to seize this opportunity, but he could not allow this flagrant attempt by that old coward to hold onto his power. If they couldn't challenge him then that meant that strength no longer ruled here, but treachery and cowardice. If Drex truly expected to run this group until his natural death then he truly was a fool, as were any who would still follow him. The old man didn't go on raids with them anymore, so how soon did they think he would pass on naturally?

"When you hear what we have to say, you will think otherwise," a weak voice rasped from behind Drex.

The frail form of Quake stepped out of the shadows into the light of the fire. The flickering of the flames twisted his already horrid features into a mask of dread, not unlike what Teo imagined the Gods of Darkness to look like. His face was pointed like that of rat, while his front teeth were filed to look more like fangs than what could be deemed a natural birth defect. The sight of the sickly man made Teo's skin crawl.

Drex nodded and the men released Jin as he spoke. "You will put that weapon away or I will rape and gut you, whore."

To Teo's surprise, Jin clasped her axe back at her side and crossed her arms over her chest, remaining silent. Blood still stained around her mouth from Dickless Jack. No doubt she realized that no fight with Drex in this moment would be a fair one. No amount of insults was worth foolishly dying over.

"I didn't kill Teo for his failure for one reason, and one reason alone. I have a plan that will prevent us from ever needing to scrape by from raid to raid again. Quake."

The snake of a man nodded as he stepped forward.

"The Gods of Darkness have finally spoken to me. They have finally answered my prayers after all this time. They have often blessed our little band with good killings and plentiful bounties. We have sacrificed many an innocent in their name, and they will finally reward us for our faith."

Teo wasn't the only one who snorted. Over the last few months Quake had begun converting some of the other members of their group to his worship of the Gods of Darkness, but not all had been receptive to his preaching. Few here had been pious in their old lives, and fewer still wished to take up the practice now, no matter which gods demanded worship. Evil men needed no help committing evil deeds, it seemed.

"Let him finish or I'll cut out your tongues!" Drex shouted.

"They have ordained a place for us to meet them in the wilderness, not far from here," Quake continued. "Once at this holy site they will present us with their messenger and give us the holy power of Demons!"

Teo thought that he saw the flames jump more hungrily out of the corner of his eye when Quake spoke. It seemed that his words had some effect on the mind. Jin and some of the other men began to gather around Teo, the epicenter of resistance in such matters of faith.

"We will leave at dawn," Drex said.

"You can't believe this shit?" Teo asked.

"I do. Why would the Gods of Darkness not watch over their servants?" the bandit leader asked.

"Their servants?" Teo snorted. "I see no servants here but Quake. And what is his service but the gibbering of a madman that he mistakes as prayers? Just because I kill and rape and rob doesn't make me a servant to Vardic, Rhenaris or Lio. It simply makes me a wanted man. This talk is madness. I say we have a vote."

"There will be no vote!" Drex slammed his fist on the throne and stood, drawing his swords. "We are being given the opportunity to gain real power. And we are going to take it!"

It was then that lines seemed to truly have been drawn. The camp had been split down the middle, with the likes of Quake and Dickless Jack standing behind Drex, while Teo had Jin and others behind him. If this came to blood it would be a close fight, and would leave little left in the way of survivors. Even if Teo could hope for his side to win with no losses—an impossible prospect—the company would lose half of its strength. It would be impossible to fend off any Paladin attacks, or even to raid the larger shipments to Illux. It would only be a matter of time before they were all captured or killed.

Teo couldn't bring himself to believe that Quake had actually spoken to the gods. He had no Divine Blood in his veins. How could such a man know what the Gods of Darkness wished? It truly was madness, but could Teo really throw away so many lives to fight against it?

Finally, Teo stood down. He lowered his dirk and stepped back from the battle-line. Those behind him slowly did the same, though some continued to grumble their dissent. Drex eyed Teo cautiously while Quake inched closer and whispered in his ear, smiling wickedly the whole time.

"Lead the way old man," Teo spat, stalking off to his tent.

Jin followed him shortly after and helped him work out his frustrations.

The next morning, with a slight drizzle starting, they broke camp for the first time in several months. Misty clouds rolled down from the mountains, blanketing the sky in a grey malaise that hid the sun and its sister, Aenna, opening to the world of the gods. With stomachs full of horse meat and bodies rested from a night's sleep it seemed that fewer men backed the religious fervor that had split the camp the night before. Hunger and boredom can lead men to seek out comfort, from any source it seemed. For a moment Teo thought that he could capitalize on this lapse and take control of the camp again, ending this farce before it began. He found that he still couldn't see how they would survive with so many of their number dead after the fighting, even if he had more men on his side this day.

Teo rolled his bedding and tied it to the saddle of his horse, making sure that the inside roll stayed dry. He had begun taking the time to disassemble his tent when he realized that they would no longer need such things, if Quake was to be believed. If he really was to become a Demon what better way to spend his last night than looking up at the open sky? The bandit left the half-collapsed shelter and returned to gathering what gear he would need over the next few days.

My last few days as a man.

Looking past his blade as he cleaned it, Teo watched Jin bent over, picking up a change of clothes and rolling it into her bedroll. According to Quake the location that the Gods of Darkness had ordained to meet them was only a day and a half ride away at the most, so why would Jin think that she needed a change of clothes? Unless she didn't intend to see this fool's errand to the end. Would it be possible for them to really escape this madness that Drex was leading them into? Perhaps if they rode out together during the night...

"Not having second thoughts, are you?" a snake-voice hissed in his ear.

Teo deftly twisted his dirk and pressed the point into Quake's throat without even looking at the man.

"I don't know how you were able to commit the others to this folly, but don't expect all of us to go in so blindly," Teo replied coldly.

"Just a warning, friend," Quake said as he pushed the blade away. "The Gods of Darkness do not forgive treachery against them or their servants. We are all committed to them now. Demons retain their memories, especially the bad ones. Do not think that Drex and the others won't come after you if you try and leave before the ordained time."

"Drex and the others?" Teo asked. "But not you, it seems."

Quake seemed to look shocked before he replied. "I do not hold grudges Teo. I speak for the gods. They whisper to me while men dream. There is no time for grudges then."

"What is their purpose then? Tell me, what could they possibly whisper to a worm such as you?"

"Their wishes are simple. They like to deceive and twist the hearts of men to do wicked things. To betray your fellows is the greatest act of worship to them. One day they will overcome the Gods of Light and return the Grey God to their side, casting out the false Fallen One. Then those who serve them will be rewarded."

With that final pronouncement, the sickly man scurried away like a rat caught in the light. His words bothered Teo more than he would have liked to admit. Quake had always been a weak and cowardly little fool, but now there was a new arrogance in his words. Something about what he had said did not bode well for the future of these men. He certainly knew more than he was letting on about what was in store for them. Teo's eyes flitted about the camp before finally settling on Drex. The bandit chieftain was lounging in his wooden throne, watching as the others packed up the camp for him. He had never once seemed to be a religious man before, so what had changed?

He has finally realized that he is getting too old to lead us.

That must have been what happened. With Quake whispering in his ear, it was only a matter of time before his fears had been played against him. The old man knew that it was inevitable that either Teo or Jin would end him and take the reins, something that his pride could not allow. There was no retiring from a life like this. No bandits made it into old age, drifting off in their sleep with a roof over their head and a woman at their side. Even so that old bastard sat in that throne like he still ruled the world, as if he were the High God himself.

Teo decided then that he had to take one more opportunity to make Drex see reason. He stood and found some dry pieces of wood that they had kept in one of the tents to use for torches or fire kindling. Teo wrapped the end of the wood in some cloth that was still dry torn from his own tent and dipped it in pitch that was kept beside the pile of wood. Taking a piece of flint and igniting the torch, Teo returned to the outside, still damp from the now waning drizzle. Before the others could take notice, he was upon his horse and riding about the camp, touching the flame to the various tents and fabric structures around its circumference, starting with his own. Even damp the animal skins and fabrics began to burn in just a matter of moments.

This threw the camp into chaos as men ran back and forth, trying desperately to stop the fires as they spread from tent to tent. Drex jumped to his feet, drawing his swords and shouting over the uproar in an attempt to gather men to him. It looked as though the old man thought that Teo was finally going to challenge his leadership. Teo couldn't help but smirk, for this would not go how Drex would expect. By the time Teo rode to meet his leader the battle-line from the night before had again been drawn, though this time several of the men who had just hours before been grumbling in dissent now stood behind Drex. Even Jin was behind the man, although her axe was not yet drawn.

"What is the meaning of this?" Drex called out.

"Do you really wish to lead us down this path?" Teo asked. "Are you truly this mad?"

"We will have more power than any of you can imagine! What fool would turn that down?"

"So be it," Teo whispered, throwing the torch onto the wooden throne. It took longer than the tents, but soon the fire was ignited and no one was able to put it out.

Teo pulled free his dirk and tossed it into the dirt at the old man's feet.

"Let's be off then," he said. "We have no need for the things that have been burned. Lead us to this power, old man, or whatever end we march toward."

He turned his horse and rode to the edge of the burning camp, waiting for the others to follow.

LATER THAT DAY Jin returned his blade to him, handing the dirk to Teo while none of the others were watching. They rode through the low hills of the Rim now, following Drex and Quake at head of the small column. It wasn't a hard ride, but they didn't waste any time stopping to rest their animals either. Quake claimed that if they kept up the current pace they would arrive at the ordained place sometime during the following day. Teo didn't care either way. He had decided that he would see this to the end now, whatever end that may be. What other choice did he have? He couldn't explain why, but he had never felt so defeated in all of his life.

Teo cast a sideways glance at Jin who also seemed troubled, but was silent in her saddle, keeping her eyes ahead. She was uncharacteristically quiet, and he noticed that her fingers twitched over the handle of her axe. The weapon seemed small now, as if it had shrunken since the last time the female warrior had brandished it. Her eyes never met his, darting this way and that, always scanning the area as if she felt that they were being watched. It was obvious to Teo that Jin was planning something, but what? Killing Drex at this point wouldn't avert the course that they were on; it was far too late for that.

The Rim almost looked menacing at their left, ancient sentinels that held dark secrets. Teo had often wished that he could explore the mountain range, but the lack of any known human settlement besides the Grey Temple would make any trek meaningless for a man like him. There weren't many riches to be found in wild places like that. Monsters were still thought to prowl the upper reaches, far beyond any of the lower grazing grounds of the farming villages. The stories were just that, but they were enough to keep most away, making them the perfect place for a fugitive to hide.

Hills rose and fell beneath them, carrying on for as far as they could see. Somewhere in the distance would be the great expanse of shimmering blue that made up the largest body of water known to man. Its gentle waves had been mesmerizing when he had first visited the coastline. Seatown was another place where a man could lose himself, hidden among the stinking wharfs and fishing ships. Teo sometimes went there to sell stolen goods and disappear again, never alerting any Paladins.

I must not think of those times. If Quake is right, think of the power I will gain.

He looked at Jin again and then spurred his horse forward, riding up to the head of the small band to settle in beside Drex and Quake. The smaller man cowered away from Teo, slinking deeper into his saddle. Drex tried to ignore Teo, but the look of fear that flickered behind his eyes was impossible to miss. Behind them, the sun had finally begun to drop past the hills at their back. The shadows pooled in Quake's hollow face, hiding his eyes even further behind his stringy hair.

"Tell me," Teo said after a time, "where is this supposed meeting to take place? How will we know when we've arrived?"

Drex chewed his lip but said nothing, nodding at Quake to answer. The small man sank even lower into his saddle before he did so.

"The gods will tell me when we have arrived. It is just past the river…"

He averted his eyes and trailed off, looking over his shoulder suddenly and then falling back further in the party to ride beside Dickless Jack. Teo snorted and continued on in silence beside his leader, Drex never looking him in the face. They continued on this way for some time, the shadows of the setting sun finally creeping over them, changing the color of the grasses from green to grey.

"Why didn't you make your move?" Drex asked, his face a skull. "If I had been ten years younger I would have been able to take you, but now? We both know how it would have ended."

"What would that have gotten me? Quake has converted too many of us to his bullshit faith," Teo spat. "Even if me and mine had killed all of your men we would have been too weak to survive another winter."

"It pains me to admit, but you aren't a dumb man, Teo. Neither am I. I know that I am gambling with our future, but what other choice do I have? I have never been a pious man, even when I lived in Illux. What have the gods ever given me? Stillborn daughters and sons who died of the pox? A wife who killed herself in her grief? What have they ever given any of us but war and death? Quake's belief about our raiding and pillaging being akin to sacrifice to the Gods of Darkness never meant anything at all to me. They could all go and fuck themselves for all I cared. But once he told me that the gods did watch our actions, that they had spoken to him of power and immortality, I listened. Not because I want to believe him, but because I have to."

You poor fool.

For the first time that he could remember, Teo pitied Drex more than he disliked him. For once he understood. Rather than responding he simply nodded and fell back in line, keeping away from any other companions, while still keeping his eyes locked on Quake. One way or another Teo was sure that he would see that man die. The snake was whispering to Dickless Jack, but quickly stopped and spurred his steed on to return him to Drex's side. He almost faded into the darkness like a ghost beside the larger man. In another few minutes, they had made camp in a small copse of fir trees, rolling out bedding over the floor of needles.

Teo looked for Jin, hoping to experience her body one last time, but she was sleeping alone at the edge of the trees. He fell asleep mildly irritated.

THE NEXT MORNING when the first fingers of sunlight cut between the towering firs they broke camp for the final time and loaded their horses. Jin was nowhere to be found. It seemed that she had slipped out sometime during the night, taking her horse and what food they had left. Some of the others were missing too, one of which was found with his throat slashed just outside of the trees. There was momentary discussion of hunting Jin and the others down, but Drex decided that it would be more prudent for them to reach the meeting place with the gods' emissary as quickly as possible. Teo felt anger that she would leave him and take others, but he knew that he would have rejected her offer had she given it. The pit of his stomach ached as he thought of her for the rest of the morning.

They continued on for the next few hours until they finally reached the banks of a river flowing from higher in the mountains into the sea to the distant east. It was wide and fast flowing, but not too deep to make a crossing. The bandits leapt from their horses and began fording the river. Teo carefully felt along the riverbed with his feet, making sure not to slip and fall, lest he be wet from more than the waist down. The swift moving water was ice cold, even in this season, and it cut across his flesh like a thousand tiny blades. His horse seemed to be even more uncomfortable with the crossing than he did.

This better be worth it.

Once they were across, they stood silently for several minutes, shivering and shaking the water from their bodies. Before mounting up again Teo noticed that the horses seemed considerably more agitated on this side of the river than they had been before. His own mount pawed nervously at the earth and continued to twist against its reigns, trying to make its way back toward the water. He kicked the beast in its sides and forcibly corrected it, pushing his way toward the front of the group.

They must be close.

It didn't take long for them to come to the place where they were to meet the emissary of the Gods of Darkness. After another hour of riding past the river they crested a small hill and descended into a shallow valley. Teo noticed that the valley was empty other than a sizable boulder on one of the far hills. The ground was rocky and barren here, more like the wastes to the south than the fertile grass-lands of the north. Once they reached the bottom, Quake rode to the front of the group and turned his horse about.

"We are here!" he screeched, waving his arms. "This is the anointed place."

The men dismounted, the horses galloping away as soon as they were unburdened. Teo looked around uneasily, keeping his hand upon his dirk. It seemed as if the world around them had gone totally silent once the sounds of the fleeing horses faded into the distance. Quake stood in the middle of the group quivering and swaying back and forth with his eyes closed. Finally, Teo grew tired of waiting and shook the little man by the arm.

"Where is the emissary of the gods?"

"He is here. I am he," Quake whispered, pulling himself away from the other bandit.

Just then three Demons appeared on the hilltop, making their way down to the valley floor. They were hulking giants, at least a head taller than any of the bandits. Each was adorned in spike-covered plate mail colored like coal. Most chilling of all was the fact that no helm upon any of their heads had any openings for eyes.

"I have brought them. I have brought the sacrifice!"

"What did you say, worm?" Drex spat, pulling free one of his swords and shouldering his way through the others toward Quake.

Teo pulled his dirk free and twisted about, checking the advance of the three Demons. It was then that he saw the other two coming from the opposite side. They had been surrounded without even noticing. A flash of red light turned a fleeing man to ash. Teo hadn't seen who it had been, nor did he care. He looked back and saw Quake running from Drex toward the embrace of the three Demons. Once the coward reached the dark behemoths he threw himself to his knees and began to pray loudly.

You will pay for this Quake. That I promise you.

"Protect your servant! Protect your servant!"

The lead Demon stepped past Quake as if it didn't even notice him, lifting its massive black blade above its head. Drex swung once and missed. The Demon's blade flashed out. Drex fell to his knees while desperately trying to keep his innards from spilling onto the ground. His killer reached down and grabbed a handful of intestine and wrapped it about the old man's neck, using the organ to choke the air from him. His blood-choked gurgles could be heard even from where Teo stood. Teo struggled with the bile at the back of his throat, his mind racing. Quake crawled out from behind the Demons and stood, posturing himself as if he was an equal.

"Drop your weapons and kneel!" Quake shouted. "Give yourselves to the Gods of Darkness. Otherwise you will die."

"You coward! You knew this would happen. We were never to become Demons!" Dickless Jack slurred.

"No, not Demons, but true servants of Darkness."

The other men turned to look at Teo, only now deciding that he would have made a better leader than Drex or Quake. The looks of fear across their faces mirrored what Teo felt within. He scanned the hillside, looking for any last desperate chance of escape. There were none. It seemed that they must either fight or die, or give themselves over to Quake and his Demons. It wasn't much of a choice. He dropped his dirk and fell to his knees, placing his hands on his head. The others did the same.

Quake produced a link of thick cord that he must have been carrying since they had left their camp at the base of the mountains. After he reached the kneeling men, he began to slowly bind all of their hands before them, cutting off the cord with a curved knife. The rope bit into Teo's flesh like a razor, burning and causing his skin to itch. When each man was securely bound, they were placed in a line for the Demons to survey. By now, two of the brutes had carried in a cart that was filled with rusted iron blades.

Teo barely noticed. Even when the first man started to scream.

Quake grabbed Dickless Jack by the hands, pulling his arms out in front of him. One of the Demons stood beside with its sword raised. The sword came down, severing both of Dickless Jack's arms just below the elbow in one, clean stroke. Blood fountained out, splattering the men closest to him. Before he could slump over Quake grabbed onto him and held the man upright while the Demon jammed an iron blade onto each bloodied stump, fusing flesh and bone with iron from a crimson glow that emanated from its gauntleted hands. The smell of cooked meat wafted to Teo's nostrils. When the glow faded Dickless Jack was finally allowed to collapse onto the ground.

Somewhere in line, one of the other men tried to flee, forcing himself to his feet as fast as he could. He was cut down a moment later.

Quake returned to the cart and grabbed a large hook and twine to begin sewing Dickless Jack's mouth. One of the Demons grabbed him and threw him aside, motioning at the next man in line. He dropped the hook and twine back into the cart. The snake-like bandit muttered to himself and nodded, grabbing the next man by the arms as before.

The screaming continued, getting closer and closer to Teo, who simply stared at the ground in front of him. He racked his brain, trying to think of something, anything that would free him from this madness. Why hadn't he fought them? At least he would have died a man, like Drex had. Finally, his eyes drifted to a small stone, just within his reach. The bandit looked around for the first time since Dickless Jack had been mutilated, the clarity returning to his thoughts. He noticed that all of the Demons watched the men who were being turned into Accursed; none paid any attention to the few kneeling men who remained. It was in this moment that Teo quickly grabbed the rock and tossed it over his back at the boulder on the hill behind them.

The Demons heard the sound of the smaller stone striking the larger one, even over the screaming and sizzling hiss of melted flesh. To Teo's surprise, four of them left the screaming man who they had gathered around and began trudging up the hill to see what had made the noise. Quake and the other Demon continued their grim work, now only a few men down the line from Teo.

This is taking too long.

Teo knew that the other four Demons would find nothing by the boulder and return long before Quake made it to his place in the line. He wouldn't get an opportunity like this again. He turned to the man beside him, Jerrick, one of the more recent recruits. He was gentler than many of the others, refusing to rape or kill women or children. Teo struck him over the head as hard as he was able, sending the man onto his face. His garbled cry caught the attention of Quake and the last Demon.

"Are you afraid to try your luck with me, snake?" he spat.

The other man looked smug, but said nothing. Quake and the Demon walked over to where Teo knelt, passing several other men who audibly sighed in relief. Teo tried not to cringe as he heard the crack of Jerrick's spine from the heel of the Demon. Quake grabbed Teo by the hands and pulled his arms taut, smiling wickedly. The Demon raised its sword high above its head.

It was then that Teo smiled.

He twisted his wrists, gripping onto Quake. Teo pulled the other man downwards as the sword stroke fell, severing one of Quake's hands at the wrist. As Quake collapsed, Teo slit the cord that bound him on the Demon's blade and grabbed Quake's knife from the wounded man's belt. Jumping to his feet, Teo jammed the knife into the gap between helm and breastplate of the behemoth beside him. The Demon staggered back, stumbling over the bodies of the half-Accursed scattered on the ground behind it. Men moaned weakly as they were crushed beneath its weight.

Teo turned and sprinted up the hillside. He crested the rise just as the ground behind him erupted in a shower of Demon-fire. He stumbled through the shower of flame and stone over the top of the hill and kept running, the sound of angry pursuit behind him. There was no way that he could lose those things, but at least he would die a man. To his great pleasure, he could just make out the distant whimpering of Quake far behind him.

Then he saw her.

Jin galloped up to him on horseback, barely slowing long enough for Teo to jump onto the saddle. He wrapped his arms around her as they rode toward the river, never looking back.

III.

Hours after she had rescued him, Teo still hadn't let go of Jin. Everything about her was a gift from the gods, whichever ones had decided to take pity upon him. The smell of her hair was intoxicating as he buried his head in it. He wished that he could lose himself in that smell, without the distant cries of disfigured men echoing in his mind.

They had forded the river several hours ago, continuing west from there without stopping once. Neither of them had any idea if the Demons would follow them this far. Teo had wounded one, and had maimed Quake, which certainly hadn't helped their cause. If the treacherous bandit was half as important to the Gods of Darkness as he claimed, then they might be running for the rest of their lives. He had intended for the wound to be fatal, but there was no guarantee of that. If Demons had the same healing powers as the Paladins, then the little snake could still possibly draw breath.

Out of all of the things that Teo's mind considered, he still didn't know why Jin had been there when she was. Had she changed her mind about joining them in that mad quest to become Demons? Hoping somehow that they would forgive her at the final hour? Or was she simply sating her curiosity?

I never thought I would owe her like this.

Finally, after the day was drawing to a close, and the darkness in Teo's heart was reflected in the clouds, Jin turned her horse and urged it toward the Rim. It was clear that she wanted to take refuge in the shelter of the trees of those mountains, far from any pathway that the Demons would assume that they had taken. They passed between towering trees on either side that hid birds and animals that chirped and chittered with the setting of the sun. Just above the lowest of the hills, where they were sheltered from any prying eyes from above or below, they made camp. It wasn't until Jin was unrolling the bedding that she spoke.

"What in the High God's name happened down there?"

"That bastard Quake fucked us," Teo whispered. "We were never meant to become Demons. He was simply using us as some kind of sacrifice to curry favor with them. They were making us into Accursed."

Jin shuddered as she spoke. "At least Drex got what he deserved. That old bastard can limp around forever now, living out the ruin that he brought on us for an eternity."

"He didn't get turned. They killed him. He was choked with his own innards."

"Do you really think that would stop them from turning him? Not by the stories I've heard."

Everyone had heard the stories. It was rumored that some of the corpse-warriors were actually corpses, reanimated by the dark powers from the Demons and Heralds, their souls ripped from the side of the High God and shackled into the mindless bodies until they could again be struck down. Teo didn't know if he had ever believed that, but after what he had seen today he knew that he could not discount it.

"Where will we go?" he asked finally.

"Let's discuss that in the morning," she said quietly.

Teo looked up at the sky, seeing Aenna faintly glowing beside the moon. Perhaps those wicked gods were looking down at him now, laughing at the misery that they had caused. How often did any of the gods look down upon the mortals anymore? How often had they ever? When his gaze returned earthward, Jin had already removed her tunic and most of her breeches. The moonlight illuminated the curves of her naked body as she crawled toward him. He had never wanted her more than in that moment.

Somewhere above them an owl called as it began its nightly hunt.

THE SUN WAS DRIFTING LAZILY over the horizon when Teo awakened with Jin, still naked but holding her knife against his throat. The blade had already bitten him lightly, causing his neck to almost itch. He blinked slowly, hoping that the image before him would shimmer and disappear, a remnant of some wicked dream. To his dismay his companion remained where she was when his eyes opened again. He opened his mouth to speak but then closed it again, his eyes getting hot. Jin's eyes betrayed a hint of sadness, but a moment later they were flint again.

Jin eased back onto the balls of her feet so that Teo could sit slightly upright, the point of the knife now resting at his groin. He was still in shock, just barely taking note of his surroundings. His clothes were piled nearby, just out of reach. Carefully she leaned over and grabbed them, tossing them to him.

"Get dressed slowly. Then I am going to bind your hands," she said calmly.

"Why?" he asked, the tenor of his voice betraying his rage. The word was harder to get out than it should have been, but his tongue had begun to stick to the roof of his mouth.

Slowly, he began to dress.

"I have always respected you Teo. You were a good fighter and a good lover. When Drex and Quake started this damned crusade, I knew that it would be the death of us, of all of us. But I also knew that there would be no convincing you to run; you are no coward after all. It was far easier for me to escape alone, in any case. One of the Jakobs tried to stop me when he noticed what was happening and I slit his throat. It wasn't until later the next day that I decided to track you and see what had happened. That's when I found you."

"You went through all of that trouble to kill me after one last night together?" He clenched his fists.

"No. I had hoped that you would have had some money on you," she began. "Some of the spoils that I couldn't grab when I ran. I was only able to make it away with some food and a few coins. When I went through your clothes this morning and found that you had nothing, I made up my mind. A few years before I joined up with you a man tried to rob me. Needless to say, I was fine, and he wasn't. I dragged his half-dead ass to Seatown where I sold him to the Paladins as a bandit, even though he was nothing like us. They gave me several gold pieces, the blessings of the faith and hung the bastard on the wharf. I didn't want you to die Teo, I still don't, but I need money. I will never sell myself on the streets, and I don't think I have it in me to join up with another group like we had. I'm tired of running. I need a fresh start. I'm sorry."

He was fully clothed now, crouched directly across from her. She was still naked. It seemed that she had decided against clothing herself until his hands were bound, lest he seize the opportunity to free himself. She was holding the knife looser now, he noticed, though it was still just a few inches away from cutting him in the wrong place. Her brown eyes seemed black in the shadows of the trees. The breeze blowing past didn't bring her scent on it. Teo must have been upwind. That made what he had decided to do easier.

Teo lunged at Jin, wrapping his hands tight around her throat. He felt the knife bite deep into his leg, just below his waist but mercifully missing any major blood vessels. The pain of the wound only made him squeeze tighter, his fingers digging into the soft flesh of her neck. She tried to pull the knife free, but he pinned her arm with his knee, shattering bone.

Her silent screams continued for several minutes until her blue lips finally stopped quivering. Her eyes were bulging from her skull now, making her face a hideous mockery of what it had once been. It was then that he felt the pain in his leg. Looking down Teo saw that her body was covered in his blood where it seeped from his wound. He shuddered as he pulled the blade free, putting as much weight on the opening as he could to desperately try and stem the flow. The pain was becoming unbearable now, not just in his leg but somewhere in his stomach as well. Finally after groping around he was able to find her clothes and force some of them into the wound. He bound it with the cord that she had intended to bind him with, then he collapsed beside her.

Why did you make me do this? Why didn't I just let you do what you wanted? I didn't want this.

"Damn you," he whispered. "Damn you all."

How long he laid there he did not know. When he eventually stood he grabbed the bedroll and threw it over her body, covering her from the elements as much as he was willing. He would have buried her if he had the stomach, but he could not bear to be around her any longer. He wasn't sure why, but he began walking north, ignoring the horse that was still hitched further down the slope. No doubt something would eat the poor beast if he didn't free it, but he no longer cared.

Teo walked up through the hills toward the peaks of the mountains, his unshod feet pricking and bleeding from every loose stone. He didn't notice, nor did he stop to think of why he even continued to climb the mountain slope. Perhaps he finally decided to sate his curiosity about what truly lay beyond the borders of those mountains before he took his own life. Perhaps he didn't have the courage to actually end his own miserable existence and he hoped that something of the dangerous creatures that prowled the upper slopes would do it for him. Either way he continued on without rest.

Hours passed, and still he stumbled on navigating the treacherous stones and footholds, crawling over fallen logs and squeezing between tight trees. The smells of the wood reminded him of hunting with his father once when he was a boy. At one point he thought that he could hear talking off in the distance, beyond the pines to his left, hidden under the sounds of running water. The thought of seeing other people, no matter who they might have been, frightened him more than he ever could have imagined. His pace quickened as fast he could manage so that he could be rid of the voices. Teo's lips became dry and they cracked under the weight of his tongue when he tried to wet them. His leg ached from the wound that still leaked blood down the leg of his pants. Deep down he knew that it would not be long until he found death and returned to the High God.

After an eternity of climbing through the mountain forest the corpse that had been Teo stumbled out of the trees into a clearing. The clearing looked as if half of the mountainside had been scooped away by some giant hand. In the middle of the empty space was an immense stone structure the likes of which Teo had never before seen. It was wide and low, easily larger than any building in Illux other than the Grand Cathedral. The building was cut from a smooth grey stone that seemed more polished than weathered, even though he knew that it was ancient. Other than the windows that were cut into its sides at various intervals, its face held only a set of giant iron doors. Off to the side of the building was a dirt field in which many men and women in grey were sparring.

The Grey Temple.

It seemed that the stories he had heard his entire life of the Temple, in which the servants of Ravim—the God of Balance—lived, had been true. Here in the mountains, at the roof of the world, was a collection of people who did not owe allegiance to either the Gods of Darkness or the Gods of Light. The forces of evil dared not tread here, nor did the laws of Illux hold sway. Even so, the wildness of the Rim had been replaced by order, and from what Teo could feel deep inside: power.

Almost numbly, he continued toward the iron gates of the Temple, awestruck by the very sight of it. He was drawn toward those gates in a trance-like state, forgoing the fear of being seen by other humans that he had so strongly felt further down the slope. When he got nearer a man in grey robes stepped out from within the shadows of the building to address him. The man was bald, his dark skin covered in swirling grey tattoos that matched the fabric of his dress. In one hand, he held a wooden staff that looked solid enough to break bone.

The man looked old and young at the same time, and his expression was calmer than Teo would have thought possible.

"Welcome, servant of Darkness," he boomed.

Teo stood speechless. After a time he croaked. "How?"

"Our scouts near the fields below spotted you and sent up word," the man replied almost softly now. "You are the bandit Teo. The Grey God was told of your approach and he spoke of your crimes. Some more recent than others."

That is not possible. The gods cannot truly see us.

"How do you know my name?" Teo asked.

"The Grey God has seen you, would-be bandit king. Your group hid on the steps of his mountains. Did you truly think that we did not watch your actions from afar? The Grey God only allowed you to continue raiding because it did little to disrupt the Balance of the world. He has gazed through Aenna above to look upon your suffering and guide you on the path that would lead to him. But you must accept his ways to achieve balance."

Teo looked down at himself and saw that he was covered in blood from the waist down. In his hand, he still dumbly clutched at the knife that Jin had tried to kill him with. With his other hand, he instinctively pulled out his own knife that had hung from his belt, forgotten until that moment.

"Who did you kill today, servant of Darkness?" the man asked.

"That isn't your concern. Give me some water and I will be one my way."

"We would never turn away a traveler, nor would we welcome a killer," the man said firmly. "Name the man you killed today."

"It was a woman," Teo whispered. "Her name…She was going to sell me to the Paladins. I…I had no choice."

"We always have a choice, Teo of the spilled blood. You have one before you now. What was her name?"

"Jin."

Teo looked at the bloody knife again, and then back at the man before him. He lifted the blade slowly, not thinking of what he would do with it. His mind still struggled to accept where he was and who he was speaking with, but something about that blade grounded him and brought him comfort. Before he could even see it move, the staff in the man's hand flashed out and shattered Teo's fingers, sending the blade flying out of sight. The staff flashed past twice more, sending the other knife to the ground and dropping Teo to his knees.

"You will never again say her name or see her face. She is of your old life, a life that is no more. Not until you are ready to rejoin the High God will 'Jin' again pass your lips. All men may change. Even our Grey God was a servant of Darkness once," the man said. "You too may find peace in the balance of things. The same peace that he himself has found."

Teo felt tears welling up in his eyes. Whether they were from the pain of his broken hand or something else he could not be sure. Something in back of his mind began to whisper to him, a voice that urged him to give himself over and be free of his pain.

"I want to be free of her. Of the guilt of what I have done. I have nothing left."

"Then come."

The Balance Monk outstretched his hand and Teo took it. The man pulled Teo to his feet and led him into the Temple behind them, out of the blinding light of the late-day sun. Even as they passed through the threshold, Teo felt a feeling that he hadn't felt since he was a child.

For the first time in over a decade, he was at peace.

DISCIPLES OF
THE FIRST CYCLE

DISCIPLES OF THE FIRST CYCLE

1042 AP

The two Balance Monks fled the Grey Temple on horseback. Behind them followed seven others. Tyrek leaned into his horse as he urged it down the mountainside into the towering trees of the forests below. This was suicide. He could feel the presence of Ravim, the Grey God, pressing down on his soul. It felt as if the disapproval of the divine being could crush him.

A bola flew from behind, nearly catching the legs of his horse. He knew the deft hand that would have thrown the weapon: Chell.

The huntress.

Chell was the foremost Balance Monk tasked with enforcing the Balance of the world with violence. It was Chell some sixteen years before who had helped defeat the rogue Paladin Cecilia as she tried to raze Seatown. She had nearly killed Tyrek then, as well. If she caught up to the two of them, they were as good as dead.

Just to his side, Elra slumped in her saddle, blood dripping from her bald head. Clutched tightly to her chest was the reason for their departure: *The First Cycle*, a codex that she had stolen from the most sacred section of the temple library.

The contents of this book had nearly driven her to madness. When she shared what she had learned with Tyrek, he knew that he could stay a Balance Monk no longer. Ravim be damned.

"Apostates!" Chell shouted. "Stop and face justice!"

Two monks lay dead in the Grey Temple because of them. But how many untold thousands were dead because of what was in this book?

The feeling of Ravim pressed on him again. Unlike the Seraphs and Heralds of the Light and Darkness, communication with the Divine Plane came not from Divine Blood, but from the harmony that Balance Monks shared with the world. For Tyrek, that harmony had been shattered, and therefore his connection to the Grey God would be severed. That didn't stop the disappointed deity from focusing on the runaway with his incredible will.

Above, Aenna, the opening to the Divine Plane, leered at him ominously. It was likely that Ravim watched the pair through it.

Leave us alone. Your lies hold no power on us any longer!

Tyrek's horse shrieked as it stumbled over the uneven terrain, throwing him to the ground.

THE FIRES of Seatown raged around him. The city was in chaos. Women and children ran in front of him, their clothing in flames. His stomach churned. Cecilia had led them here to raze the entire settlement. He knew that. Killing hadn't been a problem before. But seeing it like this...

He struck down the first child to make it to him, a little boy barely able to walk.

A mercy.

The quick cut of steel was better than the slow death of fire. That is what he told himself again and again and he sought out and finished the helpless villagers that were dying from Cecilia's wrath. The Paladin woman was crazed. Tyrek doubted that she even wanted to survive this onslaught.

He was barely a man himself, having joined up with her band shortly after running away from home. He followed her for the same reason the rest of them did: her raw power meant they would be rich.

If he had to kill a few travelers here and there, so be it. It was better than eking out a squalid existence in the slums of Illux. But this?

A man with a sword charged him, swinging wildly.

"My son!" the man shouted, tears streaming down his face.

Tyrek gutted him with the same blade, still slick with the boy's blood. The bandit began to go numb. He thought of his parents. He thought of his sister and the pain he had caused her. For a brief moment, his guilt threatened to overtake him. Then he saw the Balance Monk.

He had never seen a Balance Monk before, but he had heard the stories. She wore grey flowing robes, and her body was covered in tattoos of the same dull color. The woman moved faster than anything he had ever seen. Faster even than Cecilia.

The Balance Monk quickly dispatched her enemy and prepared to fight others just as she was surrounded. Even though fear gripped him, Tyrek was drawn toward this adversary.

Better than a child, at least.

He joined the throng of bandits preparing to strike. Some of them seemed to have gone mad, just like their leader. They were baying at the woman like hounds. She seemed nonplussed at their far superior numbers. Tyrek swallowed. His initial courage began to ebb.

"Flee if you value your lives," a deep voice said.

Tyrek turned to see the Admiral of Seatown and a host of organized guards streaming into the courtyard like a wave from the ocean. The bandit line broke before the city's defenders even reached them. Tyrek turned to flee, his bravery completely broken, when he felt the sharp pain of his arm snapping in two.

He cried out, but his ears rang so loudly he couldn't ever hear himself. The bronze-skinned Balance Monk locked eyes with him for a moment before tossing him aside like a rag doll. Fire and darkness overtook him.

TYREK CAUGHT HIMSELF, rolling from the fall and back to his feet in the same fluid motion. He spun around to see his horse lying on its side, one leg broken. It whinnied weakly as it lifted its head to look at him. He spat.

This is where it ends. At least I will die a free man.

"Face me, bitch!" he shouted.

Elra rode past him, not even looking back. Some small part of him felt abandoned. Then he had another thought, an almost chivalrous one; to hold their pursuers off so that she might escape with the book. Perhaps she could tell others about the lies of the Grey Temple and the Fourth Spire. That fleeting moment of bravery faltered as his innate desire for self-preservation again took hold.

Four of the riders flew past him, while Chell and two others pulled to a stop and sprang from their saddles. They each took aggressive stances, raising staffs and fists alike. Tyrek lowered himself to a crouch and bared his teeth like a wild animal.

"You think you can be victorious today?" he asked. "Even if you kill me, I've broken free."

"You speak madness," Chell whispered. "The same madness of your former master. I thought you were free of her. Clearly, I was mistaken."

"You think this is madness? You think I hold the same taint as that Paladin bitch? No, the opposite, huntress. I have clarity that has been shared with me by Elra. She showed me the truth of the Mortal Plane. The lies are falling away. Just ask your Grey God!"

As if summoned by name, the weight of Ravim grew suddenly more oppressive. It threw Tyrek off balance, just as Chell and the others attacked. The first blow came from a staff that connected with his shoulder, knocking it out of place. Next, a flurry of punches sent him tumbling backward.

The former bandit regained his footing and caught the next strike from the staff. He yanked it from the hands of its owner, a newer member of the order. Tyrek jammed the staff back into the man's chest so hard he collapsed in a heap.

Unfazed, Chell sprang onto him, unleashing another flurry of blows. Tyrek twisted away from her, sprinting down the mountainside. His base nature had returned, after all.

. . .

"Don't linger, someone will notice," Elra whispered.

Tyrek sighed and followed her deeper into the library. When she had asked him to meet her here in the middle of the night, he had hoped that it was because she wanted to have sex with him inside the Grey Temple for a change. Instead, she seemed to want to show him something she had found that they wouldn't have been allowed to view during the day.

She led him to the rear of the library, past the room where monks toiled during the day to make copies of the great tomes within the library. Here in the deepest recess, was where the restricted books were kept. Some were stored here for their content; deemed too dangerous for the average scholar, while others were kept here out of reverence because they were thought to have originated from the hands of Ravim himself.

The book that Elra wanted to show him was a combination of both kinds.

"*The First Cycle,*" she said, almost fervently.

The ancient-looking text seemed almost as if it would crumble into dust as she slid it off the shelf. Careful so as not to get it too near the candle she held in her other hand, she lowered it to the floor and opened the metal fastening holding the cover closed.

"I started coming here a few months ago. At first, I just wanted to see what a book written by a god looked like. But then I started to notice titles that weren't in the library proper. *The Name of the High God, Journals of Nocta the Seraph, What Lies Beyond the Nameless Sea?*, and finally, this."

"Get to the point, Elra," Tyrek said.

I don't want to get caught back here.

"The point is that this book contradicts everything we have been told about the creation and history of the Mortal Plane! Don't you get it? I think they have been hiding this because it tells the truth of the world!"

Tyrek sighed and rubbed his temples. He had grown close to this woman over the last few years in the temple, but her penchant for exaggeration and her desire to spend her free time poring over old books had always grated on him. He knew he was a poor excuse for a Balance Monk, but he was safe here, at least. No fear of Demons or bandits in the Temple. No judgment for past sins. That is what had kept him for the better part of two decades. The studies, the meditation, the training, it was all a chore to him at best. He imagined that for Elra it was the same, at least as far as the commitment to the Balance was. She did sleep with him, after all.

"None of what you are saying makes any sense." He turned away.

"Wait!" She exclaimed, her whisper almost becoming a shout. The woman gripped his arm like a band of iron. "Look for yourself."

Something in his mind told him to listen to her. Something told him to look. The light of her candle flickered across the old page and the neat script written on it.

THE BOULDERS and fallen trees on this patch of the mountain had slowed the horses. Tyrek was nearly upon them. He shook off the fear that had overtaken him earlier and sprang through the air, knocking one of the riders to the ground. Gripping the reins, Tyrek angled the horse for Elra, who was slowing in front of them.

"Elra!" he shouted. "Keep going!"

The woman looked over her shoulder at him, blood mingling with the tattoos on her face. She flashed a weak smile and turned back around. The other three riders closed in on him as she pulled ahead.

Gods. I'm a fool.

Tyrek jumped from his fresh mount, focusing all of his strength into a single kick. He broke the neck of another horse, throwing the rider face-first into a fallen tree. A woman jumped onto Tyrek as he tried to stand. His cruelty from his short stint as a bandit came flooding back into him. He blocked her initial blows and followed his defense up by gouging out her left eye. As she recoiled, screaming, he wiped the gore from her eye on his robe and returned to his sprint down the mountain.

Behind him, Chell and her companion were getting closer. Ahead, Elra and her pursuer pulled away as the ground began to clear of obstacles. All around the forest grew silent, save the sounds of the chase.

His body was beginning to tire. Even imbued with the energy of the Grey God, Balance Monks didn't have unlimited stamina. Tyrek knew that he would start to slow soon, and once he did, he was as good as dead.

What he was hoping for, he wasn't sure. But just as something had compelled him to listen to Elra and read that blasted codex those many nights ago, something kept him running now, even as the presence of the Grey God began to fade in his mind. He had made the decision to survive this, no matter the cost.

He had returned to read the book with Elra every night since the first. Now, as he approached the final pages, he felt an emptiness creep into his soul. Something told him that what he had been reading was no fabrication, no matter how outlandish it sounded. They were reading a true accounting of the Mortal Plane, long before the war between the Gods of Light and the Gods of Darkness.

When he finished the last page, Tyrek closed the book and leaned back against the wall. Beside him, the candle was nothing more than a stump. Outside, the sun would soon be rising over the neighboring peaks and lighting the windows of the library.

Elra lay next to him, asleep. She had passed out an hour before, finally unable to fight her drowsiness while he read in silence. He studied her form through her robes. The curve of her breasts as her chest rose and fell. Not for the first time she reminded him of his sister.

Forgive me.

He turned away, suddenly filled with great shame. He had forgiven himself most of his sins during his time at the Grey Temple, but some specters refused to stop haunting him. His mind wandering back to his short time following the Paladin Cecilia as they raided and razed villages. He had killed countless innocents during that time, for the promise of riches and power that had never come.

Truth be told, he missed the freedom of his old life. Or at least, the promise of freedom that it had held. Life under Cecilia had been anything but free. He had traded the stern rule of his father for the ravings of a madwoman who was just as likely to kill one of her own as she was an enemy. Still, since reading this tome, he was beginning to wish for his old life. Why stay committed to the ideals of Balance if they were built on a lie? Ravim wasn't keeping the Forces of Light and the Forces of Darkness apart for the reasons that he claimed.

Out of the corner of his eye, the book caught his attention again in the fading light of the candle. Just as it sputtered out, he knew what he wanted to do.

"Elra," he whispered. "Wake up. Grab the book. We're getting out of here."

"What?" she asked sleepily.

"You heard me. We have to move quickly, before we are seen. You and I can't stay here any longer."

She nodded as she sat up, pulling the book close.

Just then, voices from another part of the library set them both on edge. Tyrek crouched, holding a finger to his mouth and motioning for Elra to follow him. Together, they crept between bookshelves and tried to make their escape from the rear of the library.

At first, all went well. Then Tyrek stumbled into another monk who was rounding a corner with a candle in hand. The hot wax spilled, burning Elra's hand and causing her to scream and drop the book. The other monk tried to cry out at well, but Tyrek clamped a hand over his mouth and pressed him against the row of books. The man looked confused at first, but then his eyes fell on *The First Cycle*. He grew very pale and tried to struggle under Tyrek's grip. His old life returned him again as he snapped the monk's neck.

He thought Elra would scream, but she simply picked up the book, her face expressionless. Then the presence of Ravim filled his mind, and he collapsed to his knees. Elra tried to help him up when a staff caught her across the forehead, sending her spinning into a bookshelf.

"Murderers! Apostates! What have you done?" The woman shouted.

Knowing he would have to kill again, Tyrek sprang.

CHELL WAS on his back before he even realized she had caught him. Her fury was palpable as she bore him to the ground with a flurry of blows. Tyrek spun from beneath her, his body writhing in agony as he did so.

Another Balance Monk sprang at Tyrek as he broke free of Chell's grasp. Instinctively, he aimed a blow at the man's throat, catching him unawares. The monk dropped to the ground, gasping for his last breath. Tyrek dropped as a kick from Chell passed over his head. Her face, normally calm and collected, contorted into rage.

"I should have killed you in Seatown! How could the Grey God have willed this?"

"Ravim's power is built on lies! I never truly believed them. And now I know why!"

They attacked each other at nearly the same time, each matching the blows from the other with masterful precision. His command of hand-to-hand combat had been gleaned from the tutelage of the very woman he tried to kill.

I want you to regret ever finding me.

One of his punches made it through her defenses and connected with her jaw. The Balance Monk collapsed. Tyrek used the momentary pause to run once more. He knew that he had merely gotten lucky, as his strength was rapidly failing. If she caught up to him again, he wouldn't survive the encounter.

Ahead, two horses rushed past him from beneath the trees. Elra and her pursuer were no longer mounted. With her injuries, Tyrek doubted she would last long. He paused to consider heading after her, but quickly headed in the opposite direction.

I can't risk slowing.

Tyrek jumped over a fallen log and nearly lost his footing. He had almost tumbled over a ledge into a deep ravine.

"Fuck sake," he swore.

Chell sprang from the side, sweeping his legs and sending him sprawling. At the last moment, he caught the ledge. He didn't have the strength to pull himself up. This was surely going to be his end.

Just then, out of the corner of his eye, Tyrek saw a shadowy figure emerge from the trees behind Chell. His breath caught in his throat. It was Elra, but she looked completely changed. She no longer slouched, and her eyes burned with hatred.

"You serve the God of Deceit," she whispered. Her voice made Tyrek shiver. "No longer will you hold sway in these ancient mountains. The Primordial Ones speak through me, and I am their vengeance."

Chell tried to turn on Elra, but she was quickly tossed aside. The huntress slammed against a boulder, and her head slumped to the side. Elra, it seemed, had gained more strength than Tyrek knew was possible.

"How?" he sputtered as she grabbed his arm.

"Faith," she replied.

Suddenly, Chell was behind Elra, pulling free *The First Cycle* from the distracted woman's grasp. Both Elra and Tyrek tried to call out but the world fell away as they tumbled together into the ravine.

WHEN TYREK OPENED HIS EYES, the smell of smoke still filled the air. The sun had turned the morning sky the color of blood. A spear-point pressed against his throat.

"This one lives!" a voice shouted.

Every part of his body ached. He was certain that at least one leg was broken. Rough hands gripped him by the arms and pulled him to his feet. Tyrek was dragged over to a line of familiar faces. They were the last surviving bandits of Cecelia's raid. The Seatown guards stood with weapons at the ready.

"They will meet the sea's justice," a man said. "Bind them and drop them in the ocean."

"No!" one of the bandits cried. "Please, have mercy! Use a blade at least!"

"Mercy?" the man growled. "I'll show you the same mercy you showed my folk."

He grabbed the bandit who had been speaking and hacked off the man's hand at the wrist.

"Admiral!" a woman shouted.

Tyrek turned to see the Balance Monk looking on disapprovingly. She glowered at the guards and bandits in equal measure.

"Ravim has uses for these," she said, coolly. "They only need to ask to be taken in by the Grey Temple."

"Nonsense!" the Admiral shouted. "The Grey God has no power here. I appreciate your help protecting my people, but I'll see these men drowned."

This is my only chance.

Tyrek fell to his knees. The guards closest to him lifted their swords.

"Please, I wish to join the Balance Monks. Take me to the Grey Temple. I wish to change my fate."

"Silence!" the Admiral yelled over him. "Long have your people taken in those who flee to your temple in the mountains, but I do not recall the followers of the Light ever being forced to give them prisoners. Be gone, lest you have even more blood on your hands, *monk.*"

Chell stepped between the line of bandits and the Admiral. She raised her hands to fight him.

"The Pact keeps the Balance in the world, Admiral. It keeps the peace. And in this moment, it keeps those who would forsake their old ways and follow Ravim safe. Stand down, or we will purge Seatown as we did Illux in ages past."

The Admiral cut off the head of the wounded man in front of him with one clean stroke. Then he motioned to his men, and they left the Balance Monks and bandits alone.

"Those of you who will not give their lives to Ravim, speak now," she said. "If any of you attempt to go back on your pledge to the Grey God, I will show you no mercy."

Tyrek swallowed hard but nodded. What choice did he have?

He laid at the bottom of the ravine for what felt like a lifetime. His fall had been broken by several tree branches that caught him on his way to the bottom. Though he had not died, as it was likely that Chell assumed, he was certain that his injuries would be severe. When the sun began to creep lower behind the tree line, casting the ravine into shadows, he tried sitting up.

That's when he saw Elra crouched and staring at him. Her expression was one of concern. Indeed, her features were more familiar to him than they had been on the cliff above. Whatever had come over her seemed to have passed—for now.

"You live," she whispered.

"Aye," he said. "As do you."

"A blessing," she said, distantly.

Tyrek slowly stood, his entire body aching. Miraculously, nothing seemed to be broken. He scanned the growing darkness above for any signs of Chell. It seemed that she had truly taken them for dead and moved on. Above, Aenna still hung overhead menacingly. If Ravim watched them, he would know the truth, and it wouldn't be long before the pursuit continued.

"She has the book," Elra said.

"She does, and all the better."

"I thought you wanted to share it with the world, like I did?" she asked.

I just want to live.

"Not anymore. I don't care about the truth or the gods, I only care about survival. Unfortunately, now that my body bears these tattoos, I won't be able to hide in a village or even Illux. Gods be good, my only hope is to become a bandit again, and live off of caravans until the Grey Temple comes for me."

"I can't believe that you could know the truth about the Mortal Plane and choose to go back to *that*." Elra glared at him, some of the fire returning to her eyes. "You are a fool, Tyrek. A fool and a coward.

I will regain that book, find my way to Artorus, and free the true gods."

Tyrek turned and started walking away from her. There was no use talking any longer. She had lost her mind. How could he blame her, though? They had both read the same words in that book, and somehow they both knew them to be true. The Gods of Light and the Gods of Darkness were not the first divine beings sent to the Mortal Plane by the High God. There were other, far older beings in the world, and they were imprisoned beyond the Rim, and if they were ever let loose, the entire Mortal Plane would burn.

Let it burn, then.

Tyrek left without saying another word, and he tried to forget the Primordial Gods of *The First Cycle*, but he knew, just as the Grey Temple would eventually come for him, so too would the nightmares.

I'd best have all the fun I can, then.

THE GREY GOD'S EDICT

I.

1042 AP

The heavy tome pulled on the Balance Monk's saddlebag so much that she feared it would unbalance the horse. Somehow, what she had thought was just a simple book stolen by two apostates had become a burden to her in the days that she followed her quarry. It was as if it got heavier the deeper into the Rim she traveled. How could that be so? Even being from the restricted area of the Grey Temple, it was just a book.

You will understand in time.

Ravim's voice reverberated through her mind. Normally, Chell would need to meditate to hear the words that came from the Divine Plane. But ever since Tyrek and Elra had killed two of their brethren and run from the Grey Temple, it seemed as though Ravim had begun speaking to Chell unheeded. Something about these apostates had stirred an interest in the God of Balance—something about these apostates, and *that book.*

She had burned the image of the book into her mind's eye when she had recovered it from Elra. It was mostly unassuming: a traditional leather cover with gold clasps holding it together. The cover was beginning to show its age and several of the pages crumbled to the touch. Written on the cover in the relatively neat script of most of the Balance Monks was the title: *The First Cycle*. Yet the simple-looking book filled Chell with unease. So far, she had refused to look at it these past few days that she tracked her quarry, but she knew that she wouldn't be able to resist its call for long.

Chell had mistakenly thought that Elra and Tyrek had fallen to their deaths the week before. During their struggle, she had recovered the tome and both apostates had tumbled from the edge of a cliff. Gathering her wounded, Chell made her way back to the Grey Temple to mourn and meditate. No sooner had she arrived did Ravim's voice fill her mind: the apostates lived, and if she didn't catch them, the entire Mortal Plane was in grave danger. Chell would have assembled another hunting party, but she was instructed to go after them alone. It was the Grey God's edict, and she would not disobey.

Her horse picked its way through the rocky trail that headed to the north. Ravim had instructed her to follow this ancient path to a pass that would lead through the Rim of Paradise to the lands beyond. There was no record of what lay beyond the mountains. It was said that none who ventured there ever returned.

Towering oaks and pines shaded her bronze skin from the sun, leaving a mottled path of lights and darks on the path ahead of her. Her tracking skills had told her that the two apostates had split up very near to where they had fallen. Ravim told her that Tyrek could be ignored. It was the woman, Elra, who was the threat to the Balance.

It was something about this book.

Chell again fought the urge to rest her horse and read whatever had started her on this quest. She sighed and whispered words of encouragement to her mount. Her resolve would last until the evening, at least. She had never before been one to question the commands of her superiors or her god. Never before had she questioned the Balance of the world. Not when she had fought Paladins and bandits in Seatown, nor when she brought a Paladin into the Grey Temple, nor even again when that Paladin rejoined the Fourth Spire in Illux. She knew that everything happened for a reason, and all things served to bring about the Balance. So why was her desire to read this book so strong? Ravim hadn't directly forbidden it to her, but the book had been stored in the restricted section of the library, and therefore she had no right to look into its pages.

The path suddenly terminated at a large boulder. She could see it begin again higher up the slope where the trees had started to thin. Hopefully, this meant that she was nearing the mouth of the pass. If the terrain was rougher on the other side, she might have to abandon her horse to continue her hunt on foot. If for no other reason, she hoped that wasn't the case so that she could more easily overtake Elra once they reached open ground.

The Balance Monk dismounted and inspected the end of the trail for any signs of her quarry. Ravim had continued to watch her through the Basin and Aenna, so she assumed that if she was heading in the wrong direction the Grey God would surely have let her know. Still, it was hard for her to track only by faith, so she chose to rely on her mortal senses as well. It seemed that the apostate had rested here after all.

In her previous life, Chell had been a tracker by trade, first of game for villages that didn't have enough livestock, then of bandits that the Paladins didn't want to spend the manpower hunting down themselves. She had been paid well and greatly enjoyed plying her trade. Then she stumbled across a band of Demons and Accursed that quickly overpowered her. Nearly blind from the wounds left on her face, she waited with several others to be turned into Accursed and face a lifetime of damnation. This was when she had been saved by the servants of Ravim.

Chell led her horse around the boulder and back onto the trail above. Once they were back on the trail, she climbed back onto her mount and continued ahead, trying vainly to push the doubts and memories from her mind.

The trees began to give way to scrub grass and smaller shrubs. The air was much cooler here. She hoped that the pass would cut through the mountains before she reached the snow line. In the distance, a wolf howled. Chell smiled in spite of herself; she hadn't felt the thrill of a wolf hunt since before she was a Balance Monk.

By the time the sun had set behind the mountains to the west of her, she had gained entry to the mountain pass. The makeshift trail cut between two peaks and curved back on itself in a series of switchbacks that descended the slope into the distance. Near the mouth of the pass was a cleft in the rock that made for a suitable campsite. Once she had bedded down her horse, she went about searching for wood to make a small fire. Normally she wouldn't risk being seen, but as the night grew darker, she knew that it would get much colder and she couldn't risk sickness coming to her or her horse.

You are close, Chell. It's time you read the book.

She shivered at the sound of Ravim in her mind. He was telling her to read it. There was nothing stopping her now. So why did fear grip her still? Chell reached into the saddlebag and pulled the book free. The firelight danced along its surface, making the letters of the title seem to come alive. *The First Cycle.* Leaning back into her horse for warmth, Chell opened the book.

II.

Chell had to give extra care so as not to destroy the pages as she read the ancient tome. She found that no matter how tired she got, she couldn't put the book down. What she saw on those pages both horrified and excited her:

This is an accounting of the First Cycle of the world now known as the Mortal Plane, as taken down by Ravim, previously a God of Darkness, and now the God of Balance. What is written here is not for mortal eyes, lest they find themselves living in fear of the true nature of the High God's creation, but I take this account down at His request so that if something should happen to disrupt the Balance, Artorus can still be protected by those who shall come after me.

The Lesser Gods, those of us created to give mortals the choice between good and evil so that they might earn their place on the Astral Plane by the High God's side, were not, in fact, the first deities created by the High God. What we had been told, and what the mortals had been taught, was a complete lie. What follows is the truth:

In the beginning, the High God created the Mortal Plane, first of all of the Realms of Creation. The Mortal Plane was created to lock out those who stood in opposition to the High God: the Empty Gods.

The very act of creation was an anathema to them, and it shackled them outside of the Realms. Yet unbeknownst to even the High God, their powers would seep into creation in an attempt to corrupt it and lead all back to the void before creation.

After locking His enemies Outside, the High God sought to bring life and order to the Mortal Plane to ensure that it would keep the Empty Gods sapped of power for all time. To do this, He created the first gods below himself: the Primordial Gods. These were fashioned after the very elements of creation, and imbued with the High God's own power to create from nothing. This new pantheon went about creating the Mortal Plane as the High God desired. To help them in their task, each of the Primordial Gods created their own servants, species of great power that surpassed that of the mortals that live on the Mortal Plane today. Seeing that this was good, the High God left the ancient world to create other worlds even more beautiful and strange.

This was when the Empty Gods began to seep into the young world.

None of the Primordial Gods knew of the Empty Gods or the dangers that they posed, so when the avatars of the old enemies began to walk among them, they thought they had been joined by new creations of the High God, and they rejoiced. The Primordial Gods shared their powers with those creatures, and even as it harmed them, the Empty Gods used this power to corrupt creation.

The servitor species began to wage war against one another in an attempt to unmake creation. Their fighting reshaped the ancient world from what it had been when the High God had left it. Soon, just as it seemed that the Empty Gods had won and they would be free to return all to the void, the High God returned and set His creation in order.

There was much bloodshed as the Primordial Gods and their servants turned against the creator that they once worshiped so fever-ishly. Nearly all of them were wiped out in the fighting which left much of the Mortal Plane in ruin. It was then that the High God sought to begin anew, learning from some of His mistakes in the ancient world.

Though their creations were by and large destroyed, the Primordial Gods themselves were saved, for the High God saw them as His first children. He shaped a prison for them, Artorus, and placed it in a remote part of the Mortal Plane. This prison would hold them for all time, so long as none who were corrupted by their madness sought to free them. To ensure their eternal damnation, the High God empowered one of the servitors who had been untouched by the taint of the Empty Gods to stand as the eternal guardian of Artorus.

Then the High God raised a mountain range to block Artorus from the lands to the south where He planned to begin anew. It was only then, after the Primordial Gods had been imprisoned, and their servants scattered around the world, that the High God first created humanity, and thus the Second Cycle of the world began.

We Lesser Gods were made not in the High God's image, but in humanity's, to give the mortals the chance to choose righteousness over wickedness, and in the hope that by having this choice of their own desires, they would be hardier against the whispers of the Empty Gods. Another lesson that He had learned, was not to give the Lesser Gods his power of raw creation. Though we carry His Divine Blood, we cannot create whole cloth, instead, we can only change that which He has already made. He also created for us the Divine Plane, our own realm with which we could take respite from the mortals so that we did not become as connected to the Mortal Plane itself as our predecessors.

When the war between the Gods of Light and the Gods of Darkness grew to the point that one of our own was slain, the High God knew that His work was not finished, and he raised me to be His voice and the keeper of the Balance, lest the whispers of the enemy seep back into the world and the minds of mortals.

It is for this very reason that I constructed the Grey Temple where I did in the Rim, to prevent those who would do harm to creation from traveling past the Rim and into Artorus. Still, I cannot share this directly with my monks, lest curiosity or madness overtake them.

Knowledge is a dangerous thing, and simply knowing the truth of creation makes one susceptible to the whispers from Outside. To keep my mind from succumbing, I must spend most of my time in meditation while I monitor the Mortal Plane below.

If you are reading this account, it is possible that I have been killed. To my servants, seek out Artorus and aid the Eternal Guardian there, lest he be overwhelmed by the agents of the enemy. Still, this knowledge cannot become widespread, or else we risk the Primordial Gods being freed and destruction coming upon the Mortal Plane.

If I still live and you have opened your mind to this knowledge, know that it is a curse, and you will find yourself hearing them in time…

Chell was shaking when she closed the book. That had only been the introduction. It seemed that the rest of the heavy tome outlined the specific history of the First Cycle and the various cultures and histories of the Primordial God's servitors. She shuddered at the thought of the voices from outside creation whispering to her, driving her to madness.

So that is what drove Elra and Tyrek to kill and flee. They have already been tainted.

Elra has, Tyrek has not. The truth shook his already weakening convictions in our cause and placed him back on the path of wickedness, but he is not yet their pawn. Elra though, will attempt to attack the Eternal Guardian and bring down the walls of Artorus to free those she now sees as the true gods of this realm.

The voice of Ravim brought her some peace for the moment. Even as he explained the peril to her, his presence was calm and comforting.

May I ask why I was sent after her? Should we not have left this up to the Guardian? Am I not now in danger of this taint myself?

The power of the Guardian has begun to wane. Without the constant presence of the High God, he grows weak. We must ensure that he doesn't fall to this woman, for she surely has grown in power since she fled the temple. Do not despair, my child, I chose you specifically because you could resist the call of the Outside. They have little direct power over the High God's creation, so they attempt to influence and deceive. You will not fall to them.

I understand. What must I do now then?

Time grows short. Get some sleep and continue through the pass in the morning. Artorus is only a few days' ride from you.

Chell leaned back against her horse and watched the flames as they danced. As sleep came closer, she felt as though something in the fire was alive and watching her with hate-filled eyes.

III.

Ravim spoke to her less over the following days. She wasn't sure why the Grey God had abandoned her, but it made her mood grow even more dour. The path through the pass had been more treacherous than she had initially assumed, and her horse had nearly lost its life when an embankment broke way and tumbled below. Still, she carried on until the towering Rim of Paradise was behind her, and a great plain stretched onto the horizon.

She hadn't reopened *The First Cycle* since that first night. Her usually dreamless sleep had become filled with nightmares. There hadn't been any further signs of Elra since the initial campsite Chell had found. She began to worry to herself about how a woman on foot could cover so much ground so quickly.

She surely has grown in power since she fled the temple.

Ravim's words returned to her, cutting across her thoughts like a blade. Chell shuddered. What could that mean? Did the Empty Gods change her body just as surely as they had taken control of her mind?

Though warmer than the mountains had been, this plain north of the Rim was certainly colder than the lands to the south. Chell would have hated to see what the winter looked like here. The grasslands around her were sparse, with little to no large trees or scrub, but the land itself seemed much healthier than that of its southern counter-parts. The taint of the Gods of Darkness had not seeped into the earth here, and that gave Chell some reprieve from her uneasiness.

Animals darted through the grass around her horse's feet, clearly not afraid that a human was among them. The Balance Monk surmised that this was because they had never needed to run from a hunter before. She decided to allow them to keep that security, so she resorted to scavenging for roots and other edible plants to supplement what little supplies she had left. Hopefully, she would catch up to Elra or reach Artorus before she was forced to hunt.

Let these creatures at least live in peace.

That night, she settled down without a fire, deciding that the warmth of her horse would have to be enough on this exposed plain. She couldn't risk Elra knowing that she was being followed, and she didn't like the feeling that staring into the flames gave her now. As she lay there, her thoughts began to wander.

Her faith in Ravim hadn't been shaken by the contents of that book, but she couldn't declare herself as devout as she had been. Everything that mortals had been taught about creation and the cosmology of the Realms of Creation had been a lie; mortals didn't live for their own reasons but to continue to be the unwitting jailers of an ancient foe they had no knowledge of. That fact made her feel betrayed. None of the gods had asked them how they felt about that arrangement.

How much of that book was even true? If Ravim had lied to his monks about that, could anything he told them be trusted?

As the night wore on, her reservations faded into the void of sleep.

SHE RAN through the burning forest. The heat bathed her scales. She wasn't a human; she was something far older. Her tail flicked from side to side as she ran, trying to avoid the flames and giant trees that collapsed around her. She held a crude spear in her hand.

Enemies were ahead. They were the reason for this inferno. She needed to rejoin the others. She needed to find their enemies and kill them.

The whispers urged her on. They told her the truth. They told her to destroy.

A tree fell before her, its last life spent in a deafening crack. She sprang over it, her claws finding purchase on the log. Her tongue licked the air. Even through the acrid smoke, she could tell that they were close. So close.

She jumped down and continued on, the heat receding with the forest behind her.

Then she saw them. Shapes rising out of the darkness, flickering in the shadows like living flame.

She stabbed with the spear at the shapes of her enemies. One fell with a shout, spraying her with hot blood. From behind, she could hear the cries of her companions as they too emerged from the burning forest and joined the fray.

Guttural cries rose from her throat to answer theirs. She didn't recognize the sound, but she understood its fury.

An arrow glanced off of her hide. Then another. She roared again, this time in challenge. One of the shapes lumbered out of the darkness. She barely had time to take in the sight of the creature that was wreathed in flame before the light was taken from her eyes.

CHELL AWOKE SUDDENLY, covered in sweat. This nightmare had been the worst yet. She shivered, even as the light of the sun crept over the plain. Somehow, she had just seen from the eyes of another, and she knew that it had been one of the servitors of the Primordial Gods. She wondered if the Eternal Guardian would be of the same species as the reptilian creature she had been in her dream.

You will reach Artorus today.

The Grey God's voice interrupted her thoughts. He hadn't abandoned her after all.

Go quickly. Your quarry is there already.

Her pulse quickened as she climbed onto her horse. Now this would end, finally. Taking a deep breath to steady her shaking hands, Chell urged her mount into a gallop. The brown and greens of the grasslands rushed past her in a blur.

Then she saw something rising on the horizon, and she knew without a doubt what it was.

Artorus was a glass sphere that looked to be as tall as a mountain. Its surface swirled with a dark amethyst cloud. Standing to each side of the orb were two stone statues, their arms outstretched toward one another and over the top of the glass. She gritted her teeth and leaned down into the saddle, urging her horse to go even faster.

I am nearing the end.

IV.

Artorus loomed over Chell, growing ever larger. Now that she was closer and it filled her field of vision, she could see that not just clouds roamed under the surface of the polished glass; lightning arced across the face of the Primordial Prison, as did gouts of flame and water, bursts of stone, and the swirling of cyclones. She wasn't sure if it always looked this ominous, but it seemed to her that the Primordial Gods were agitated. Perhaps they sensed that one who could free them was close at hand.

There is a temple at the base of the orb. This is where you will find Elra and the Eternal Guardian. Quickly, while there is still time!

The God of Balance filled Chell with renewed vigor. She could tell that he was lending her a portion of his strength for the coming battle. The power was intoxicating. For the first time in weeks, she felt good again. The heavy tome that bounced up and down inside her saddlebag was all but forgotten.

As the Primordial Prison grew closer and dominated Chell's field of vision, she saw the small temple built at the base of the sphere. It was a squat, unassuming structure that almost looked as if it were keeping the glass prison from rolling away. On the sides of the building appeared to be smaller statues like the ones on either end of

Artorus. She also noticed that the structure lacked any kind of windows.

The Balance Monk again had to wonder what manner of creature this Eternal Guardian would be. Were they a lizard as she had been in her dream, or one of the fire creatures perhaps? Would they speak her language? Would they know her to be a friend sent by a servant of the High God or would they think her another disciple of the Empty Gods like Elra?

There was only one way to be sure.

High God, watch over me. Ravim, God of Balance, watch over me.

As Chell got near the entrance to the temple, she saw no signs of Elra or the Eternal Guardian outside. She dismounted her horse and hitched him to the side of the temple, where he would be less noticed from a distance. She doubted that Elra was anywhere but inside the temple by now, but at least the prison had not been destroyed yet.

Taking one final breath to steel herself, Chell walked through the cavernous opening and into the blackness beyond.

INSIDE THE TEMPLE was at first only darkness. Then, after a few short and twisting corridors that she navigated by touch, she found herself bathed in the faint light of a torch. That was when she saw the other figure and gasped. Regaining her composure, Chell sprang into action, hammering the other Balance Monk with a quick punch. She was met with the crack of breaking glass as she realized too late that she had punched a mirror that ran from floor to ceiling before the corridor again turned out of the torchlight.

"Gods be good," she muttered. What had become of her these last few days?

Chell ignored the mirror and followed the hall around into darkness again. This time, another torch was placed closer than the last had been, helping her move more quickly through the maze-like corridor. It continued to wrap in on itself, taking her right then left, through darkness and light, and past the tapestries that she couldn't quite make out, for what seemed like an impossibly long time.

Based on the size of the temple from the outside, I should have reached the end by now...

Then she heard voices and slowed her progress through another portion of darkness.

"I know why you have come," boomed the first voice, like a peal of thunder.

"Then step aside, old man," Elra hissed, though she sounded like many people talking at once.

They were both here then, just as Ravim had said they would be, and she was not too late.

"I am older even than your gods," the Eternal Guardian rumbled, "yet I am not weak. I am Turuk, formerly of Mellon, servant of the god Nemia, and Eternal Guardian of Artorus. I step aside for no one, mortal or divine."

"So be it," the multitude within Elra said. "The true gods shall return by my hand, and they shall herald the return of those trapped Outside."

Chell shivered and crawled around the corner. Ahead of her, the light from the outside illuminated the tunnel. It seemed that the temple opened into an atrium at the base of the glass sphere. She sprinted into the open and raised her hands, preparing herself to fight.

In front of the lavender surface of glass stood a giant, some eight feet tall. He looked to be made of stones held together by roots and branches. His arms were logs, and his face a stump that had broken to look as if a crown adorned his head. In his large hands he held an axe, the blade of which was a black stone that shone like glass in the light. She knew it to be obsidian from her studies in the Grey Temple. Set back in his head were two eyes that seemed to glow with an internal flame. Those eyes fell on her as she landed in the light.

Elra, or what had once been Elra turned to face her as well. The apostate Balance Monk hunched over like her back had been broken. Her grey robes hung from her body in tatters, showing a patchwork of scabs and bloody wounds all over her body. Chell stifled a gasp when she realized that the woman had cut away most of the tattoos that marked her as a servant of Ravim. The skin on her face was pallid and hung loose like it no longer fit her skull, and her eyes—her eyes were black and dotted with hundreds of small white dots like the sky was full of stars.

"I knew you'd come," Elra said.

"Turuk!" Chell shouted. "I am Chell, a servant of Ravim, the God of Balance. I come to help prevent this one from opening Artorus and endangering creation!"

"It remains to be seen," Turuk said. "Come then, servant of the enemy. Let us finish this."

Elra hissed and sprang through the air at the Guardian, shouting a curse in a language Chell did not recognize. Turuk swung his great axe with such force that it would have cloven a horse in two. Elra kicked off of the flat side of the weapon and spun through the air, landing in a crouch beside the giant.

Chell jumped at Elra herself now, her hands curled into claws that intended to hammer and gouge at the face of her foe. Elra moved with an inhuman speed that was even difficult for the other Balance Monk to follow. She caught Chell by her left wrist and twisted, snapping the bone.

Chell cried out, "How!?"

"I am a servant of greater ones than you," Elra said, her voice sounding more human for a moment. Then the multitude returned, "and we are displeased with thee."

Chell twisted away just as the axe of Turuk crashed down on Elra's arm, severing it at the elbow. The woman did not cry out in pain, even as her blood sprayed over her opponents. She stepped backward, laughing. Ignoring the pain in her broken wrist, Chell stepped toward Elra, kicking and punching at the woman's head from her wounded side. The apostate struggled to block with her wounded arm, allowing most of Chell's blows to land. The sagging skin on her face began to split, though she still merely laughed.

Turuk stepped between the women and battered Elra back against the wall of the temple with the haft of his axe. He followed after with another blow that severed the woman's legs at the knees. The ground drank more of her blood as she flopped about like a dying fish. Though her appearance gave Chell shivers, the woman was done for. The power given to her by those outside had been for naught. Yet for some reason, she continued to laugh, even as the flow of blood slowed and her body stopped moving.

"Your gods," she rasped, "are weak. But mine ARE STRONG!"

Her swollen back erupted, sending bone and gore in every direction. Out of her carcass crawled a being more foul and strange than even anything created by the Gods of Darkness. It had skin that was a putrid green, with flabby growths in place of limbs that terminated in boils and flailing tentacles. Its head was eyeless but contained a maw filled with rows and rows of wicked teeth. Across its chest were dozens of heads, each resembling Elra, and all with eyes that looked like the night sky.

"At last," the multitude said. "The mortals of the Second Cycle are even weaker than those of the First. No matter, our time is finally at hand."

Then a new tentacle ripped from within the creature's abdomen, sprouting from within one of the Elra mouths. It whipped both Chell and Turuk backward with one crack. The Balance Monk was able to land on her feet, but the Eternal Guardian was not so lucky. Turuk slammed into the far wall of the temple with such force that he punched through the stone into the darkness beyond. His axe fell between Chell and the beast.

It's too late then. This is one of the Avatars of the Empty Gods. I did not think they would have been able to manifest in Elra so soon.

What do I do?

There is nothing you can do. Only the High God or the Eternal Guardian at the height of his power could have stopped one such as this. I am sorry, Chell. I have sent you to your doom.

The doubts of her patron deity disturbed her. How could the Grey God give up so easily?

Come to my aid then. Come back to the Mortal Plane and end this.

I cannot. The Pact forbids it.

You are the Pact!

Chell shook him from her mind and sprang into action. The Avatar slithered over to the glass surface of Artorus like a great slug, raising one of its tentacles to strike. Chell picked up the heavy weapon of the Eternal Guardian and swung. The axe severed the tentacle a hand's width from the creature's body. The multitude of voices all cried out once, just as each of the dozens of eyes fell upon her.

"Why do you fight us, servant of a false god?" they asked. "You know the truth. We can sense it. You read the book just as she did. Help us to free the Primordial Ones and unmake the lie that is the High God's world."

Chell lifted the axe again, resting its haft on her broken arm. She glared at the creature as best she could, though the sightless eyes unnerved her.

"Lies or not, the Mortal Plane is filled with people who deserve life. They deserve peace. They deserve Balance. I will not allow you to take that from them."

"Then return to the void," the voices said.

The creature lunged, if such a thing was possible, but it was too slow, and Chell was able to get out of the way of the sweeping tentacles. She swung the axe again, but it was too unwieldy for her to be accurate with one arm. Her blow was swept aside by a fresh tentacle from the beast, causing her to stagger back.

"My weapon," Turuk boomed, suddenly beside her.

Chell swung the haft into the great wooden hand of the Guardian. The wood and stone being looked the same as he had when she had first seen him. It seemed that the blow from the Avatar hadn't harmed him as much as Chell had assumed. The pair prepared for another attack as the creature before them let out a howl.

"We are beyond time. No mortal can contend with us."

"After today, no mortal will have to," Turuk said.

The Guardian attacked the creature from the left and Chell from the right. While she had no true weapons and only one good arm, she hoped that her attacks would at least distract the Avatar enough for Turuk to destroy it. The Balance Monk pounced onto the creature, using her fingers to gouge out as many of the star-eyes as she could in rapid succession.

The Avatar cried out again as bright green blood ran down its swollen body. Turuk swung his axe into the Avatar along its midsection, nearly cleaving it in two. The top half of the beast separated from the lower half with a wet squelch as more of the green blood poured onto the ground. The grass that the blood touched seemed to wither and die almost instantly.

The upper half of the creature shook Chell off as more tentacles burst from within its gaping wound. Boils festered on all of the Elra faces that suddenly wept pus a color similar to the creature's blood. Turuk took another swing, this time trying to bisect the creature vertically. It held him fast with several tentacles, while others lashed at the rocks that made up his chest. When that didn't seem to work, the Avatar drove one of the tentacles through the wood and soil center of Turuk's abdomen. The Guardian staggered and fell to his knees, dropping his axe.

Chell swore and rolled underneath the writhing mass of arms to grab the weapon with her good arm. She swung upward wildly. Her strength wasn't enough to sever them all, but she did cut the tentacle that pierced the Eternal Guardian. Turuk pushed himself to his feet, grabbing the beast by the arms and tossing it into the wall of the temple just as it had done to him. Then he took the axe from Chell and threw the black-bladed weapon into the center of the mass of Elra faces. The creature howled in pain, its tentacles grabbed in random directions.

The Balance Monk sprinted toward the beast, jumping at just the right moment to avoid the writhing mass of its arms and land with her feet planted firmly on either side of the axe. The blubbery hide of the creature was slick with blood and slime, but she held herself in place. Then Chell leaned into the axe with all of her weight, pressing it deeper and deeper into the middle of the beast. Its tentacles gripped her, but she could already feel their strength waning.

Suddenly, Turuk was there, beating on each of the Elra faces in turn, pounding them all into a ruinous pulp. The Avatar of the Empty

Gods began to shudder and moan. When it spoke again, the voices seemed less numerous than before.

"We are eternal. We are not finished. Already, we have other plans in motion. You have lost. Your High God has abandoned you. There is no hope."

Turuk yanked the axe free and raised it for the killing blow. He hesitated and handed the haft of the weapon to Chell.

"Destroy it," he said, softly.

Chell raised the weapon as best she could, bringing it back down on the cluster of faces. The Avatar of the Empty Gods went still. Then its blubbery mass seemed to melt into a puddle of green blood, leaving no trace of its body behind.

Turuk took his weapon back from the Balance Monk and walked over to the edge of Artorus. There he fell to his knees.

V.

Chell stood beside the fallen Guardian, who even on his knees seemed to tower over her. His wooden fingers gripped the wound in his midsection. To Chell, it looked like sap rather than blood flowed from within. She wasn't sure how to treat the wound on such a creature, so she simply stood near and waited for instruction.

"I will survive," he said at last, "though my time as the Eternal Guardian has finished. I haven't truly felt the High God's strength for an age..."

He trailed off, and for a moment, Chell thought that he was mistaken and he was passing from this plane. Then he looked at her and spoke again.

"There is still hope, I think. The High God sent you to me for a reason. That is why I gave you the final blow."

"What do you mean?" Chell asked. "I was sent by Ravim, the God of Balance, known by some as the Grey God. The High God has been missing since the creation of the Pact and the death of Xyxax, nearly a thousand years past."

"The High God has her hands in all things," he said cryptically.

"She?" Chell asked.

The Guardian smiled and looked up at Aenna longingly.

"She used to sit and talk with me," he said. "The conversations we used to have. She told me a great many things that I swore I would never reveal to another mortal. She also told me what to do once my time had passed. Go back into the temple. Near the entrance, there is a mirror..."

"I know of it," Chell replied. "I cracked it when I came in. I'm ashamed to say in the darkness I thought my own reflection was Elra."

Then Turuk seemed to laugh, though the sound was more akin to wind rustling leaves than the mirth of a mortal.

"You will be surprised what you find there. Go to the mirror and then return to me."

Chell nodded and returned to the shadows of the temple entrance. Already, the halls were lighter than they had been before, as several walls to the atrium had broken during the battle. Still, she took her time threading her way back toward the entrance.

What is he having me do? Do you have any idea?

Ravim didn't answer her.

Finally, she found herself back at the corner on which the mirror was set. To her surprise, it looked as though there wasn't a single crack on it. Chell swore and looked over the seamless surface of glass. It was impossible. She knew that she had nearly shattered the thing with her strike. The Balance Monk leaned in to inspect it more. Her hand grazed the part of the mirror where she knew that she had punched it previously. Suddenly, Chell felt herself pulled into the surface of the mirror, and she fell into a silver darkness.

She ran through the burning forest again, but this time she wasn't a lizard, but a being made of tree and stone. In her hand, she gripped an axe made of obsidian. Normally, the volcanic glass would shatter on contact with something hard, but her weapon had been blessed.

Ahead, the fires had taken a part of the forest that she had been the most attached to. These trees she had felt a kinship with, for she had fashioned them at Nemia's direction.

And now they burned.

She cried out in rage. Around her, she sensed her enemies running through the burning forest, yet these were not the ones who had burned it. These were not creatures of flame.

Bursting through the trees, she stood in front of those who had destroyed her grove. She shuddered at the thought of the trees burning to death as she raised her axe...

CHELL WAS FALLING *through an endless silver expanse. She couldn't tell which way was up or from where she had come. She remembered the Guardian, though she couldn't remember their name. She only knew that she had somehow fallen into the mirror in the temple...*

HER AXE CONNECTED *with one of the flaming beasts, and she shuddered in the exaltation her revenge bore. Another came at her from the side, and she batted them away like an insect. None would stop her vengeance.*

Arrows buried themselves harmlessly into her bark. She laughed at them, and her laughter sounded like the wind rustling the leaves of the trees they had burned.

Then the lizards sprang from inside the burning wood, attacking the same enemies that she attacked.

She could not allow them to take her vengeance. They would have cut down the trees themselves if given the chance.

Her axe buried itself in the back of the head of one such creature just after a hail of arrows glanced off of its squamous hide.

The fire creatures swarmed her then, but she was filled with a rage far hotter than their flesh...

CHELL WAS BEGINNING *to struggle to remember anything. Her own name came and went like a piece of down blown on a spring wind. She tried to grasp at it, at any memory of her past, but they all slipped through her fingers. Breaksword. Elra. Tyrek. Ravim. The names flitted by and she no longer knew if one of them was her own...*

*T*OSSING ASIDE *those who would have burned her, she bellowed a challenge to all within earshot. She would not be cowed by these beasts. She was a champion of Nemia, the greatest goddess of the Realm.*

She swung her axe, decapitating a foe and spraying the field with the fluid that ran throughout its body.

The warrior bellowed again, daring any to come and face her when she saw it...

*T*HE WOMAN *who couldn't remember her name floated over a battlefield that she felt like she had fought on. Below her, swarms of lizard men and fire creatures fought, with giants made of trees and stone lumbering between them. Still others she didn't recognize joined the fray, causing a deluge of destruction that seemed to damage the very earth below them. Suddenly, a large creature that looked like an insect covered in writhing, worm-like tentacles was among them...*

*T*HE AVATAR THREW ASIDE ALL *of those that she faced. The whispers told her that this was good. They told her that this was as it should be. Had not Nemia told them that one from Outside would come in their darkest hour?*

Yet she knew that thing should not be. It did not belong in the forests and the groves. This thing would unmake them as surely as the fires would burn them away.

So she sprang...

*T*HE WOMAN WATCHED *as a warrior that she thought she recognized from somewhere jumped onto the back of the lumbering monster, hacking away at its compound eyes. The creature shuddered and let out a howl that sounded like the cries of dozens of voices at once...*

. . .

CHELL FELL BACKWARD OUT of the mirror in a heap. Her breathing was ragged, and her flesh felt oddly tight. She stood and began stumbling back toward Turuk. He had told her to visit the mirror, though for what purpose she still couldn't guess. The memories of what she had seen in there flooded her mind, and still Ravim was silent.

When the Balance Monk stumbled back into the light of the atrium, the Eternal Guardian was standing in its center, waiting for her. He looked better, as if his wound had begun to heal. When he saw her, his wooden face formed a faint smile.

"I was right then. It is done," he said.

"What is done?" Chell rasped. Her voice sounded foreign to her, like the grinding of stone.

"You have seen what I have seen. You are now the Eternal Guardian, filled with the strength that I once had."

Chell stepped back from him in spite of herself.

"W-what do you mean?" she asked.

"Look at yourself."

She looked down at her hands and saw that they were as stone. Startled, she cried out.

"Don't be alarmed," Turuk said. "The mirror has given you the power that the High God once granted to me. In you, it is renewed. Your human form wasn't as strong as mine was then, so it had to be changed. Now Artorus is your charge."

"But-but," she stammered. "What of Ravim? What of my commitment to Balance?"

"You fight to save *creation* now," Turuk replied. "No doubt your connection to Ravim has been severed. You now serve none but the High God."

Chell sat on the ground suddenly, the new weight of her body feeling foreign and wrong to her. She shuddered again in spite of herself.

"W-will I be alone?" she asked, finally.

"For a time, I would think so," Turuk said, sadly. "I cannot stay here. I very well may be the last of my kind. I wish to explore the Mortal Plane and see its forests and groves until my spark is spent and I rejoin the High God on the Astral Plane."

Chell looked at her hands again. She slowly felt her resolve returning.

"What of my horse? And *The First Cycle*? I brought the book with me that started all of this."

"I will see both returned to your Grey Temple before I begin my journey, though none within the temple walls may see me. Mortals cannot yet know the truth of the world, lest the enemy seep in. I fear it will be a lonely life for us both for a time, but I believe it will not always be so. Be good, Eternal Guardian Chell."

He shouldered his axe and walked from the atrium back into the temple, leaving Chell alone. After a time, she stood and walked over to the surface of Artorus. The new Guardian placed her stone hand on the glass. She immediately felt a surge of hateful energy from within.

So long as I draw breath, this prison shall hold.

Chell sat on the ground and crossed her legs. She would meditate until she was needed again. Somehow, she knew she would be.

IN THE SHADOW OF LIGHT

IN THE SHADOW OF LIGHT

1044 AP

"**D**rink," Grant said, laughing.

Tess rolled her eyes. She hated this game but swallowed the mead anyway. The large tavern was filled with games and revelry on such nights. After a week of training exercises alternating with standing around and doing nothing, the soldiers of Illux's army were allowed to return home and take a few days of personal time. Such was the way for a standing army that never expected to go to war. It was better than the alternative, she supposed.

"Alright, alright, it's my turn now you idiot," Tess snickered.

She looked over her drinking companion closely, studying him for some weakness that she wouldn't have noticed before. She supposed he was a handsome man, though he wasn't her type. His eyes were an icy blue, and his skin tanned from his time in the sun. Grant had no tell that Tess could find, not yet anyway.

"You've regretted nearly every woman you've ever bedded, for one reason or another," Tess said.

"So have you," Grant shot back.

"That's not the game."

"Fine. No, I have not," he said confidently.

There was a pause. Tess looked at his face again, searching for some sign that he was lying. The other soldier stared at her, unblinking, his confidence palpable. Maybe she had guessed wrong. Not likely. Then it came to her.

"Drink," she said.

"What?" Grant asked. "I wasn't lying."

"You were, otherwise you would have told me to drink almost instantly. You didn't. You might be a bad liar, but you aren't a cheat."

"Damn," he said, gripping the mug with both hands and tipping it back. "Okay, one more round."

"I'm tired of this. I'm just tired, really."

The man forged ahead over her protests. "You wish you were a Paladin like your sisters."

"Fuck off," Tess said, standing. She turned and walked out of the tavern after throwing her coins on the bar.

"Tess wait!" Grant shouted as he drained his cup and ran after her.

She ignored him, running her fingers through her short, raven-colored hair. She had let it grow out longer than normal, just enough that she had something she could tie back while in uniform. She planned to cut it back down closer to her scalp again, but Tamai liked it this way, so perhaps she would keep it this length.

The muddy streets in this part of Illux were in especially poor shape. A deep puddle hidden in the darkness filled her boot as she splashed into it, causing more curses to flow from her lips. It had been Grant's idea to go to that *shit-hole*.

That blowhard owes me new boots.

Grant was beside her suddenly, huffing and puffing like he was out of shape. He avoided the puddle altogether, which angered Tess even more. Once he caught his breath, Grant tried to light his pipe with little success. When that failed, he threw his pipeweed into his mouth and chewed it some before spitting it out in frustration.

"Look, Tess," he began, "I didn't mean any harm. It was a stupid joke. I wasn't trying to open an old wound, you know that."

"That's exactly what you were doing, Grant. It's not an old wound, it's a fresh one. My twenty-first birthday is in less than a month, and I haven't heard a word from them. They know I live in the city now, and they still don't see me? They are too *important* for some dumb bitch from the army, even if she is their sister. I expected that much from Gwen, but Ariana too?"

Tess spat. Thinking of her Paladin sisters often made her unreasonably angry. All of them had grown up together in Strega, far from the niceties of Illux or even the larger villages. They had been closer then, but Tess usually found herself left out, being the youngest. Then one day, Gwen and Ariana went off the join the Paladin Order together, leaving Tess behind. She had seen them a few times since then, but it was mostly while they looked down their noses at her.

"It can't be that bad, I mean..." he trailed off.

"Have you ever talked to a Paladin?" Tess asked.

"Of course I have. Gods be good I'm nearly ten years older than you."

"And half as smart, half as string, and not even half as good with women. What's your point?"

Grant rooted around in his pockets again before giving up. He looked more melancholy than anything.

"I don't know how Tamai puts up with you."

"She usually doesn't."

Tess reached into her pocket and produced fresh pipeweed for him. She even helped him light it.

"It'd be different if things were like the old days," he said after letting out a puff of smoke. "Back when Jerrok was Seraph. The army actually did something back then. Even when they weren't marching out in force, smaller battalions got dispatched to the villages all of the time. They helped keep the peace, they helped keep Seatown in check. Now? We just play at war. Where's the honor in that?"

"Where's the honor in any killing, Grant?" Tess asked.

And what does honor matter anyhow?

Grant shrugged. He was right of course. Tess joined the army because she had been one of the best brawlers in the village growing up. Fighting came naturally to her. But when she enlisted, she realized how different being a soldier was from the stories. Long gone were the days when Illux needed a standing army. The Lady Ren only kept one out of tradition, it seemed. She wasn't willing to use them as Jerrok had, and the attacks on the villages had slowed to the point of being nearly non-existent under her reign. Though she had been disappointed at first, Tess supposed that she should be thankful that she wasn't killing. Still, she did wonder what her life would have been like if she had followed in her sisters' footsteps.

Tess waved farewell and they both went their separate ways. Grant lived closer to the middle of the city than Tess did, though he wasn't from any better family than her, either. He was just luckier. Grant was from Amel, originally. His only claim to fame was that he had lived down the street from the Lady Ren for a time when he was a child. Tess had no such luck. Unfortunately, the only people of note from her village had been her sisters.

Ahead, the lights in the windows of her small cottage were glowing welcomingly. Tamai liked to call it a cottage because it sounded cuter to her, but the reality is that it was a hovel like every home in the slums. She was hopelessly romantic at times. Tess knew that would hurt her someday. She paused, trying to collect her thoughts and leave her anger toward her sisters at the door. Tamai deserved someone better, so Tess would try to be that person as much as she could.

She pushed the door open and walked in, dropping her bag by the door. Food was already on the table, the fire was crackling, and Tamai was lying on the bed suggestively. Tamai had dusky skin like Tess, and at that moment, Tess could see all of it.

"Well, soldier," Tamai said, "what would you like to eat first?"

The food was undoubtedly cold by the time they finished. Tess held Tamai in her arms, both women cuddling by the fire. Tess should have been the happiest she had been in days, but her mind kept twisting Grant's words around, leaving her restless.

You wish you were a Paladin just like your sisters. I should kick his ass for that.

Tamai stopped tracking her finders on Tess's thigh. She looked up, and at that moment Tess knew that she had been doing a shit job masking her expression. The soldier swallowed and tried to give a weak smile.

"What?" Tamai asked. "What's wrong?"

"Nothing. I'm just thinking."

"I can see that. And you most certainly aren't thinking about me, otherwise, you wouldn't have to fake a smile. You came home to a hot meal and a naked woman and you are thinking about something else?"

"It's Grant, he—" Tess began.

"Grant!" Tamai sat upright. "You interrupted our night alone to think about that idiot? Seriously, I swear to the High God I will kill him. What could he possibly have done to draw your attention away from this?"

"I'm sorry," Tess lied. "He just said that I wished that I had become a Paladin, and it pissed me off, that's all."

"Sweetheart, I hate to say this, I really do, but he's right. The way you feel about Gwen and Ariana is unhealthy, to say the least. Look, we both know that you will never bring yourself to be a Paladin, no matter how much you want to. I've said this before: you need to leave the army. Join the City Watch if you can't stop being a fighter, but get out of the army. It leaves you too far in their shadow."

"You think I'm a coward, don't you?" Tess asked, her voice ice.

"I never said that. You'd see more action in the Watch. Stop being like this."

"I will be however I want. I'm not going to wash clothes or mend shoes my whole life, Tamai. I deserve better."

And so do you.

The fire began to burn low. Tess felt her stomach rumble. Now she wished she had eaten before starting a fight. If things continued, she'd have to go sleep at Grant's place, and he was no cook. She tried to reach out and touch Tamai's face, to stop this before it went any further, but her partner recoiled.

A sharp knock at the door startled them both. Tamai grabbed one of the blankets off of the bed and covered herself. Tess stood and picked up one of the knives from the table, slowly moving her hand to the doorknob.

"Tess, it's me, Grant. It's, uh, kind of a big deal. Open up, please?"

Tess opened the door, grabbed Grant by the arm, and threw him inside where he clattered against the table, sending the cold meal to the floor. She pointed the knife at him accusingly. When his eyes fell to her exposed breasts, she placed the point of her knife in his chin, lifting his head.

"What do you want? We were in the middle of something!"

Tamai began cleaning up the floor with her free hand. She scowled at both Tess and Grant but said nothing. Tess noticed that Grant looked hardly more dressed than she was. His shirt was unbuttoned and his pants were on backward.

"Look, it's about your sisters…" Grant trailed off.

"This again?" Tess sneered. "You already ruined my night Grant, and it had the best sex I've had in months. Why can't you let this go?"

"It's not about before. I swear," Grant said. He held his hand up defensively. Tess lowered the knife. Tamai clicked her tongue. "I had a, uh, friend over tonight. A Paladin woman named, well, it doesn't matter. So while we were—talking—she mentioned that two rangers had gone missing in the Rim. Two sisters, I guess the Lady Ren is sending more Paladins to look for them, but that won't be for a few days. I asked their names, and she said Gwen and Ar—"

Tess opened the door again, shoving Grant out before he could finish.

"Go home and get dressed. I'll meet you there."

"What?" Grant asked.

Tess slammed the door in his face. She quickly started pulling her clothes back on while Tamai glared at her in silence. Once she was dressed, Tess put her bow and quiver on her back before grabbing some food and shoveling it into her mouth. The soldier walked over to Tamai and leaned in to kiss her, food still overflowing from her lips. The other woman shoved her away.

"What are you doing, Tess? You can't chase after them."

"I'll figure out something."

"Are you even thinking about this?" Tamai asked.

"No time," Tess replied.

"This is stupid. At least wait until morning. You just let Grant barge in here while neither of us were wearing clothes, and now you are gonna run off in the middle of the night while we are still in the middle of a fight? Are you serious?"

You deserve better.

"It's my sisters, Tamai. I can't sit here and do nothing!"

"You aren't a Paladin!"

"You keep reminding me," Tess said, turning.

She walked out the door and didn't look back.

GRANT WAS outside and dressed by the time Tess got to his front door. He had a row of dirks strapped to his leg and a sword across his back. He looked ready for a war that would likely never come. Tess smiled. Grant might have been an ass, but he was a loyal ass.

"What now?" He asked. "The Rim would take months to traverse, and we don't even know where they were last seen. Add that to the fact that we would be branded as deserters in less than two days, and that sneaking out of Illux in the middle of the night is nigh impossible—"

"The Lady," was all Tess said.

Grant put his face in his hands for a moment.

"You've gone daft. Mad. I should have stayed with that woman. Gods be good. Do you suppose Tamai would be willing to give men a try? I'm sure we can bond over the loss of your mind."

Tess ignored him.

"Come on," she said. "We're losing moonlight."

They cut through the city as quickly as they could, moving at a brisk pace while not outright running to not attract the attention of the City Watch. Tess still wasn't quite as confident navigating the city as Grant was, so she frequently deferred to him when it came time to decide which streets to take.

Finally, by the middle of the night, they entered the central plaza of the city and the home of the Grand Cathedral. The pale moon hung behind the white spires, rimming them with a halo of light. Tess eyed the upper reaches of the Fourth Spire: the home of the Seraph. No doubt the Lady Ren had been asleep for hours by this point like any sane person would have been. That meant that Tess would need to get creative to get her attention.

Grant isn't going to like this.

They crossed the plaza to the Paladin training grounds and walked to the base of the steps leading into the Fourth Spire. Above, bathed in torchlight, were two Paladin guards who placed their hands upon their weapons as soon as they saw the pair. Tess set her bow and her knives down in front of her. Grant undid his dirks and sword. With their hands raised, the pair walked up the steps.

"What in the High God's name are you two doing here at this time of night?" Asked one.

"The Grand Cathedral is closed for worship," said the other.

Grant shot Tess a venomous glance. She elbowed him before speaking up.

"We've come to have an audience with the Seraph," she said, calmly. "I imagine that the Lady is sleeping. Would you be so kind as to wake her?"

Even in the limited light, Tess could see Grant roll his eyes. The guards drew their blades.

"You have one chance," the first one said. "Turn back now, or we will cut you down right here."

"This is urgent," Tess pleaded. "It's about the Paladin rangers, Gwen and Ariana."

"I don't care if it's about Daniel-fucking-Nightbreaker," the second one said. "Leave now, or I swear to the gods you'll wish you had."

Grant pulled on her arm to lead her away. Tess shook him off and stepped higher up the stair.

"They are my sisters, and I request permission to go look for them —please."

"Go look then! Why would the Lady care?"

"I'm in the army. I can't abandon my post."

"Too bad," said the second one. "Now, leave."

Grant grabbed her by both arms and pulled her back down the steps. Tess tried to shake him off again and she began to shout.

"I want to see the Lady Ren! I want to see the Seraph!"

"Tess," Grant whispered. "Stop, before you get us killed. This'll have to wait until morning."

"No!" She elbowed Grant in the face. "I'm not leaving until I see her! I demand that you wake the Lady!"

"That's enough," the first Paladin said, walking toward her.

"Ren! Seraph of Illux! I am in need!"

A crackling blast of energy struck the steps between the soldier and the Paladin. Both stepped backward, covering their eyes from the sudden flash of brilliance. Tess heard what sounded like the flapping wings of a large bird overhead. When she looked up, she saw the silhouette of the Seraph descending from above.

The Lady Ren landed on the steps between them, Nightbreaker clutched in her hand. She wore a silk dress that showed off her figure. The moonlight shone off her ebony skin like liquid silver. Tess felt her mouth go dry as she nearly swooned. She had only ever seen the Seraph from a distance before. Ren was beautiful.

I'm sorry Tamai.

"What is the meaning of this?" Ren boomed. Her voice was soft but held the weight of thunder. Lightning arced across the surface of Nightbreaker, making the hair on Tess's arms stand on end.

Out of the corner of her eye, Tess saw Grant drop to one knee, just as the Paladins behind the Seraph did. Taking a gamble, the soldier stood her ground.

"My lady," she said, "I am sorry that my shouts woke you. My name is Tess."

Tess took a curt bow. When her head lifted back up she saw the dark eyes of the Seraph boring into her.

"Why are you shouting on the steps of the Fourth Spire, Tess of the midnight hour?" The Seraph asked.

"The Paladins, Gwen, and Ariana. The rangers who went missing in the Rim. They—they're my sisters, my lady. I wish to ask permission to go look for them with my companion here. We are enlisted, so we cannot leave without the permission of our commander, or, well, you."

"And did you go to your commander?"

"No, my lady. I figured I had one shot, so I took the biggest target. I hope my aim was true."

Tess smirked at the Seraph. She thought that she saw the woman blush.

"I understand your concern. I'm worried about them too. They were sent from Rinwaithe to check the surrounding area for a caravan that went missing shortly after leaving the village. They haven't returned in weeks. Even so, they are two of my most capable rangers. If anyone could survive the danger of those mountains, it's them. You must understand that I can't send two mortal soldiers alone into the wilderness. More lives could be lost for no reason. I promise you that I am sending the best Paladins to go looking for them. Broderick Breaksword will lead a rescue expedition once he returns from—"

"That's too long!" Tess blurted. The Paladins' mouths hung agape. Even Ren looked taken about at the forwardness of this woman. "If we weren't soldiers we could go looking for them without your leave, and we would be less equipped to do so. Please, don't deny me this. I need to find them. I cannot live thinking that I could have done something but didn't.

"I know what it is like to lose one who was as a sister to me," Ren said, pensively. "Fine, you two have my leave to go looking for them. As I said, they were last seen in the foothills below Rinwaithe. Bryant, fetch these two some horses. Chet, go tell Commander Stokes that these two have been sent on a mission by the Seraph."

"Thank you, my lady," Tess said, bowing.

"Don't lose yourself to grief, soldier. You may not like what you find in those mountains."

AFTER A FEW DAYS OF RIDING, they reached the foothills of the Rim. The mountains rose to brush the sky sending the green sea of trees tumbling down from snow-capped peaks. The road continued up into the hills and through the trees to the only village in the Rim of Paradise.

Rinwaithe was located far to the northwest of Illux. While other villages grazed cattle in the lower hills farther from the untamed forests of the Rim, Rinwaithe was a logging community. It provided the majority of the lumber that Illux needed, rather than the food tithes that the rest of the villages sent to the City of Light. The two soldiers paused before entering the wood. A jay darted through the shadows of the tree line. Tess followed the bird's movements until it was out of sight.

"Well?" Grant asked. "What now? Rinwaithe is above, most likely another day's ride into the forest. Whatever got—whatever your sisters went looking for is probably in those trees."

"Obviously Grant," Tess grumped. "Gods be good that's why we're here. We continue up until we hit the village. Hopefully, they can give us some insight into what direction they last headed."

"I just want to remind you that I said this was hopeless."

"I just want to remind you to shut the fuck up."

Grant spurred his horse into a trot, disappearing into the wall of trees. Tess watched for any other signs of movement before she followed. There were all kinds of stories about these mountains. The Rim of Paradise was said to hold creatures that were not found in the lands below. Ancient creatures from before the Age of the Pact. Her horse whinnied quietly as she advanced and the sunlight was replaced with a canopy of trees.

Based on what Grant remembered from his last visit to the village, he said it would take a least a day to work their way deep enough into the forest to get to Rinwaithe. The trees in the Rim were massive, towering over the riders like the buildings in the inner-city of Illux. Though there was beauty here, she knew what darkness could be creeping about a forest such as this.

Demons.

Though Tess didn't want to admit it, she knew that it was likely that the caravan had been attacked by a band of Demons and

Accursed. If it had been bandits, they would have left the bodies to rot on the road, and her sisters wouldn't have gone missing. If it had been Demons though, every man and woman in that caravan would have been taken and *turned*. Rumors abounded about how that happened, but everyone knew that Accursed had to come from somewhere.

She shivered. How could people live all of the way out here, so far from the safety of Illux or Seatown?

Not unlike Strega.

The village of her youth was the closest to the Great Chasm, located far to the west of Illux. Strega was often said to be the edge of the world. Although it was isolated, and built on the outskirts of one of the evilest places on the Mortal Plane, it was relatively safe. Demons tended to shy away from the place, or at least they had the entire time that she was growing up. Even they feared what was lying at the bottom of that crater.

In those days Gwen and Ariana were inseparable, and little Tess followed them on all of their adventures, but never actually took part in them. It didn't help that her mother and father favored the older girls as well. They weren't as impetuous, they didn't curse as often, and they certainly didn't pick fights with the boys of the village. Tess had broken more than a few noses in her day, after all. The other kids around the village had started calling the red stains on their shirts "Tess Flowers" before she left town to follow her sisters.

Ariana had been more understanding of who Tess was, and of what she wanted to be. Gwen, on the other hand, felt like she needed to be a surrogate parent and reel Tess in. It was often Gwen who chastised the younger girl more often than their parents ever did. And although no one but Ariana ever learned the truth, it had been Gwen who had broken Tess's arm when she was fighting the boy Jakson.

Gwen had a crush on Jakson, and the two would sneak off in the middle of the night to fool around. Ariana would whisper to Tess about it, telling her that her older sister wasn't a maiden anymore. One of those nights, Tess got curious and followed them. She found Gwen crying alone. Tess didn't ever find out what the boy had done. Truth be told, she didn't care. Instead, she found him walking back to his house and she pounced on him. His eyes were swollen shut by the time Gwen found them. Then Gwen attacked Tess of all people.

Not two years later, her older sisters were gone. They left for Illux to become Paladins; heroes empowered by the blessing of the Gods of Light. Their parents had been so proud. As they were leaving, Tess told them that she wanted them to stay with her. She wanted them to wait for all three of them to be old enough to become Paladins together. Ariana hugged her and told her to follow when she was able. Gwen had laughed and told that she would never have the discipline that it took to be a Paladin.

Tess spent the next few years learning to shoot a bow. Her targets were two dolls that she had made when she was younger. In the middle of the night, just before her seventeenth birthday, she stole a horse and fled Strega alone. By the time she reached Illux, she had made up her mind. If her sisters were Paladins, she would never willingly choose to be that. Instead, she would join the army and put her fighting skills to use defending the Light differently.

And instead of fighting, I get to drink and disappoint Tamai.

Ahead, the path began to get steeper as the first of the hills rose beneath them. The shadows of the trees became more oppressive, throwing the riders into an early twilight. They still hadn't seen any signs of other riders on the road. It seemed that no one else had thought it prudent to leave Rinwaithe after the caravan and two Paladins went missing.

"Tess," Grant said. "What are you going to do if we don't find them?"

"I'm not stopping until we do."

"The army will expect—"

"You heard the Seraph," she said. "We will take however long it takes. I won't return to Strega to tell my parents their favorite girls are dead."

"You can't honestly think—"

"Shh!" Tess interrupted.

Both horses came to an abrupt halt. There were deep ruts in the mud here, from a wagon by the looks of it, heading off of the trail deeper into the forest to the west. Tess hopped down and studied the markings. They looked like they could have been weeks old. The rain had washed moth other signs away, but these tracks had remained.

Then she saw it.

Burned into the bark of one of the trees was a symbol. It looked like a crude sword or arrow, and it pointed in the same direction that the tracks seemed to be heading. Tess ran her fingers over it. Something very hot had gone into this tree to make this mark. Something like the fire a Paladin could produce.

"My sisters went this way after the wagon tracks," she said as she mounted her horse.

"Why would the wagon have gone off the trail?"

"That's why," Tess replied, pointing. A lone arrow was lodged in a trunk at the opposite side of the trail.

"That's no Accursed bolt," Grant observed. "We are dealing with men."

"Aye."

Tess urged her horse onward through the brush and off of the road.

THE PAIR FOUND the body not two hours later. They had what signs of passage they could, along with the occasional Paladin mark, when they came across it hanging from a tree. It was bloated and rotten, nearly beyond recognition. Birds and other scavengers had removed most of the flesh from its face. Even so, it was still recognizable as a child.

The horses nearly panicked when they came across it, and both soldiers had to spend the next few minutes calming their mounts. Finally, Grant unhorsed and climbed the tree, cutting the rope while Tess gently lowered the poor child to the ground. She cursed when she realized that they couldn't have been more than ten years old.

"This is evil," Grant said, hopping back down.

"We have to bury her," Tess whispered.

"I agree, but with what? We have no shovels."

"Then gather rocks."

They spent the better part of an hour gathering suitable stones to make a cairn for the girl. When they were done, they watered the horses and sat at the base of the tree. Neither spoke for quite some time. Tess listened to her own ragged breathing as the sounds of the forest died away. Her stomach was a tempest of disgust and rage.

"It's almost nightfall. We should camp here for the night and then head back. This is too much for us, Tess. I don't know your sisters, but I do know Paladins, and I know women. Neither would have seen that girl in the tree and left her there. That means she was strung up after they came this way."

"I know," Tess said.

She stood and removed her weapons from her horse. Grant shot her a quizzical look.

"We're close. I can feel it. This was a warning of some kind, no doubt for anyone else who would dare to come looking for this caravan. We leave the horses and go on foot. This ends tonight, one way or another."

Grant's eyes fell to the cairn. He didn't say a word, but he tied both horses to a tree and took a water skin from his pack.

Gods of Light, watch over your daughters. Tonight they will be forced to kill.

Tess led the way through the trees, creeping low to the ground on cat's feet. She had her bow at the ready, her arm reaching over her shoulder to the quiver on her back. Every sound drew her attention, causing her fingers to caress the fletching on her arrows. Beside her, Grant held a dirk in each hand. She supposed that his face might have been even grimmer than hers. Was he a father himself? He was certainly old enough and slept around enough. If they survived this, she would ask him. If they survived this, she would consider taking Tamai up on her offer to adopt an orphan.

When the darkness was finally absolute, the smell of burning logs and the faint murmur of voices reached them from ahead. A faint orange glow rimmed the trees in the distance. The two soldiers circled around so as to not come upon the fires directly. Each of them kept their eyes open for any sign of scouts that could alert the camp to their presence.

They nearly stumbled into one while he was taking a piss. He was a big man, but the arrow in his eye dropped him all the same. Grant caught the body before it could make a sound from crashing into the brush. The soldier gently laid the dead scout down and they continued.

Finally, they came upon the edge of the camp, still staying a good distance back in the nighttime shadows where they would remain unseen. The camp was sizable for a bandit camp, with several tents and even crude lean-tos cobbled together from fallen logs and lumber stolen from the caravan. Tess counted at least twelve bandits wandering the camp. Most had a child or young woman trailing them. The prisoners were held by a rope that was tied around their necks and to the waist of the bandits. In the center of the camp just near the fire were the few male prisoners tied to the trunk of a massive tree. Beside them were two large women with matching braids.

Tess's breath caught in her throat. Gwen and Ariana were alive, though both looked like they had been beaten regularly. Ariana's head was slumped into her chest, and her breathing looked shallow. Gwen seemed to be eying one bandit in particular, a bald man with swirling grey tattoos all over his body.

"A Balance Monk?" Grant hissed. "What in the High God's name is happening here? How could these bandits hold two Paladins hostage, even with a Balance Monk among them?"

Tess pointed at the child bound to the man. He was a toddler that followed the monk around like a kicked dog.

"That girl wasn't a message for us. She was a message to my sisters. If they try anything, the men kill the villagers."

"Gods be good, what do we do?"

"We kill them, Grant. We kill them all."

Tess nocked an arrow and paused her mind racing. She quickly counted the bandits again. There were thirteen bandits in the camp and possibly more scouts in the wood. She and Grant were hopelessly outnumbered. This was an impossible task. But it needed to be done.

The one who looked to be a Balance Monk walked over to Ariana and kicked her in the ribs. This woman shook herself awake. He smiled, his mouth missing most of his front teeth.

Probably from Gwen.

The man took a pot of water and doused the fire, reducing much of the camp to darkness. Several of the children began to cry. The only light came from a few scattered torches on the edge of camp. Tess struggled to see what was happening.

"Go on bitch," the monk said. "I'm going to free your hands. Use your magic to relight my fire."

"Light it yourself," Gwen said.

Do as you're told or I'll gut this boy."

Tess could see the man leaning over Gwen with a dagger. He cut her loose from the tree and she collapsed onto the ground. After a moment collecting herself, Gwen got to her knees.

"Go around," Tess whispered. "When it starts, cut as many people loose as you can."

Grant grimly nodded and disappeared into the shadows. Just then, a flash of blue and the fire reignited amid of shower of sparks and bits of wood that exploded into the air. The monk stepped back, clearly startled.

"Too much," he said. "Were you hoping to singe me, I wonder?"

He grabbed Gwen by the hair and lifted her to her feet. Tess slowly stood, preparing to draw back her bowstring. The monk wrapped a noose around Gwen's neck, laughing.

"What are you doing?" Ariana screamed, weakly.

Several of the other bandits moved in closer. A few of them grabbed their hostages and held them aloft.

"I decided I only want one Paladin prize. She has more spirit than you, which means she will get into the most trouble, I think."

"No!" Ariana yelled, her vigor returning as she tried to wrestle her hands free.

"Ah, ah, ah," the monk said, tapping the small boy on the head with his knife.

"Don't," Gwen said. "Sister, don't let him kill another child because of me. Please. Just let this happen."

The monk waved some of his men over to grab the rope and pull. Gwen was lifted into the air, her feet kicking wildly. The Paladin's face quickly began to contort as she gasped for air. Ariana started to cry, burying her face in her arm.

Luna, Goddess of Light, protect me. Arra, Goddess of Light, give me strength. Samson, God of Light, guide my arm.

Tess stepped out of the shadows.

"Get your hands off of my sister or I'll give them to her as a gift!"

She let her first arrow fly. It cut the rope binding the toddler to the monk. Her next arrow dropped her sister to the ground. Her third struck the bonds holding Ariana to the tree. The fourth flew right at the face of the still-stunned bandit leader. He recovered himself and snatched it from the air.

Cursing, she switched targets, launching another missile at the closest bandit to her. It took him through the windpipe, dropping the man to his knees. Then she saw Grant diving into the confusion, slicing rope and throats alike with masterful efficiency. Gwen still rolled on the ground, clawing at her neck to get rid of the noose. Ariana stood, blasting the monk with a burst of blue flame. Tess could tell that she had been too weak to make it count, but at least he had been knocked off his feet for a moment.

The soldier stepped further into the camp, turning and loosing another arrow into a man who moved to kill his hostage. Ariana pulled Gwen to her feet and the women converged on the fallen monk together. The free villagers began gathering the children, cowering together beneath the largest of the lean-tos. Tess nocked another arrow. Her bow was struck from her hand by a small man holding a hatchet. He sprung on her, hacking wildly at her face. Tess used his momentum to fling him from the top of her just as she hit the ground. She pulled her knife and pounced on the bandit, stabbing his stomach over and over.

In the distance, Grant now sparred with a bandit large enough to be a Paladin. The man swung a warhammer that shattered the wooden structures around him. Tess recovered her bow and sank an arrow between his shoulder blades. He barely paused before knocking Grant off his feet. Her next arrow took him in the back of the knee. That caused him to collapse just long enough for Grant to roll out of the way.

A scream drew Tess's attention to her sisters. Gwen was cradling a broken arm as the monk pummeled them each with a flurry of blows. She took a deep breath and aimed her next arrow at him again. She loosed. The monk twisted Ariana in front of himself, burying the arrow in her side. She screamed and collapsed.

"No!" Tess shouted.

Then the monk was sprinting at her. She sent another arrow his way. He dodged it with ease and seemed to snicker at her. Halfway to her, he picked up a broken pole, twisting it behind his back like a staff. The next arrow she aimed ahead of the man. He had no trouble batting it out of the air with his new weapon.

"Tess!" Gwen shouted. "Run!"

"Fuck," Tess said.

In the distance, a flying dirk took out another bandit. The child tied to him looked dead from this distance. Tess reached back to her quiver. Her hand came up empty. Then the monk was upon her. His makeshift staff broke two of her fingers as it swept the bow from her hands. His next strike took her in the gut. The monk kicked her legs out from under her.

"Those are your sisters, hmm?" He asked. "These poor people will hate your family when I'm done with them."

A blast of energy took him from behind, sending him sprawling. Tess quickly rolled over. She saw Gwen and Ariana both coming up toward her. Each looked pale, but their arms were alight with energy.

"Get out of there!" Ariana yelled.

Tess pulled free her knife.

What am I going to do with this?

She threw the knife away and groped for her bow. Once she had it in her hands she ducked down to where the other bandit had knocked her from her feet. Desperately, she searched around his corpse for any fallen arrows. She found two. Behind her, the monk was pulling himself to his feet.

"Tess!" Gwen shouted.

Tess took a deep breath, nocked an arrow, and stood. She turned, just as the monk made his way toward her. The soldier loosed the first arrow just to the left of his head. The monk easily grabbed it from the air. A moment later, her second arrow was sprouting from his chest. Shocked, he dropped to his knees. Tess approached the man, pushing him over with her boot.

The blood from the arrow blossomed across his shirt. Up close, Tess could admire the swirls of grey that marked him as a previous Balance Monk. His eyes, full of hate, looked up at her as they glossed over.

"That's a Tess flower you have on your shirt," she said.

"I can't believe we did it," Grant said. "It was like one of the old tales of Ash Company or something! I mean, did you count how many of them there were?"

"I did," Tess replied.

They were riding south again, the hills and peaks of the Rim receding behind them. The two soldiers returned to Illux as they had left it: alone. Gwen, Ariana, and the villagers were recovering in Rinwaithe.

"Are you sure you don't want to stay and wait for them?" Grant asked for what must have been the third time.

"I'm sure. They think I should be a Paladin now. Like I earned it somehow. I don't want to have that conversation over and over again."

Her sisters had been proud. They hugged her and kissed her like she was a child. That didn't matter. She hadn't wanted any of that. She only wanted them to be safe. And now they were. A lone tear rolled down her face.

"Were those the first men you've ever killed?" Grant asked.

"No," Tess lied.

"That's good," he said. "Because the first ones haunt you. You don't forget them easily, whether they deserved it or not."

"It's that little girl who I won't forget. Those men deserve nothing more from me."

Those men had been led by a runaway Balance Monk named Tyrek. He had been a man of Illux once, Ariana had told Tess on the way back to Rinwaithe. He had been a bandit before, and for one reason or another, he had fallen back into that life. When the caravan went missing, the sisters had been dispatched to find out what had happened. They stumbled across the camp and could do nothing, or else the children would have been killed. Gwen attacked anyway, and Tess had buried the consequences of that mistake.

He had escaped a Balance Monk party that had been hunting him, he had told the sisters. Eventually, more would have come for him, though. Very few monks in history had ever left the Grey Temple. What had driven him back to such depravity none could say.

He got what he deserved.

Tess patted her horse on the neck. In a few days, she would be back in Illux and everything would be back to normal. Her sisters said that people would call her a hero. She didn't feel like one. She was just Tess. That was all she wanted to be now. Tamai would still be mad at her if Tess even went home. That woman deserved so much better than Tess could give her.

Tess of the broken promises.

Tess sighed. She would let Tamai down gently. She was a killer now—not a lover.

"Tamai will be happy to see you in one piece, I'd wager," Grant mused.

Her resolve melted. Not yet. She couldn't give her up yet.

"I hope so. I have some making up to do," Tess said.

She thought back to the cairn in the mountains and the little girl who lay beneath it. No one would place flowers on her grave, but Tess had gotten her a flower all the same.

THE SONS OF LIGHTHAMMER

THE SONS OF LIGHTHAMMER

1047 AP

The ceiling of his family's manor looked especially interesting at that moment. The ancient stone was finally starting to crack. Arkos Lighthammer was trying to look anywhere but at his father, who was droning on about the history of their family. Tonight, his usually dry manner of speech had been replaced with uncharacteristically dramatic flair. This was often the case when they had guests, and tonight was a special occasion indeed. It had been just days since the most recent Initiation of the Paladins, the Initiation that Arkos and his cousin Devin has taken part in, and as such, Arkon Lighthammer was hosting half of the families of the inner city.

"And that tapestry depicts when our progenitor, Killian the Lighthammer, slew two Heralds in open combat during the Northern Campaign," the old man went on. "For his bravery, Fiora Godschosen named him the Supreme Commander of the Paladin Order after her ascension, and all of that before his first son was born."

The tapestry in question was actually newer than all of the others in the foyer. Arkos had been small boy when his father had it commissioned. The story it depicted was likely shit. He doubted most of what his father claimed about their lineage, storied as it was. Nothing pleased the old man more than having people think that they came from superior stock.

Where is Devin?

His thoughts turned to his cousin. Devin often butted heads with the Lighthammer patriarch, but even he wouldn't miss this party—or any party, for that matter. Devin enjoyed drinking almost as much as he enjoyed fighting, and it was said that he might have even been the most promising of all of the recruits.

As if by magic, Devin seemed to materialize in the center of the crowd, making himself seen by those gathered to listen to Arkon. He was a big man, with a tight black beard and dark skin; a spitting image of the man on the tapestry that the crowd gathered below. Devin wore the shining ivory plate of the Paladin Order this night. On his back was strapped a giant white and gold hammer. *The* hammer. It had been a gift to Devin from Arkon for his performance during training. Though Arkos knew that it had been a slight against him as well. Perhaps even more so.

"Gods be good!" Devin shouted. "They sure got my likeness when they finished this one, didn't they?"

The crowd laughed. Arkon's expression, however, seemed to sour. The old man didn't like to be shown up, especially not by his sister's son.

"Yes," he said, drawing attention away from his nephew, "both sons of the house of Lighthammer are throwbacks to Killian! And that is why we gather here! Now, please follow Miranda for refreshments."

The crowd followed Arkos's other cousin—from his mother's side —into the next room, where food and drink had been set out. Several prominent guests had still not arrived, and far-be-it from Arkon to waste his best showmanship on the rabble. There were still toasts to made, wine to drink, and revelry that would continue late into the night.

The shriveled up old man was dressed in his nicest fineries: silken robes draped over purely-ornamental armor for Arkon Lighthammer had never been initiated.

"What was that about?" Arkon grumped at Devin once the guests were out of earshot.

"What? I was just having a little fun," Devin replied.

"You have *too much* fun, I've been told. You're an embarrassment. If I had known you'd make a mockery of our family name, I would have never given you that hammer."

Devin rolled his eyes. He tried to leave the room, but his uncle shot out an arm to block his retreat.

The newly-made Paladin let out a low growl and said, "Give the hammer to Arkos, then. The High God knows he actually *wanted* the damn thing."

Here we go.

"Don't tell me what to do with my own son!" the patriarch shouted.

Devin pushed the old man out of the way and walked into the other room. Arkos tried to quietly remove himself as well, but then his father's gaze fell upon him.

"And you," Arkon said through gritted teeth. "You are the biggest embarrassment of all. If you were half the man your cousin is, I could have given you the hammer. I would have gladly done so! Instead, by some cruel joke, I am forced to give it to my sister's son. If only you had a brother..."

"Yes father," Arkos whispered, "I'm nothing but a failure and a fool. You don't even like Devin, and yet you compare me to him. I live in the shadow of a man you can't stand the sight of. I did well in training, too. In fact—"

"That's enough! Castille is the only one that favors you. The Lady hasn't noticed you, nor has Broderick Breaksword."

"As if you care for the opinions of *either* of them. When have they been friends to our family?"

"I care for what improves the status of my son!"

Just then, one of their guests, Julius Silvershield, tried to sneak past the bickering pair. Julius's parents were dead, leaving the young man with one of the largest manors in the city. Arkos knew that his father coveted that property, and as such had taken to watching over the young heir. He was often a guest in their home, though Arkos tended to give him a wide berth.

"Where are you going, Julius? The festivities have just begun," Arkos said.

"I have my own festivities to partake in tonight," the younger man replied.

"Don't get into too much trouble," the Lighthammer patriarch said, flashing a knowing smile.

Julius bowed deeper than was necessary and scurried out the front door. When the servant opened it, Arkos could hear the familiar voice of Castille Denost, the highest ranked Paladin in the Order.

"Ah, Julius, how good to see you."

"Go," Arkon said, his voice already turning back to ice. "Your mother will be missing you."

Arkos nodded and fled the room. In the great hall, he saw the guests were now enjoying the best wine and ales that his father could afford—which meant the best on the Mortal Plane. Devin had a small crowd gathered around himself as he told them of the Initiation. Most of these were from Paladin families, which meant that they already knew all of the details of the ceremony, but they listened with rapt attention anyway. Devin had that effect on people.

Seated near the head of the table, Arkos found his mother playing with a plate of cheese and blood sausage. She looked especially bored. He sat down beside her, motioning for a goblet to be brought over. It would take several cups to enter the stupor required to escape this night.

"These slums servants are especially slow," she said.

"Yes, but it helps to pay the less fortunate, doesn't it?" Arkos replied.

"You sound like your cousin. Don't let your father hear you talk like that." She gave him a weak smile.

"It couldn't hurt. I've already drawn his ire tonight, simply by existing. So much for celebrating my great achievement."

"Your father...he means well. I know he draws attention to Devin in public, but you know he favors you. You have always been such a good boy. You make him proud."

"Honestly mother, I don't care if I make him sick. I won't have to see him soon, in any case. I decided to move to the barracks."

Just now.

"What!?" His mother sputtered.

The barracks were the home of the Paladins while they were in active service to the Light. The great structure sat opposite the Grand Cathedral in the very center of Illux. It was tradition that Paladins live there their entire lives, leaving only if they were to start a family. Inner city families, however, who were of famous and rich bloodlines, were often allowed to continue to keep their Paladin offspring in their ancestral homes, as they were close to the Fourth Spire already. It had been assumed that Arkos would stay at home, as his grandfather had before him. Devin, on the other hand, had already moved to the barracks to live with his lover Gil and to be close to his friend Trent.

"Does your father know?" She asked.

"Not yet."

Arkos stood and walked over to join his cousin who was entertaining a new audience. Devin was a better storyteller than Arkon, at least. Arkos recognized several of Devin's listeners: Yan and Hunt, two Paladin recruits who weren't due to be initiated for a few months at least, the Whitehorn girl whose name he couldn't remember, and the youngest Darksend boy. Devin had attracted a better crowd than Arkon ever could if he didn't have food and drink to bribe them with. Arkos sipped his ale as his cousin told them all of how he had bested Trent, Gil, and a dozen others under the watchful eye of Broderick Breaksword. The Paladin Ranger and one-time Balance Monk was highly respected by most of the city, even as he was disliked by many of the elite.

The young man called Yan visibly rolled his eyes and wandered off after a time. No doubt he had seen the skirmish in question and disliked Devin's embellishments.

You aren't as popular as you think, cousin.

By now, Arkon and Castille had wandered in, followed closely by

Redrick, the Captain of the City Watch. They moved to a corner, talking in hushed tones. Even among the best of Illux, they considered themselves greater than the rest. Soon they would toast the sons of Lighthammer, and the true feast would begin. That meant that Arkos only had to deal with this for another few hours at most.

"So, Arkos," a voice said.

The newly-made Paladin turned to see his cousin Miranda sipping wine behind him.

"Yes?" He asked.

"Awfully quiet tonight. Are you purposely hiding in your cousin's shadow, or your father's?"

Arkos laugh. "I'm actually just enjoying the quiet."

"I've always assumed you didn't speak up because you didn't want to end up like your namesake."

Arkos swallowed. The last famous bearer of that name was a Seraph who had gone mad, ruling Illux with an iron fist for a generation before being killed by the Paladin Arendt, during his rebellion. Why his father had chosen that name for him, he would never know.

"You're funny cousin," Arkos said. "And you've had too much wine already."

"I just pay attention," She seemed to be ignoring his comment. "Devin is loud because he wants to stand out. He doesn't like silence, because his father is dead. You, on the other hand, are quiet and like to hide because yours is still living."

Arkos simply nodded and turned around, trying to find somewhere he could drink without interruption. He heard Miranda snicker as he slinked away. She was right, of course. Devin's father had taken ill when they were younger. His mother never quite recovered from the loss, and secluded herself to the east wing of the manor. No doubt she was there even now, unaware that her son had just become a holy warrior.

"Attention, please!" Castille shouted over the din. "I would like to raise a goblet to our fine host, Arkon Lighthammer! And to the sons of this family, Arkos and Devin!"

A cheer rose up from the crowd.

"May they produce many more sons for this storied house!"

The cheering fell to a low rumble, punctuated by with a few snickers. They all knew that Devin wouldn't be producing any heirs. Castille knew it too. Was he putting Arkon in his place or getting back at him for some sleight? Why make a scene now?

"I'll let my cousin produce enough for the two of us," Devin laughed. "If Gil learns how to get pregnant, I'll let you all know."

The guests laughed again. Everyone, it seemed, but Arkon. He grimly nursed on a large goblet of wine that stained the white of his mustache and beard. He walked over to his nephew, motioning for those standing near to move away. Arkos tried to move with them, but he wasn't fast enough.

"You can't help yourself, can you?" Arkon asked. "Even in public, you shame me. After I took you and your mother in. After I let you take my name even though she married a man from lesser stock."

"Don't talk about my parents like that!" Devin growled.

"Or what? You've already shamed me enough by taking up with a man and spending more time with that boy from the slums than your own flesh and blood! Castille has told me all about Gil and this Trent—"

"They are each twice the man you are!" Devin shouted, drawing looks and hushed gasps from the guests. "You are a coward! Have any of you wondered why the old bastard never became a Paladin himself? He's too afraid to get his hands dirty. You disgust me, old man."

Devin shoved past his uncle and stormed out, leaving the party far less lively than it had been before.

THE GUESTS STAYED LONG ENOUGH to eat, but all of them filtered out shortly after Devin's display. By the end, Arkon sat at the head of the table with several spilled goblets of wine all around him. The other members of the Lighthammer family had all retired to their rooms long ago, leaving the patriarch to his drink in silence.

Arkos sat opposite his father at the far end of the table, watching as Arkon sank further and further into drunken despair. Arkos wasn't sure why he sat there; if it was out of loyalty or morbid curiosity. The old man hadn't spoken to him in hours. In fact, he had done nothing other than drink and hang his head. Finally, when it seemed that he had passed out for good, Arkos stood and made to leave the hall.

"Leaving me already, eh son?" Arkon slurred.

"I'll help you to your room," Arkos said.

"You were always such a loyal boy. I love you for that, I do. Come, help me up."

It's just the wine. That's all.

Arkos tried to ignore the praise from his father. He knew how this would go just like it had every time before. But even so, part of him couldn't help but bask in it during these short outbursts. Once, before Devin had come to live with them, his father had been loving. But that was so long ago that he hardly remembered it.

"There, that's a good boy," his father said. "You always do what you're told. You don't stand up for yourself like your cousin. You don't have the spine. That's a good boy."

Arkos dropped his father. The old man cursed as he hit the floor with the crunch of old bones. The Paladin ignored the whines of the drunken old man as he made for the exit of the manor. He kicked open the front door with such force that one of the hinges ripped from the wall. The night air that accosted him was cool, shocking him back to reality. What was he going to do? Run away like petulant child?

You don't stand up for yourself like your cousin.

Then he knew.

LUCKILY FOR ARKOS, Devin Lighthammer had yet to return to the barracks. The Paladin was nearly drunk, stumbling back that direction from his favorite tavern in the middle ring of the city. Arkos had been there with him once or twice, and headed straight that way once he was outside.

Overhead Aenna, the opening to the Divine Plane, shone through the clouds that partially covered the moon. The streets of Illux were cast in a silvery-grey light, making the city seem empty and dead. At least that was how it looked to the Paladin as he gained on his quarry.

It was once Devin rounded the corner into an alley to relieve himself that his cousin sprang. Arkos jumped onto Devin's back, forcing him to the ground. He brought his fists down onto his cousin again and again before the dazed warrior even realized what was happening. Finally, Devin snapped out of it and roared, grabbing Arkos by the shoulders and throwing him into the side of the building.

"Arkos?" What in the High God's name are you doing?" Devin spat, wiping blood from his mouth as he stood. "You could have gotten yourself killed. I would have blasted you if I hadn't seen who it was."

"Good," Arkos said. "Then you would have finally been done with your family once and for all, just like you've always wanted."

"What are you talking about?"

"You love Trent more than your own flesh and blood! More than me. And Gil—"

Devin unclasped his hammer and cape, casting them aside. His hands started to glow a faint blue and the air in the small alley crackled with energy.

"You want my love? Maybe you should stop being so much like your father!

Magic erupted out of Devin, slamming Arkos back into the wall. Bricks and other rubble showered the alley. Dazed, Arkos shook his head to stop the ringing. He had forgotten to bring weapons. No doubt this was why his cousin had cast aside the hammer so easily. Even in anger, he chose to fight fairly.

I'm a fool.

Arkos ignited his own magic, lancing white-hot energy at his cousin. Devin's protective magic flared to life, blocking the attack with ease and lighting the alley like daytime. Once the darkness returned, Arkos was in his face, punching him straight in the jaw. Devin staggered backward, laughing.

"There you go cousin," he said, spitting out blood. "I'd like to see your father do that."

"Shut up!" Arkos roared as he attacked again.

Devin parried each blow, following them up with some of his own. He kneed Arkos in the stomach and tossed him out of the alley and into the street. The younger Paladin hit the ground and rolled face-down into a puddle of something other than water. Arkos sputtered and pushed himself up, just in time to see two members of the City Watch pointing their way. A rough hand grabbed him by the back of the neck and pulled him to his feet.

"Let's go," Devin whispered. "We can kill each other later."

Arkos nodded dumbly and followed his cousin back down the alley. They cut across another street, ducking another pair of guards as they did so. The pair sprinted toward the center of the city. The watch would have a hard time following them in the dark, so long as they stayed off of the main roads. And besides, what drunk ruffians would be from the inner city and not the slums?

They rounded another corner, heading roughly toward home when Arkos heard more shouts. He turned and saw a much larger group of City Watch a few blocks behind them waving torches. He hissed and pushed Devin down another alley, slipping under hanging gardens that smelled of lilac. Together, they jumped over an iron fence that marked the property line of an inner city manor. In the dark, Arkos couldn't tell whose it was, so they just hunkered down in some shrubs and waited for the guards to run past.

After a few moments, the members of the City Watch seemed to disperse down different streets, looking for the fighters. When it seemed that the coast was clear, Devin stood and started to scale the fence again.

"So that's it, huh?" Arkos asked. "I attack you and you just let it go?"

Devin dropped back to the ground and spun on his cousin.

"What do you want from me, Arkos? An apology? You want to be my best friend? Follow me around like a lost dog? Is that it? I'm the best warrior this family has ever seen. What are you aside from your father's bootlicker?"

Arkos wound up to punch him again when the muffled screams of a woman cut through the night. They seemed to be coming from inside the house. Instinctively, he reached to his side, but there was no sword.

I am a fool.

Devin unclasped his hammer and nodded toward the door. They converged on it together, Devin holding the Lighthammer while Arkos tried the handle. It held fast. Arkos considered what to do next when he heard the woman again. This time she clearly cried: *HELP!* Devin didn't hesitate. He slammed the door with his warhammer, knocking it inward.

The two Paladins rushed inside, searching for the woman and the danger. No servants rushed to stop them or see what the sound of broken door was. In fact, the manor seemed deathly still other than the sounds of struggle in another room. They moved further into the house, searching for the source of the sounds.

Then they found it, and Devin swore, "Gods be good!"

Julius Silvershield had a woman pinned to his table. She was crying and trying to get free of him while he tore at her clothes. Arkos blinked in shock. This sin was one of the foulest.

"Unhand her," he heard himself say.

"What the fuck is this?" Julius asked, looking up.

"This is a rescue," Devin said.

The larger Paladin swung the hammer, striking Julius in the shoulder and sending him sprawling. Arkos could tell that his cousin had been holding back, or else Julius would have likely been killed. Devin helped the crying woman to her feet, shielding her from her attacker with his body. Arkos still didn't know what to do. He searched the room for anything that could make sense of what he had just seen. Devin said something to get his attention. Arkos saw him pointing at Julius. Arkos nodded dumbly and jumped onto the man. He struck Julius in the face again and again. Teeth and bits of gore splattered onto the marble floor. He didn't stop. Nothing made sense to him in that moment. His body felt as if it was a conduit for senseless rage.

"Arkos!" Devin shouted from far away. "That's enough! Leave him."

When the Paladin stood, the man who had just been a guest in his home hours ago now shuddered on the floor, covering the ruins of his face. Arkos turned and followed Devin out the door and back into the night.

"I'M PROUD OF YOU."

Devin had said that at some point the previous night, between returning the woman to her home in the slums and when they had finally parted for the night, just before sunrise. Proud of what, Arkos wasn't sure. They hadn't fought again, nor even spoke of their previous argument. Instead, they decided that they would approach Arkon in the morning, together. Even though they had prevented Julius from raping that woman, they had assaulted him while evading the City Watch. Reporting this crime would require a little finesse or else they risked their positions in the Paladin Order, and they hoped that the Lighthammer patriarch would use his connection to Redrick to see it done.

When Arkos awoke later in the morning, he found his father and Devin downstairs, already deep in argument.

"You can't be serious!" Devin bellowed. Half-eaten biscuits littered the table in front of him like corpses.

"I am," Arkos replied coolly. "I'll hear no more about it."

"What's going on?" Arkos asked.

"Your father says to forget what we saw last night. Julius Silver-shield was raping that woman, Arkon! She deserves justice! I'm not going to sit idly by, while that monster gets to stay in his comfortable manor and could possibly do that again!"

"What would you have me do?"

"Go to the City Watch! Have him arrested." Devin slammed his fist on the table for emphasis.

Arkon laughed.

"No, I will not. And neither will you," he said. "Do you think this is the first time this has happened? Gods be good, this isn't even the first time Julius has been caught. Haven't you ever wondered why he never became a Paladin? Or did you boys notice that he had no servants? That his house was nearly empty? The boy is out of money. I've been paying these women to keep them quiet every time he gets carried away like this. Soon, he'll owe me so much I can take his house."

Arkos felt sick. He knew his father was capable of justifying cruelty, but this?

"Father," he whispered finally, "you couldn't. He is guilty of serious crimes."

"That's for the High God to decide," the old man said, leaning back in his chair. "Besides, the women always take the money."

"This is foul," Devin said as he pushed himself up. "Those women deserved more than your coin. They should take every piece of gold you give them, and even *then* his manhood should still be ripped off. I'm part of this house no longer!"

He took his hammer and threw it onto the table. Arkos stared at his cousin, mouth agape.

"If you don't pick that hammer up right now, I swear to the gods I'll have you disinherited. I'll throw your mother onto the street. Now *sit down* and calm yourself."

"No. Cousin, come with me."

Forgive me.

"I-I can't."

"Then you *are* just like him."

Devin stormed out of the Lighthammer Manor for the last time.

Arkos sat alone in his room for hours, trying to decide if he would ever get the courage to speak to anyone ever again. He was ashamed of himself. He was ashamed of his father. He was ashamed of the name Lighthammer. Devin had been the only member of his family to show a single shred of honor. The Paladin paced back and forth, considering what his options were. A light knock at his door signaled that his mother had finally come to check on him.

"Arkos," she called, "may I come in?"

"Yes."

She entered slowly, closing the door behind herself. She was wearing all black today. Fitting, considering the loss of Devin that morning. He doubted that was the reason, however.

"Did you know?" He asked.

"About the women from the slums?" She looked away. "I did."

"And you let this go on?"

"It wasn't like they were from good families, Arkos. Think about it. They got money from your father. Gods, perhaps one of them would get pregnant and the boy would have been forced to marry the poor wretch…"

"A *sinspawn?*" Arkos whispered, clenching his fists. "I've heard you both use the word. Don't pretend that you would show a child of such a union any grace, mother. You are just as guilty as father is. Both of you…"

She walked closer, putting a hand on his face. Arkos could feel the tears welling up in his eyes.

"Those girls aren't your responsibility, Arkos. Forget them."

Arkos recoiled from her touch.

"Devin was right," he spat. "This family is fouler than any Demon."

Arkos was sure to grab his sword this time, strapping it to his side before he walked out the door. If he moved quickly, he could find Redrick and report Julius to the City Watch before shame completely overtook him.

THE GATES of Illux loomed overhead. Their glittering golden surface reflected a beam of sunlight onto the lone Paladin walking toward them. He should have gone to the practice grounds today. He should have checked in with his superiors at the barracks or the Fourth Spire for instruction. His absence would be noticed. He would face punishment of some kind.

Hopefully my actions today will atone for it.

He had been told that Redrick was inspecting the guards at the gatehouses today, and by now would be at the eastern gate. This was it. The time for Arkos Lighthammer to stand up to his father and make his ancestors proud. It was time for Arkos Lighthammer to earn his place on a tapestry. As a boy, he had believed that all Paladins were heroes. Now he knew otherwise.

He stopped short of walking inside the gatehouse. If he did this, his father would be furious. He could be disowned. Even as disgusting as his parents' behavior had been, they were still his family. Could he really cast them off as quickly as his cousin had? His stomach churned. This wasn't noble or brave. He was being a coward. But cowardice felt safe.

Forgive me.

Arkos turned to return home, his shame overwhelming. His anger had subsided, replaced now with fear. He could never be half the man Devin was, and he knew it.

"Cousin!" A familiar voice boomed.

His heart sank. Arkos turned to see Devin walking out of the gatehouse. His cousin grinned from ear to ear. It even looked like he was proud. When Devin got close, he took Arkos in with a swallowing hug.

"I knew you would make the right decision. Forgive me for what I said earlier. Your father doesn't have the courage you do. I'm proud of you, Arkos." Devin released Arkos from his embrace. "Come with me, let's go to the barracks and get you moved over. You don't need to stay with those fools anymore."

"I-I think I'll stay there one more night, at least. For my mother's sake," Arkos stammered.

Devin's smile lessened. "Suit yourself. Would you get a drink with me, at least?"

"We shouldn't," Arkos said. "You need to check back in. I need to take a walk alone."

Devin nodded, letting Arkos wander off in the opposite direction. A sickness washed over him. Now he was a liar as well as a coward. His cousin thought better of him than he deserved. With any luck, the city would swallow him up on his walk back to Lighthammer Manor.

. . .

ARKOS ATE his dinner in silence. His father and mother sat at the opposite end of the table, quietly digging through their own plates as well. The servants hadn't made anything special tonight; his father claimed to be saving money after the extravagance of the night before.

"Your mother tells me that you plan to leave," Arkon said.

"I did," Arkos replied.

"Ah, so you've changed your mind? Good. I'd hate to see you follow in your idiot cousin's footsteps. Perhaps you are smarter than I give you credit for."

Arkos snorted but said nothing.

"Speaking of which," his father continued, "Redrick paid me a visit today while you were wandering the city. He told me that your cousin came to see him." Arkos swallowed hard, but never looked up from his plate. "The woman has already been paid. Redrick gave Julius a tongue lashing, though from what he told me it was *nothing* compared to the beating that you gave the boy. In any case, he is willing to overlook a little fun for an old family.

"The little miscreant will have to give me his manor, now. Once the paperwork for that is complete, I will give the word and he'll be arrested. We don't want your cousin loosing his lips to the Seraph. The gods know she doesn't appreciate our bloodlines the way her predecessor did. See son, we both get what we want."

"And what if he does it again in the meantime?" Arkos croaked.

"Then I suppose I pay a little more for the property than I wanted," Arkon chuckled.

Arkos stood, toppling his chair.

"More of these theatrics?" His father asked, clearly annoyed.

"Dear, sit down," his mother pleaded.

"No," was all he could muster.

Arkos stormed out of his parents' presence once again. The fire that burned in his belly threatened to ignite the world around him. He saw that his father had affixed the family hammer above the entrance. The Paladin yanked the weapon down.

The Lighthammer will pass justice once again.

He slipped out of his house and snuck through the night like a thief. It didn't take long for him to reach his destination: Silvershield Manor. The light of candles still flickered in the windows. Arkos busted open the front gate with his hammer, the twisted metal falling away from him as he stepped through, its remnants curving up toward the sky like raised spears.

This was the property that his father coveted so much that he would cover up a heinous sin. All of that would change tonight.

The door hung askew from the previous night. It didn't take much to break it from its hinges. Just as before, no one rushed to see the source of the sound. Arkos moved quickly from room to room, hunting for his prey. He was nowhere to be seen on the lower level, so the Paladin made his way up the staircase to the second floor.

Julius was lying on a feather bed with several empty bottles of wine scattered about the room. His broken face was covered by his hands, so he didn't see Arkos enter the room.

"How many?" Arkos spat.

Julius nearly tumbled from the bed.

"What? Why are you back again? Your father paid her!" The wretched man scrambled backward, clutching a bottle before him like it was a knife.

"How many women have you raped?"

"I—"

"Answer me!" Arkos shouted. He swung his hammer, demolishing the end of the bed in an explosion of feathers and wood shards.

"I don't know! Ten, eleven, a dozen, I think! I don't know!"

"*Twelve*, then," Arkos said.

The Paladin advanced on the rapist, knocking the bottle from his trembling hands easily.

"Please," Julius pleaded. "I've never killed anyone!"

"Paladins seek out evil, Julius. We mete out justice. If you can survive twelve blows from the Lighthammer, I'll consider your debt paid."

Before the man could speak again, he was struck by a blow from the hammer that sent him spinning into the wall. The wet crunch of broken bones was nearly drowned out by his screams. Arkos raised the hammer again. His rage started to wane as he saw the bloodied man cowering beneath him.

You don't have the spine. That's a good boy.

His father's words echoed in his mind. That was all the encouragement that he needed. Julius Silvershield stopped making any sound after the third blow. Stopped breathing after the fifth. The twelfth sent his broken corpse out the window to the fence below, where it was impaled by the broken iron gate.

Arkos didn't blink. He walked back down through the house that would have belonged to his father, taking in the history of the family that he had just extinguished. Paintings of great heroes decorated the walls, but beyond that, the house was mostly empty. There was nothing here worth saving.

Outside, the Paladin approached the body of Julius Silvershield. What was left of the man was being held up by the remains of the gate in a macabre fashion. Arkos bent down and wrote the word *rapist* on the ground in the man's blood. When he was finished, he ignited the dormant magic in his body and turned it on the manor.

THE PATRIARCH of the Lighthammer family sat in his favorite chair by the fire when his son entered the room. Arkon was sipping from a goblet and leafing through a copy of the *Canticle of the Forsaken Ones*. Arkos considered killing him as well, but the thought was fleeting. He had already gone too far tonight. Devin would never have done such a thing. Still, his anger burned like the Silvershield Manor, and he needed to turn it on something.

Father," he said. "I want to show you something."

Arkon looked at him in confusion. Arkos was sure that his father would notice the gore that streaked his armor, as well as the still-dripping hammer that he clutched in his hand.

"What have you done?" The old man whispered.

"Come and see."

His father followed him outside, where an orange glow danced in the distance. Shouts filled the streets as the City Watch rushed to contain the blaze. It took his father a few moments to process what he was seeing, but once he did, he faltered and grabbed onto the railing of their porch to steady himself.

"What have you done?" He asked again.

"You won't be getting your *investment* back, father. And you'd best see if Redrick is willing to overlook a little fun for an old family."

Arkos shoved the warhammer into his father's hands and walked back inside, leaving the old man to shiver alone in the cool night air.

TEN OF SEATOWN

I.

1049 AP

The salt in the air mingled with the salt in Wyn's tears. The ship rocked in the surf as the unusually choppy waves buffeted the ship that housed her father above the ocean's surface for the last time. The body of Admiral Titus Thacker sat on the deck of the ship, draped in a blue and green shroud. He had died the night before from an illness that he had caught the past winter and never quite shaken.

His only child stood over him like a sentinel, waiting for the place in the ocean waters that felt right to her. Then she would give the order, and the crew would commit her father to The Nameless Sea that he loved so well. Titus would finally rejoin his wife, Althea, whose ship had gone down nearly a decade before.

Wyn looked out toward the horizon, imagining the lands that her mother had discovered. Rich, fertile shores untainted by the Darkness of the Mortal Plane. Ever since the raid on Seatown by the rogue Paladin Cecilia, when Wyn had been just a girl, her mother had taken to The Nameless Sea on a ship named *Wyn* to search for a new home for their people. Althea had found many suitable places, but Titus, ever the pragmatist, feared what would happen if the powers in Illux felt as if Seatown were abandoning them.

The young Thacker had planned to be just like her mother when she was grown, sailing beyond the horizon and laying eyes on places no mortal had ever seen. Then Althea had sailed off one day and never returned. The mast of her ship washed ashore some weeks later, and they knew what had become of her. Titus had fallen into a deep depression that he had never truly climbed out of, and his sour mood nearly drowned his daughter as well. Looking out at the water, she felt guilt creep into her belly as she admitted to herself that she had some modicum of relief that he was gone. Now she could live her life as she saw fit, not suffocating under the protective gaze of the Admiral.

The call of the gulls overhead returned her to the moment, and she again gazed at the shroud that covered her father. Now the Seraph would need to be summoned to choose his successor. The government of Seatown would be reeling in the interim, and Wyn would undoubtedly be forced to step in for the time being to lead her people. Once the Lady Ren arrived, Wyn would be free to make her own destiny, and it wouldn't involve being in charge of the largest mortal settlement outside of the City of Light.

Gods be good, a month from now and I'll never see this place again.

The water here, though still a tumult, was a serene blue that reminded her of her mother's eyes. She knew that her father would have liked that. A wisp of cloud above was the only thing that separated the sky from the sea at that moment. Shielding her eyes from the light of the sun, Wyn breathed in the salt air and gathered her senses, willing her tears to stop.

"Here!" she shouted, stronger than she felt.

"This is the spot!" the bosun confirmed to the crew. "Prepare the Admiral!"

Fighting the waves, the crew gathered around the bier and lifted the shrouded man toward the railing on the starboard side, preparing to commit him to the depths. The priest from the church that her father favored started a sermon, and once again Wyn felt her mind drift.

When the sermon was over, the crew heaved and Admiral Titus Thacker rejoined his wife beneath the waves.

"Be well, father," Wynn whispered. "May you find her quickly."

Wyn turned and walked back to the cabin of the ship. The ocean held less allure to her in that moment.

BACK AT THE PORT, the ship docked with the usual flurry of activity. Wyn wasn't sure why she expected anything different, but the crew certainly didn't seem as somber as she would have expected for a burial voyage.

They've all lost someone before. Even being their Admiral, my father was just another man.

She tried to disembark discreetly, but Chrysta was already waiting for her, waving in a cheerful way that seemed unbecoming of the moment. When she drew close, and grabbed Wyn by the arm her expression soured, however.

"It's been a busy day," she whispered. "Already the city cries out for a successor to your father. There have been crowds in the town square all morning."

"Gods above, can't they let him rest for a single day?" Wyn sighed. "Well, I'll make certain that a messenger is sent to Illux by tomorrow. It will be weeks before the Seraph comes, in any case."

Chrysta rubbed her palms together. That was when Wyn noticed that her cheeks were rosier than usual. The woman's greying hair started to shake loose as she spoke, her voice dropping even lower.

"That's the issue, dear. They don't want to wait."

Wyn looked sidelong at her mother's oldest friend.

"What did you say? The Seraph has always chosen the Admiral since Arendt founded Seatown. That isn't changing because—it's Hyrum, isn't it? That fucking cur couldn't even wait for the sea to take my father."

Her fingernails bit deep into her palms. Chrysta looked concerned, but quickly smiled at a passerby. Wyn noticed then that they weren't heading toward the Overlook, the tower that always housed the Admiral and their family. Instead, the older woman was leading her somewhere else, farther from the docks than she wanted to be at that moment.

"It's not just Hyrum. There were dozens of voices at these meetings. Not all of them support that wily bastard. Your father, rest his spark, was a great man. But Seatown has needed sterner stuff since your mother died. They—we—don't want Illux to be in charge anymore. Catering to the City of Light is what prevented us from following your mother across the sea—"

Wyn reeled on her. "Don't start that again! I wished a thousand times that my father would have listened to her and allowed his people to flee this accursed place, but don't lay her death at his feet. He did that enough for the last ten years!"

"I was only meaning—"

"I know what you meant. Illux hasn't given two shits about us my entire life. Just because Jerrok is gone and the Lady Ren is in charge now doesn't mean that things have changed. I know this. My father was many things, but he was no fool. If we cast off Illux in one motion, we possibly bring about the wrath of all of the Light on us. These things have to be done in stages, with compromise!"

Chrysta was smiling then.

"You are right, of course. And what better way to take one small step toward independence than choosing an Admiral of our own? And who better than someone whom the people trust and who understands the nuances required when dealing with Illux? Someone who also has the adventurer spirit that we need to move our people to new lands?"

Realization washed over her like the tide.

"No," Wyn said.

"The people of Seatown need someone like your father to keep them from being crushed by Illux. But they also need someone like your mother to lead them over the horizon. Who better than their daughter?"

Wyn abruptly turned to walk back toward the wharf and the Overlook.

"Not me, Chrysta. Find someone else. I'll be sending a messenger in the morning."

"What of Hyrum, then?" the older woman asked, her voice like ice. "Do you really want to entrust your father's people to that man? Your mother's legacy? What do you think he will do with the power? Because if you don't step up, he will take it."

Wyn paused a moment, then shook her head. She continued on her way, calling back, "If they are foolish enough to follow him, let them. Once the Seraph arrives, I plan to gather a crew and pick up where my mother left off."

She spent the walk back to her home sulking in the midday sun.

Damn that woman.

Still, she couldn't shake the feeling that Chrysta was right. Who was Ren to the people of Seatown? Why shouldn't they have a say in who governed them, rather than some distant mouthpiece, divine or otherwise? And she knew Hyrum was no good for this town. He was one of the wealthiest merchants outside of Illux, and he used his coffers not to help the people of Seatown, but to fleece them. Her father had often butted heads with the man, and more than once she was sure that he contemplated having him arrested on one charge or another.

"Not all servants of the Gods of Darkness live in the wilderness and prey on caravans," he had told her once.

Even so, there was no reason for her to get involved. Wyn still had some of her mother's old maps, her most cherished possessions, and she intended to fill in the blank spots or die trying. She couldn't do that if she was shackled to the Overlook, governing the people of Seatown. Certainly not if she was engaged in a power struggle with Illux at the same time. Yet how many more lands could a fleet of ships discover than a single one? Althea's legacy could live on in more than just the memory of one motherless little girl.

Damn that woman.

II.

The following day, no messenger had been sent to Illux. As far as the City of Light and the Lady Ren knew, Seatown was still ruled by Titus Thacker. Wyn supposed that if the gods were watching they might have told the Seraph, but she was unconvinced that they worried themselves with such petty things.

Wyn stood in the center of a crowd that had gathered to hear Hyrum speak from a makeshift platform at the base of the statue of the Seraph Arendt. The merchant was dressed in even more extravagant finery than normal; his cloak was cloth of gold, and rings with dazzling jewels mined from caves in the Rim adorned his fingers. He looked richer than anyone from Illux, even. Wyn held back her disgust. She just hoped that his gaudiness would not sway the people of her city.

"And what do the people of Illux know of us? Of our struggles?" he shouted, his voice confident and sonorous. "What can some inner city family know of the dangers of a squall or the tragedy of an empty net? How can they hope to govern us from so far away? The Seraph's hands are already full with one city, she has no time for another!"

"He's right!" someone yelled from the crowd.

"Fuck them!" another continued.

"Now that the Admiral has rejoined the sea, it's time for us to chart our own course. It's time for the people of Seatown to choose their own leader. It's time that we govern ourselves!"

The crowd erupted in applause. Wyn grimaced. Even though she agreed with his words, she knew what would come next, and she knew just how terrible for her people that would be.

"As the foremost merchant in Seatown, and a prominent member of this community, I humbly request the honor of serving this place that I love as the new Admiral! I will make sure that the wealth this city has given me is returned tenfold!"

The roar of the crowd was deafening. Wyn looked around at the faces of those screaming support for Hyrum. She saw real admiration there, and it made her sick. Her eyes fell upon a Paladin named Kellan, who was barely hiding a grimace, not far from where she stood. Some near the man cast wary glances at him. No one knew exactly how the Paladins of Seatown would react to criticisms of Illux.

Kellan turned and shouldered his way through the crowd, toward the large building that housed the eight Paladins that were stationed here. Wyn looked back up at Hyrum and saw that the merchant watched the Paladin go, his confident facade cracking for just a moment.

That's my opening.

Wyn pulled her hood back on and crept through the crowd as it started to swarm the platform Hyrum stood on. She made it out of the crush and approached the Paladin's home, hoping that Hyrum was too distracted by his supporters to notice the cloaked woman.

"Wyn," a voice hissed from beside the building.

Startled, Wyn spun to see Chrysta motioning her to come off to the side.

"What are you doing here?" Wyn asked.

"I was looking for you. I heard that no messenger went to Illux this morning, so I came to find you. When you weren't at the Overlook, I knew where you'd be. I'm glad to see that you gained some sense since yesterday."

Wyn shook her head, stifling a laugh.

"You're impossible. Some days I'm glad that you weren't a sailor like mother. Other days I wish you were. I'm not sure how I feel today."

Chrysta's smile widened.

"Let's see how you feel after you talk with the Paladins. I was trying to bring you here yesterday."

"You what—"

The door opened, and Kellan leaned out. His dark hair was shaved close to his head, and his icy blue eyes fell on Wyn.

"Well?" he asked. "Are you two coming in? Or do you plan to wait for Hyrum to join you?"

Wyn straightened and smoothed her cloak before nodding. Both women followed the man inside before he closed and bolted the door.

Inside, they stood in a sitting room with a hearth and nearly a dozen chairs. Wyn saw that the other eight Paladins were already in the room. Her heart caught in her throat. She didn't like being caught unawares like this. A sideways glance at Chrysta showed that the other woman was far more prepared than Wyn was.

Damn you, Chrysta.

"Welcome, Admiral," said Celeste, a woman with nut brown skin like Wyn's.

"I-I don't understand," Wyn stammered. "I'm not…"

"Not yet," Kellan said, "but the people in this room aim to change that. Take a seat."

Wyn and Chrysta each sat in a sturdy chair that was clearly meant to support more weight than that of a normal human. Wyn looked about the room. It was sparsely furnished, with nothing more than the chairs and a few old weapons adorning the walls. This wasn't a place that often welcomed guests. Kellan and Celeste sat directly across from her, with Mika, Fen, Louis, Jaimie, Caleb, and Ansel forming a semicircle to their left and right.

"By this afternoon, the eight of us will become ten," Celeste began. "Two more Seatown natives, Jok and Theo should arrive by the evening. Their initiation was a few months past. Your father requested we bolster our numbers before he took ill. It didn't take much to convince the Seraph that we needed more warriors used to the coastal climate to have them assigned here."

"This puts us in an interesting position," Kellan continued. "There haven't been this many Paladins stationed in one location outside of Illux since the Pact. Especially ten united in…purpose, such as we are."

Wyn fidgeted nervously in her seat. His voice had taken on a chilling aspect.

"What purpose is that?" she asked.

"Independence from Illux, and from the Fourth Spire," Fen interjected. "We wish for the authority of the so-called Lady Ren to be a distant memory for not only us, but the people of Seatown."

"But why?" Wyn asked, her voice shaking.

"Long have the people of Illux cared only for themselves. This is a tale told in every tavern from here to the Great Chasm. But there is more than that." Kellan leaned forward, a wicked smile crossing his face. "Don't tell me that you never chafed under the rule of your father? What child doesn't wish to be free of their parents? We only want the right to make our own decisions, to chart our own course. We cannot do that if we are constantly under the thumb of the Seraph. This is why we want you to be the Admiral. Together, the eleven of us can lead Seatown to a prosperous future."

It can't be that simple.

"Why me?" she asked. "Why not Hyrum? I wasn't even the one to suggest that the people choose their own Admiral, he was. It seems to me that your plan would work flawlessly with him."

"Hyrum is much less…accommodating than we take you to be," Kellan said.

Less tractable, you mean.

Chrysta spoke up then, clearly having spoken with the Paladins at length already, which Wyn still wasn't sure she could forgive her for.

"Hyrum only wants to enrich himself, you know this, dear. He says that his wealth will flow to the people of Seatown, but the truth is anything but. He suggested that the people choose an Admiral so that he could secure the power that he has long coveted, not because he actually wants what's best for us. Not like you do. Not like *they* do."

The Paladins all nodded in agreement, their faces getting more solemn by the moment. Wyn felt a flash of irritation. They thought she was as easily duped as Chrysta was.

"What would you do, then? I already decided to announce to the city that I would take the title before Hyrum could tarnish it. What would the Paladins have to offer? The people will ultimately decide."

"Aye," Kellan said, "and yet here we are. Hyrum's words are like honey, and already he has crowds supporting him. With our endorsement, you would show the people that you have the Light behind you. That should be enough to sway them to our cause."

"And if it isn't?"

"We will not let that merchant control Seatown," Kellan said, firmly.

That final pronouncement made Wyn shiver. She quickly pushed away from her chair and bowed as deferentially as she was able.

"Thank you for the offer. I will certainly think about it tonight."

Without waiting for Chrysta, she walked back out into the town square.

Soon there will be ten of them.

WYN WAITED a few hours for the crowd of Hyrum supporters to disperse before taking to the makeshift stand at the base of Arendt. The Seraph loomed over her, his golden form blanketing her in shadow. His name was infamous to most outside Seatown. The Seraph who had caused the Purge of Illux nearly five hundred years ago. Yet he had also founded Seatown, and legend said he had always intended them to be a people apart from the City of Light.

What if instead of ranging through the wilderness, you had moved the Fourth Spire here? That would have been something.

Some people passing by noticed that once again there was a figure standing above them, ready to speak. It didn't take long for another crowd, though smaller than Hyrum's, to form around her. She gauged her words carefully as they filtered in, mumbling to themselves that it was the daughter of the dead Admiral before them. Wyn had been well-liked in the city, as much her mother's doing as her father's. But she had often kept to herself, so many of these folk no doubt saw her as a stranger. She needed to change that, and quickly.

"People of Seatown!" she began, "most of you know me as the quiet daughter of Admiral Titus. I am the only child of one of the greatest rulers our city has ever known! But think also of my mother Althea, a sailor and explorer who sought to take our people to new lands where the Forces of Darkness could not molest us, where the people of Illux could not take us for granted! Her blood also runs in my veins, and I am angry!"

The crowd had begun to cheer with her short genealogy before growing silent.

"No longer should we allow Illux or the inner city families or even the Seraph to choose for us an Admiral. Did not Arendt create Seatown to be a gem on the coast, filled with a people unto themselves?"

"Yes!" they answered.

"Why then do we bow down to those who have never caught a fish or hoisted a sail or even smelled the salt on the air? On this point, the estimable Hyrum and I agree. Yet we differ in the fact that I do not think he is the best choice to lead our city. Nay, I say he is the worst!"

Some cheered while others booed. Many stared at her in shock. That was when she noticed Kellan and Celeste in the crowd watching her alongside Chrysta.

"He claims the wealth Seatown has given him will return tenfold? I say, how can that be when it was stolen from you? Was it not your sweat and blood that filled the nets with the fish he sold in Illux for a dozen times what he paid you for them? How many among you have lived in squalor while he rests in a manse on the hill? Do you trust this man, whose hands are as soft as the down of his bedding, to know your struggles? When was the last time Hyrum held a rope or a net? When was the last time he has cried for a loved one lost at sea?"

The cheering continued even as more and more people joined the crowd.

"I say he belongs in Illux with the rich families of the inner city, not out here with the people of Arendt who know the sea and the value of a day's work. I ask that I should be the next Admiral of Seatown, not because of my father, but because of my mother. Because I know the ocean and the coast and the fight it takes to make them ours!"

She hopped down from the stand and was swept up in the crowd, buoyed across the top of them like she was adrift in the sea. Her eyes found Chrysta, and the older woman looked proud of her. When she looked for the two Paladins, however, it seemed that they had vanished.

THAT EVENING, Wyn retired to the Overlook thoroughly exhausted from speaking in taverns and arguing with priests about whether or not Ren should be summoned to choose her father's successor. She had done in an afternoon what Hyrum hadn't been able to do in the last two days. It seemed that all quarters of Seatown were firmly on her side.

Just as she prepared to walk the winding stairs to her bedchamber above, there was a hurried knock on the thick oak door. Wyn had carried a dirk or a sword ever since she was a child, at her mother's insistence. Nearly losing her daughter during Ceclia's raid had certainly given the woman cause to train her daughter to fight. Wyn reached to her side for her blade now, surprised by a disturbance at this late hour.

Dirk in hand, she approached the door and placed her hand on the lock.

"Who is it?" she called.

"It's Chrysta. Stop with the theatrics and let me in!"

Wyn sheathed the dirk and ushered her mother's friend inside. A storm had blown in off the Nameless Sea, blanketing the world outside with a fine mist.

"Why in the High God's name are you here this late? I'm exhausted and was about to climb into bed."

"You know as well as anyone that the Admiral has long hours,"

Chrysta said. "I came to tell you what news there is of Hyrum. It seems that word of your claim to Admiral has infuriated him. Somehow, it has been suggested that the people vote tomorrow, before the afternoon tide. There are even rumors that he has been bribing the less fortunate for votes."

"Let him force a vote then," Wyn scoffed. "He won't win, Chrysta. He's hoping that he can slide in before I can talk to any more crowds. It won't matter. He's afraid, and that's all I need to know."

"That's what I'm afraid of, dear, and why I've come so late. I heard that he was offering top coin to several experienced warriors today in bars around town. No one is sure what for, but I have my suspicions. Hyrum isn't a fool. If he is worried about you becoming Admiral, I think he might do something dangerous."

"Dangerous? Like what the Paladins implied today? Chrysta, you can't be serious. Your new friends are the only ones I'm worried about. Honestly, I don't know how I can forgive you for going behind my back like that. And Paladins of all people trying to usurp the rule of the Seraph? Have you thrown in with ten more Cecilias?"

Chrysta slapped Wyn across the face. Even though she was getting on in years, the blow was fierce.

"Shame on you, Wyn Thacker. Your mother and father raised you better than that."

Chrysta spun, tears in her eyes, and threw open the door. A quarrel from a crossbow buried itself in her eye. She fell backward, knocking Wyn to the ground.

"Chrysta!" Wyn cried.

She rolled the body of the older woman to the side and crawled out of sight from the still-open door. Another quarrel hit the stones of the wall behind her, where she had been a mere moment before. Dirk in hand once again, she tried to kick the door closed without exposing herself.

It was no use. The body of Chrysta prevented the door from closing all the way.

"Dammit," she cursed.

Forgive me, Chrysta.

Wyn pulled the body around the door just as it was forced wide. A giant of a man with a face covered by a black mask towered over her. From his belt dangled a crossbow, and in his hand was a simple club. She tried to roll away from him, but he was much faster than his size implied. With one kick, her dirk went flying across the room. The man struck her left arm with his club. She cried out as the bones burst through the flesh of her forearm.

The next blow sent her head slamming into the stone floor. Her vision darkened and the world swam around her. She knew that she would be seeing her mother and father very soon. The man lifted her up by the neck, pinning her against the wall. Wyn closed her eyes as her assassin raised his club for the final blow.

She felt a warm spray of blood, followed by the sound of a guttural scream. Then she was on the floor in a broken heap. Willing her eyes to open, Wyn saw her attacker dumbly holding the stump of his arm. Suddenly, a flash of silver removed his head from his neck and he slumped down beside the other two bodies on the ground.

The last thing she saw before the darkness took her was the glowing face of Kellan as the Paladin kneeled down by her side.

III.

Though her arm was completely healed by the Paladin's magic, her blood still stained the floor of the Overlook the following morning. As did the blood of Chrysta and her murderer. Kellan had taken the bodies to give them a burial at sea. Wyn had been too shaken up to go with him. Without his timely appearance, she would have been dead as well, and it would have been Hyrum—or someone he paid—who would be cleaning these floors.

She hunkered down with the brush and wash bucket, scouring every inch of scarlet from the floor. She had played on this floor as a child, always getting in the way of her father and mother as they came and went from the tower. There were even nights where she had fallen asleep down here on the ground floor and one of them had carried her up to bed. Now she removed the last traces of her mother's friend from these same stones.

Her resolve had been tested last night, but as she cleaned up the remaining vestiges of the attack, she felt her strength returning. This was Hyrum's doing, of that she was sure. Chrysta had come to warn her that such a thing was possible, and Wyn had ignored the warning. Now she was dead.

Thank the gods Kellan came.

The Paladin had been coming to try and warn her of what he had heard as well, and to make one last attempt at convincing her to throw in with the eight—no, ten—of them. She sighed as she dipped the brush back into the now crimson water. She now realized that even if they made her uncomfortable, she needed the Paladins for protection if nothing else. Her parents had taught her to fight, but she was no warrior. That was something she planned to rectify after Hyrum was dealt with.

The vote was to be held in a few short hours. The Paladins announced that they would gather the people together in the square just before the afternoon tide. The crowd would split into two groups, one for Wyn and one for Hyrum. The larger crowd would mean that that candidate was the new Admiral. This was when Kellan would make it known who the Paladins supported, not only to catch Hyrum off guard, but to surprise and influence the people as well. They had kept word of the assassination attempt quiet for now. Wyn had decided to hide until the vote, to allow Hyrum to hope that his plan had worked, even though he no doubt wondered why he hadn't heard from his lackey yet.

Once this is over, I'll have him tried and hanged. Gods be good, he'll pay for what he did to you Chrysta. I hope one day you can forgive me.

The thought of tying a weight to him and dropping him in the sea sounded appealing as well, but she decided that she didn't want to pollute the resting place of her parents and Chrysta. This scum deserved to die in the air and be committed to the earth. The ocean was too good for him.

Outside her window, she saw that the Nameless Sea was calm today, the complete opposite of what it had been when she laid her father to rest. She decided that she needed to gather her thoughts and prepare herself for the afternoon.

Once the last bit of blood was cleaned up, Wyn slid out the door and quickly walked down the dock to where her childhood boat still bobbed in the surf. Her father never had the heart to get rid of it and, truth be told, neither had she. It was barely bigger than a rowboat, though it did have a small mast and sail. While she would no doubt feel cramped on it today, while she had been growing up, it had felt like freedom. The pink and gold paint had long since peeled off the bow, but the name still showed on the placard hanging from the stern: *Wyn's Grace.*

Making certain that no one was looking, Wyn undid the rope that fastened the small boat to the dock and hopped in, using the child-sized oars to push her way out to sea. It didn't take long for her to get halfway between the ships on the horizon and the city at her back. There she stopped paddling and lowered the sail so that she would simply float here.

The only sounds she heard were the occasional call from the gulls and the quiet lapping of the waves against the hull of the small boat. Wyn leaned over the railing and cupped the water with her hands. This was where she felt the most at peace. For a moment, she thought she could see the reflection of both of her parents standing behind her, but they vanished with the dip of the boat.

"Am I strong enough to do this?" she asked the sea. "All I wanted was to explore and sail. But I can't leave Seatown to be ignored by Illux any longer or to be drained by Hyrum. I have to avenge Chrysta. I know all of this, but am I strong enough?"

When no one answered, Wyn splashed water on her face and lay down on the deck with a sigh. Overhead, the sun was nearing its zenith beside Aenna. Did the Gods of Light look down on her and have any knowledge to share? She wasn't a prayerful woman, and didn't plan to start today. The gods had taken her mother and father from her. It was to the sea that she owed her allegiance.

Two gulls landed on the prow and gazed at her sideways. Once they had her attention, they flew back toward Seatown before wheeling about and heading farther out to sea. Wyn followed them with her gaze until they disappeared over the horizon. If she wanted to follow them, first she needed to make certain that her home was safe.

She raised the sail and began turning her boat back to shore. It was time to end this.

. . .

CELESTE WAS WAITING for her when she returned to the dock. Wyn tied her boat and hopped ashore, standing taller than she had before. The Paladin sized her up and down with a smirk.

"We feared that you had gotten scared and run off," she said.

"Just needed to gather my thoughts," Wyn said. "I do it best out there. I think I had forgotten that until today."

"Are you ready? It's nearly time."

"Let's go."

Wyn followed her back into the heart of the city. She didn't give the Overlook another glance. It would truly be her home again soon enough and, hopefully, its ghosts would rest once it was. Ahead, the distant rumble of the crowd grew louder as they approached. Then the crowd was silenced as the voice of Hyrum carried on the breeze.

"It seems that my challenger has abandoned us," he mocked. "Not all are cut from the same cloth as me or her father. I say then that unless someone here wishes to challenge me, I am the new Admiral of Seatown!"

Wyn and Celeste picked up the pace, rounding the final corner and arriving at the back of the gathered citizens.

"I haven't gone anywhere!" she shouted.

The crowd parted, allowing Wyn to join Hyrum on the platform. She tried to ignore her would-be murderer as she waved and smiled at the crowd. From the corner of her eye, she could see her competitor clenching his fists in rage.

"Surprised to see me?" she whispered.

"Yes," he said coolly. "I thought you had decided to run away like a frightened child. No matter. I'll be sure to gift you a fine home once the Overlook is mine."

Though his words dripped with malice, she felt a pang of doubt. He didn't sound like a man who just failed to have someone killed. Perhaps he was a better politician than she had given him credit for. After a few moments, the cheering of the crowd abated to let the two candidates speak. Hyrum bowed deferentially to Wyn, but she shook her head in protest.

"You were here first," she said. "I'll allow you the honor."

Hyrum scowled at her before smoothing his cloth of gold and stepping forward. His voice was loud, but not as confident as it had seemed the day before.

"Those of you who have listened to me these past few days already know what I have to offer our great city. I propose nothing less now. Wyn Thacker has an impressive genealogy, of which there is no doubt, but what of her personal accomplishments? What has she done besides hide in the Overlook or out on a ship? I have proven my aptitude for business and politics. What has she proven besides the merits of a pretty face?"

Some of the crowd cheered again when he finished, while some booed. Wyn could tell that her last-minute appearance had left him at a loss for words. She needed to use that to her advantage.

"I appreciate the compliment Hyrum," she shouted with a smile. "I do have a pretty face. And yes, I have spent much of my time on the sea, though I wouldn't call it hiding. I would call it living, the way our people have lived for five hundred years!" The cheering dwarfed what Hyrum had mustered. "In fact, the sea is where I was this morning. I revere the gods and the Seraph like any pious woman, but the sea is where I seek guidance. It is not only my wish to make Seatown independent from the control of Illux, but for us to seek new lands and explore the High God's creation!

"Show me a ship crafted by Demons or an Accursed that can swim? If we set sail for the place my mother found, we can truly be safe from the horrors of the Darkness. What better way to honor the Light than to survive? Are we not a people apart, as envisioned by the Seraph Arendt? Is the sea not our birthright?"

She stepped back beside Hyrum, her heart swelling. For a moment, it seemed to her that the vote would be unanimous in her favor. Flanking the crowd stood the ten forms of the Paladins, the midday sun glinting off their white armor. It didn't seem that she needed their support after all, but she did owe them her life, so a deal still needed to be struck.

"Those who support Hyrum for the next Admiral, stand to the left of Arendt!" Kellan shouted. "Those who support Wyn to the right."

The crowd began to disperse into two camps. To Wyn's surprise, it was closer than she expected. Perhaps the rumors Chrysta had heard were true, and Hyrum had begun paying people to vote for him. A pang of fear struck her for a moment before she steadied herself. This wasn't over, the Paladins still needed to make their move.

Kellan nodded at the platform, and the Paladins moved to join the crowd on the right side. This caused an uproar among those on Hyrum's side. No doubt many of them had expected the champions to remain neutral. Beside her, Hyrum had begun to mutter to himself. Then he leaned in and grabbed Wyn by the arm.

"I don't know what kind of deal you made with them, but it won't work," he hissed. "If you are working with the ten of them, you will still be under the thumb of the Seraph."

She shook her arm free. Overhead, she could hear two gulls calling for one another.

"You are mistaken, Hyrum," she replied. "Just as you were last night. They hold no allegiance to Ren, only to Seatown."

Confusion washed over his face. Then he replaced it with a look of confidence as he once again smoothed his robes.

"I have no idea what you're talking about, but if you think that ten Paladins turning against the Seraph is a good thing, you must have forgotten what Cecilia's raid was like."

Wyn tried to ignore the shiver that his words gave her. Below, the crowd was nearly done splitting up, and once the Paladins had chosen their place, it seemed to sway most of the remainder to her side. It was clear even without counting that Wyn was going to be the next Admiral. She breathed a sigh of relief, even as her eyes fell on Kellan and Celeste; the Paladins regarded her with an expression not unlike that of a predator.

"It seems your ploy worked," Hyrum spat. "No matter. I shall move myself and my wealth to Illux then. Expect this town to shrivel up and die by the next winter."

He turned to leave the platform. Her mind raced. She hadn't planned to publicly accuse him of murder until this was done, but she couldn't risk him escaping to Illux. As the crowd cheered her name, her eyes fell back to the Paladins. They were already advancing on the platform. In moments, they had surrounded the pair of candidates and barred Hyrum from leaving.

"Not so fast, merchant," Mika said with a grin.

"What's going on?" Hyrum demanded as Mika grabbed him. "What is the meaning of this?"

The ten Paladins joined her on the platform, dragging the recalcitrant Hyrum with them. They quickly fanned out to flank the new Admiral.

What are they planning to do with him?

"We ten of Seatown declare Wyn Thacker the new Admiral of our city!" Kellan shouted. "Together, she will work with us to ensure that Seatown prospers the way that we have all dreamed of, and that soon, Illux will hold no power here."

Wyn's blood froze. The tone Kellan was taking was not one of servitude to the Admiral, but one of control. She looked and saw that Hyrum's face was one of confusion and fear.

"We begin this new order today," Kellan continued. "A messenger will be dispatched to Illux to inform the Lady Ren that the people of Seatown have chosen their own Admiral, and she shall not be controlled by distant leaders. For now, we will continue our face of deference to the City of Light, but this is the first step toward us breaking the shackles of the Fourth Spire permanently."

Kellan motioned, and Hyrum was dragged to the front of the platform. The Paladin drew his sword and pointed it at the chest of the now-whimpering merchant.

"This man, Hyrum Velkor, has been charged with murder and treason. Last night I intercepted an assassin hired by Hyrum to kill Wyn at the Overlook. Gods forgive me, I was too slow to get there and Lady Chrysta had already been killed. The Ten find you, Hyrum Velkor, guilty."

The Ten?

Wyn swallowed. This wasn't what she wanted. Something was wrong. Hyrum whimpered and cried out, tears streaming down his face.

"No!" he shouted. "I don't know what you're talking about. I didn't hire any assassins! I paid people to vote for me, that's all. Please, gods have mercy! I swear to the High God, I didn't do this!"

Wyn looked into his eyes and didn't think he was lying. It felt as if the world dropped out from under her. What if he was telling the truth? Who then had sent the assassin to kill her? Who was responsible for Chrysta's death?

"Wyn, please!" Hyrum pleaded.

She stepped forward to try and placate Kellan.

"Not now," she whispered urgently. "We need to hold a trial. It is customary for the Admiral to decide the fate and guilt of the charged. Take him to a cell, but I want to see what else we can find out first."

"This isn't how we do things now, Admiral," Kellan said.

His sword fell, and the head of Hyrum the merchant bounced off the platform to the crowd below. One of Wyn's supporters lifted the head and screamed in triumph.

"For the Admiral!" the man shouted. "For the Ten!"

Most of the crowd cheered, while those bribed by Hyrum began to disperse quickly, fear in their eyes. Wyn stared at the headless corpse of her rival, dumbstruck. Vaguely, she was aware of the Paladins talking to a messenger behind her. They handed the man an envelope that bore the wax seal of the Admiral.

"This is to go only to the Seraph," Celeste said. "If she has any concerns, you can bring her response to us. The Admiral is not to be disturbed with such things. Do you understand?"

"Yes, my lady," the man said. As he walked past Wyn and off the platform he nodded. "Admiral."

Wyn started to collapse to her knees when she was caught by strong hands. Kellan looked at her with faint concern.

"Come, you need rest," he said. "The burden of a leader is a heavy one. We will do whatever is necessary to help you lead Seatown efficiently."

Wyn nodded dumbly as he led her off the platform. When she looked at the statue of Arendt she saw that it had been sprayed with Hyrum's blood.

What have I done?

The Paladins left her alone at the Overlook after escorting her home. Wyn spent the remainder of the day sitting in the bedroom that had once been her father's, staring out of the window at the Nameless Sea. The Admiral didn't see a single gull from her vantage point. She hoped that it was just because of the black clouds that were moving in from the horizon.

THE BLOOD-SOAKED
SACRAMENT

I.

1050 AP

The corpse rotated left to right, suspended from a rope that was tied to the dead man's feet. Edmund still hadn't found the head by the time other members of the City Watch arrived at the killing ground. He had never seen anything like this in his short tenure as a member of the Watch. A lake of scarlet marred the white stones of the patio below the hanging garden that the body was dangling from. Written on the wall of the modest manor in yet more blood was the word: THIEF.

"Did someone call for Redrick?" Edmund asked Pike, the nearest guard.

"Aye, I sent Franz as soon as I heard what you'd found," Pike replied. "Light help us, what happened here?"

Edmund had no answers, but his eyes fell back upon the bloody message on the wall. It was not unlike the murder of Julius Silver-shield some years before. The last scion of his house, Julius had been brutally killed by an unknown assailant, and his manor burned to the ground. The word RAPIST had been written on the ground in the man's blood.

No one had ever come forward to back up that allegation against the dead man, and Captain Redrick believed that it had been a lie to justify such a brazen killing. In either case, they had never found any information about who had done the deed, and it seemed like the city had moved on. But now this had happened, and Edmund had been the one to stumble across it during his normal rounds.

"Keep them back!" Pike shouted to the other guards as a crowd started to form.

Edmund was originally from the slums and, as a result, had few positive feelings toward the rich families of the inner city. But even they didn't deserve this.

No one does. This was cruel.

Examining the corpse more closely revealed that the man had taken a lot of abuse prior to his decapitation. It was likely that the killer had tortured him first. Edmund held back the urge to vomit. He usually had a strong stomach, but the cruelty of this was too much for him. He turned away and looked at the sky toward Aenna to center himself. The opening to the Divine Plane watched, unmoving.

"Make way," a familiar voice shouted. "Let me through, you fools."

It was Captain Redrick. He must have been close to get here so quickly. Though the City Watch nominally made their home in the gatehouses around the outer wall of Illux, Redrick was known to hobnob with his friends in the inner city more than manage his force of guards. Redrick was old enough to be Edmund's father, though his black beard had yet to show it. His bushy brows furrowed in distaste.

"Gods above. Who found him like this?" Redrick asked.

"I did, sir," Edmund volunteered.

Redrick nodded and then moved to inspect the body as if he had already forgotten why he had asked the question in the first place. The captain covered his nose with one hand as he prodded the dead man with the other.

"His head?" he asked.

"Not yet, sir," Edmund said. "We've been trying to keep the crowd at bay. I will continue to search inside the home now that you've arrived."

Redrick nodded again and walked back to the edge of the forming crowd. He raised his hands high into the air and put on a forced smile.

"Good people of Illux, there is no cause for alarm. The brave members of the Watch have indeed discovered the body of a notable merchant, but we have no reason to believe anyone else is in danger. The wretched soul who committed this heinous sin was likely motivated by jealousy for the victim's good fortune. Unless you have information to share with us about this crime, please move on with your day."

I hope you are right, captain.

Edmund opened the rear door to the manor, glad to be away from the horror behind him. Inside, he found a lavish, if a bit messy, abode. It was clear that this merchant—Edmund still didn't know the man's name, though Redrick likely did—was one for parties, but not for cleaning up after them.

Past the rear entrance was the dining room, in the center of which was a large mahogany table littered with wine goblets and rotten food. The smell was sickly sweet, causing Edmund to again fight back the urge to wretch. He picked through the refuse that covered the table, looking for any clue as to what had prompted the killing. Of the head, there was no sign.

When he was satisfied that the dining room held nothing of interest, he gladly moved deeper into the house. After a few more minutes of searching the ground floor, he moved up the stairs to the floor above. That was when he found the first spot of blood inside, smeared along the railing. His pulse quickened as he continued up. For the first time, he realized that the killer might still be inside. Edmund swallowed and drew his sword.

Ahead, the door to one of the rooms hung ajar, with more blood covering the handle. The guard took a moment to steady himself before pressing on. He considered turning back to get help, but thought of the disdain he would likely have received from Captain Redrick when he did so. Using the pommel of his weapon, Edmund slowly pushed the door open.

It appeared that this had been the merchant's bedroom. A large four-poster bed sat in the center of the room, with its purple and cloth-of-gold curtains pulled closed. He was immediately greeted with the metallic smell of blood once more, though he couldn't see any beyond the door. Creeping forward on cat's feet, Edmund pulled back the curtain with the point of his sword.

Even though he knew he was looking for the remainder of a dead man's body, Edmund still let out a gasp. Sitting on the center of the blood-soaked bed atop a pile of pillows was the merchant's head. Its mouth was stuffed with gold coins, which gave the pallid cheeks a lumpy appearance and spilled out onto the pillows below.

"You must've stolen from the wrong person, my friend," Edmund whispered.

"Aye," a voice said.

Edmund jumped and spun on the visitor, his sword raised. It was just the captain. Redrick again had his nose covered with silk cloth. He looked at the grisly scene with barely concealed disdain.

"Wilfred was known for bilking his customers from the slums and often underpaying for goods purchased in the villages. He was a fool who bragged about his crimes while drunk during his parties. No doubt one of the wretches he cheated decided to get revenge."

"Forgive me for asking this, sir," Edmund said. "But if he was known for being a thief, why didn't you have him arrested?"

Redrick lowered the cloth over his face so that Edmund could see his scowl.

"I don't like your tone, Edmund. Remember who you are talking to. As for your, accusation, it's not that simple. He was from a previously respected family, though he gambled away much of his parents' wealth. They had made sizable contributions to the church in the past, and had powerful friends."

Including the Captain of the City Watch, it seems.

"I chose to council the lad, rather than throw him in irons. Besides, his so-called victims were always of a less fortunate sort. Now, if you are done blaming your commander for this disgusting crime, I want you to get your ass to the slums and start looking for anyone who

Wilfred had less-than-fair dealings with. He should have a ledger downstairs on the desk near the front door. I'll finish up here."

"Sir!" Edmund saluted before slinking away.

He knew that one of these days his mouth would get him in trouble, but he couldn't help himself. Growing up as one of the so-called "less fortunate sort" himself, he had joined the City Watch to keep his old neighborhoods safe. But he quickly discovered that the Watch was more likely to preserve the interests of the inner city families.

Maybe I would have been better off becoming a Paladin.

EDMUND SIGHED as he knocked on the fifth door that afternoon. There hadn't been a name on that list that had been what he would have considered a fair dealing. Wilfred, it seemed, was more than just a merchant, but also a money-lender, and he charged the desperate of the slums double or even triple what he would charge that of an inner city family. A few names in the ledger were families that Edmund knew or had grown up with, and several of those were now destitute. He didn't think any of them had been the killer, but he wouldn't have blamed them if they had been.

After an indeterminable amount of time, the door opened, revealing a younger woman with sunken eyes whose name Edmund guessed was Victoria. The woman looked at him with a mix of hope and disdain. Edmund cleared his throat awkwardly, but she regarded him silently.

"Ma'am," he said stiffly. "My name is Edmund, I am with the City Watch. I was hoping I could speak to you for a few minutes about a merchant named Wilfred Aglent?"

It looked for a moment like the hopeful part of her expression won out.

"Come inside, then."

Edmund followed her beckoning hand into the small hovel. The difference between this woman's home and that of the dead merchant couldn't have been more stark. The thatched roof was falling down in places, and errant beams of sunlight crept in to illuminate the modestly furnished room. The door in the back of the room held a small cot that looked like it had belonged to a child. The woman motioned for Edmund to sit, her own eyes lingering on the cot for a few moments.

"Did someone finally decide to listen to me?" she rasped.

"I beg your pardon?" Edmund asked. "I'm here because Wilfred listed you as someone he recently loaned money to. He was found killed this morning and—"

"Killed!" She shouted, jumping to her feet. "Gods be good, my prayers have been answered. What of my boy? What of my Sebastian?"

"I'm sorry, I still don't understand."

"I told everything to that guard when Sebastian went missing. You all should have been told by now!"

Edmund held his hands up in a vain attempt to calm her.

"Why don't you start at the beginning?"

The woman collapsed back into her chair, her body already wracked with sobs. When she had composed herself, she began, her sunken eyes as sharp as flint.

"My name is Victoria. I live alone with my son, Sebastian. When his father died, we were destitute. I was forced to do things I ain't proud of to survive, but I always kept to the Light and kept my son safe.

"Eventually I had to turn to Wilfred for money. At first, I was able to keep making payments to him. But then I fell behind. He said I could get caught up if I let Sebastian do some work for him cleaning up his manor. I didn't want to, but I also didn't want my boy living on the streets. This seemed fine at first, but then one day my boy never came home. When I went looking for him, Wilfred acted like he didn't even know I had a son; acted like I was crazy and just trying to get out of paying him back!"

Edmund's heart sank. He had seen no signs that the boy had been there. Perhaps this killer had taken or harmed the child as well?

Gods be good. I have to find him.

"I'm sorry, Victoria, I searched the manor myself and found no sign of Sebastian. Someone who knew what kind of man Wilfred was killed him and wrote 'thief' on the wall in blood. I have been going through the names in his ledger to see if I can track his killer down…"

Victoria spat on the floor.

"His killer did this city a service. I should've known that the City Watch would only care about keeping the rich filth of the inner city safe and not a missing slum child!"

"Calm down," Edmund said.

"No!" She shouted, standing again. "Get out of my house!"

Edmund rose and started for the door. He stopped at the threshold and turned back to face the grieving mother one final time.

"Who was the guard that you spoke to previously? Regardless of what you think of me, I'm also from the slums and won't forget your son so easily."

"He was bald and had a scar across his cheek. His name was Ackley, or Arendt or something. Find my son, or don't come back here."

Edmund nodded and walked back out into the street, his heart already sinking. He was certain that he knew the watchman in question, and he knew the man wasn't to be trusted.

ALARIC SAT in the back of the tavern, obscured by pipe smoke, alongside another less-than-reputable member of the Watch named Exley. Edmund knew Alaric by his reputation more than anything. He had tried to force himself on Edmund's friend Liara once, something the man paid for, though Liara herself had been reprimanded for striking a fellow guard. The rest Edmund knew were rumors that Alaric had once been a bandit and continued his wicked ways by taking bribes and covering up crimes.

Crimes like abducting children.

Edmund pulled up a chair and sat at the table with the men, a cold ale in his hand.

"Alaric," he said.

"Edmund, is it?" the man rasped as he puffed on his pipe again. "Don't see your type in here often."

"My type?"

The other guard simply smiled.

"I actually came here to talk to you about something Redrick set me on," Edmund sighed.

"*Captain* Redrick," Exley corrected.

"Yes, of course. Did you hear that a merchant called Wilfred Aglent was killed this morning?"

The smile faded from Alaric's face. He tipped back his mug and wiped the ale from his chin.

"Awful business, that. Beheaded, I heard."

"Just so," Edmund replied. "And the murderer wrote the word 'thief' on the wall of his manse in blood. Awful business, indeed. I'm the one who found the bloke, and his head. The *captain* asked me to follow up on the names from the man's ledger. He's certain that the killer was a man from the slums, likely cheated by Wilfred's more…irregular money-lending practices. During my inquiry, your name came up."

Alaric eyed him suspiciously while Exley buried his gaze into his mug.

"Did it now?" Alaric asked. "In what context, may I ask?"

"A woman told me that she spoke to you about her son disappearing. A boy named Sebastian who worked for Wilfred. Ring a bell?"

"It doesn't," Alaric said, pushing himself up from the table. Beside him, Exley did the same. "I'd be careful who you ask questions to, Edmund. The Watch protects its own, remember that."

The curls of smoke followed the men out of the tavern, leaving Edmund alone at the table with his now warm mug of ale.

A FEW DAYS LATER, Edmund saw Alaric again, though this time the man was barely recognizable. Both of his hands had been removed at the elbow, as had his head. Unlike Wilfred, though, the head of the City Watchman was clearly visible, impaled on the point of the man's sword where it lay propped up next to the next message from the killer. The word on the wall this time said KIDNAPPER.

Edmund hadn't been the first to find the body this time, though he had stumbled into the mass of City Watch blocking off the area when he had returned to the tavern where he had met Alaric in the preceding days. It seemed that his favored watering hole was known outside the Watch.

The Watch protects its own.

Alaric's words echoed in Edmund's mind as he stared at the mangled corpse slumped against the wall. Redrick was kneeling beside the body when Edmund got there, his fists clenched.

"This slum thug has gotten another one, and now one of us!" He muttered without looking up. "What have you found? Besides the words of crazed citizens."

"Crazed?" Edmund asked.

"You heard me. Alaric told me that you paid him a visit here with troubling questions based on the ramblings of a woman buried in debt to Wilfred. There was no missing child, but now there are two dead bodies, and you are wasting time throwing wild accusations at your fellow guards!"

"Don't you find it odd that our killer accused Alaric of being a kidnapper?"

Redrick glared at Edmund, but waited to speak until the other guards were out of earshot.

"Once again, your mouth betrays you, Edmund. I should have you expelled from the Watch for that kind of talk!" Then his tone softened. "Alaric was certainly not the best of us, I won't claim otherwise, but he wouldn't steal a child, nor ignore such a sin if he knew of it. All this bloody mess means is that our murderer has had the same flights of fancy as you, or that he has spoken to the same people. Have you considered that?"

Edmund had not.

"I—" he began.

Redrick waved at him dismissively. "I don't want to hear it, Edmund. Get back out there and talk to this woman again. We need to nip this in the bud, do you understand? I know you are a smart man, which is why I haven't set someone else on this yet. Don't make me regret that decision."

"Sir." Edmund nodded and stood. As he walked back through the crowd, he heard the whispers that connected this death to that of Wilfred. The gossips in the Watch had already named the man they now hunted for: *The Whitestone Killer.*

II.

Her body wasn't displayed like the others, nor was there writing in her blood, but her death had been just as savage. By the look of it, Victoria had been dead for a day or more. Her body was swollen, and her entire home stank of decay. Upon closer inspection, Edmund could tell that she had been stabbed nearly a dozen times by a fairly large blade.

A sword, even.

He kneeled in the blood beside her body and examined her more closely. Though she was already beginning to decompose, he could see the signs of the struggle all across her body. The wounds were as wide as a sword, but most didn't penetrate all the way out of her back, as if her attacker wanted to protect something behind her. Something or *someone*. Edmund pictured two men, one to hold her still and the other stabbing her until she stopped fighting. Her right hand was still clutched tight. Holding back his urge to retch, Edmund pried apart her fingers to find a scrap of bloodied cloth, not unlike the material that he wore on his own tunic.

His fists clenched as he thought of the woman struggling for her life, her last thoughts most likely drifting to the child she would never see again. The guard kicked the very chair he had sat in previously in disgust. It clattered into the wall, causing one of the feeble legs to snap off. He sighed and sat in the other chair, resting his head in his hands.

How could you let this happen? Is there no justice from the Gods of Light?

His silent prayer, like all others, went unanswered. Tears streamed down his face as he sat alone in the blood-soaked room for what felt like hours. Edmund had failed this woman, of that he was certain. This was no random burglary; her death had to have happened because she had spoken to him. Someone, it seemed, was tying up loose ends.

One thing he knew deep in his bones: this was not The Whitestone Killer. The two bodies that they had attributed to that murderer had been meant to draw attention to themselves. This was not. No doubt Victoria's killer had hoped that no one would come to check on some wretch from the slums for quite some time. He knew of the apathy of the rest of this city all too well.

"Forgive me," Edmund whispered to her, "I failed you. I will find out what happened to your son, and I swear to bring your killers to justice."

There was little help for the boy. Sebastian was likely dead and buried in an unmarked grave somewhere by now. The least Edmund could do was find out who had done this and why. He didn't know where his questions would lead him, but he knew where to begin.

"WHAT HAPPENED after I talked to you two?!" Edmund shouted as he struck the other guard again.

Exley spat blood and teeth onto Edmund's tunic. He hung from the ceiling of a warehouse, suspended by his wrists. Edmund had little trouble overpowering the other guard as the man stumbled home drunk that evening. It was nearly morning now; enough time had passed that Edmund expected his prisoner to have sobered up some.

"You'll hang for this, you little bastard," the man gurgled.

"I might, but not before you," Edmund sighed. "I know you or Alaric killed Victoria. The woman I mentioned to you both in the tavern. The one who alerted Alaric about her missing son. My question is, why? Did you two also kill the boy?"

"You can't prove shit, Edmund. Who saw us do the deed, eh? The gods?"

His laugh was cruel and cut short by wheezes. It reminded Edmund of the air escaping from a punctured lung.

"Captain Redrick is in her home right now, tearing it apart for any sign that you were there. Once he finds it, the Seraph herself will have your head. Now tell me what happened."

"You're a bad liar."

Exley swallowed what Edmund imagined was mostly blood. The man closed his eyes, and his head hung limp against his arms. His breaths were shallow, but he still lived.

He's right. I've made a huge mistake.

Edmund rubbed his temples and paced the warehouse, trying to decide what to do next. Exley was right. If Edmund was caught doing this, he would likely face the noose or the dungeon himself. Either way, he was committed to this path now, as rash as it was. He knew that Victoria had likely been killed by two men, by two members of the City Watch. Still, it was unlikely that anyone would think that was enough evidence to kidnap and torture another guard.

Behind him, Exley began to moan. The man lifted his swollen head and peered around the room, looking for his abductor again.

"Edmund!" he called out weakly. "You sniveling cunt, kill me or cut me loose. I'm not telling you a fucking thing."

That gave Edmund an idea. He pulled his sword from its scabbard slowly as he spoke.

"Have it your way. I'll have to display your body somewhere else, of course. What should I write with your blood? I already used kidnapper on Alaric. Maybe 'murderer' will work for you?"

Exley's eyes narrowed, but Edmund could see the man's lip begin to quiver.

"You're lying again. Y-you aren't him. You're not the Whitestone Killer."

"Aren't I? I found your friend, Wilfred, and then Alaric turns up dead after I accuse him of covering up the kidnapping of Sebastian. Think, Exley. You aren't as dumb as he was. I've been killing everyone connected to whatever happened to that little boy, and I'll kill you too unless you tell me where he is."

The other guard seemed to melt, his body shaking like he had taken on a sudden chill. It seemed that Edmund was a better liar than Exley had given him credit for.

"Alright! Alright! Don't fucking gut me here, I'll tell you what I know."

Edmund pressed the sword into Exley's chin until blood began to flow down the blade.

"Talk," he growled.

"We—Alaric and I—would help Wilfred with his schemes. Nothing too wild, mind you, he mostly just robbed people blind. But the two of us kept the Watch off his back. Any word of someone making a stink about him, and we were there to shut them up. Then one day he comes to us and says he has a kid he needs us to, ah…transport."

"Sebastian?"

"No. Not yet, anyhow. The first was a girl. But there were more. A dozen, maybe?"

Edmund felt the world fall out from under him. A dozen? His stomach was tied up in knots. This was far worse than he had even allowed himself to guess. He would need to get Redrick involved as quickly as possible.

"Where did you take them?" Edmund asked.

"We always took them into the Grand Cathedral, as instructed. We'd set them up to pray at one of the altars or in a pew someplace and leave them be. I swear to the High God I don't know what happened to them next."

"And Victoria?"

Exley looked off into the distance for a time before his gaze fell back onto Edmund. His eyes, which had once been flint, now glistened with tears.

"After you came to see us," he began, "Alaric got scared. Said we couldn't keep this under wraps much longer with you poking your nose around and her running her mouth. So, we went back to her home and, ah—"

"Say it!" Edmund commanded. "Say what you did!"

"He held her arms while I ran her through. It was a mercy, Edmund. A mercy. She'd never see her boy again. This way they can be reunited on the Astral Plane."

Edmund's sword flashed, and Exley landed on the ground with a wet crunch. The rope swung back and forth, its severed end beginning to unravel. The broken guard crawled away on his hands and knees whimpering like a child. Edmund followed him, sword raised. He thought of Sebastian, of Victoria, of the other dozen or more children whose names he didn't know. The rage that filled his body threatened to undo him, but he regained control at the last possible moment.

"Get up," he said. "I'm taking you to the captain, and from there, to the noose, gods willing."

REDRICK SAT in the corner of his rarely-used office at the Northern Gatehouse. His hands were clasped with steepled fingers in front of his face, obscuring whatever expression he bore. Edmund stood in the center of the room, recounting what he had discovered and what Exley had told him some hours before. The man in question, still blood-soaked and shaking, lay on the floor like a dog.

"Do you deny any of what I have said?" Edmund asked him.

Exley remained silent.

"Answer me you cur!" Edmund shouted, kicking the other man in the ribs.

"Aye, it's true! But sir, Captain Redrick, you must keep me away from this man. He's the Whitestone Killer."

Redrick chortled softly before standing.

"You always were dim-witted, weren't you, Exley? If Edmund is the Whitestone Killer, then I am the fucking Grey God. He no doubt told you that so you'd spill your guts, and it seemed to work marvelously." His steely gaze fell on Edmund. "Unfortunately for you,

I told you to find this killer, not root out corruption in our ranks. You directly disobeyed my orders."

"I—" Edmund began.

"You should have come to me the moment you found that woman dead. We could've handled this the proper way. Don't mistake me, Edmund, I'm glad that you've brought this embarrassment here, but I would've liked this to be more discreet. Now that everyone has seen him like this, there's no keeping his corruption under wraps. No matter, I'll tell the Lady today, and he'll be executed within the week. You, on the other hand, can no longer be trusted."

"What?" Edmund was dumbfounded.

"I'll continue the Whitestone investigation myself, as it is the current priority of the City Watch, lest the people of Illux begin to panic thinking we have a killer on the loose. Now that you have thoroughly embarrassed the Watch and myself, you are on wall duty for the time being."

Edmund clenched his fists.

"Wall duty? I embarrassed the Watch? Alaric and Exley murdered a woman! They helped kidnap children. Children who are still missing! This could need the help of the Paladins or even the Seraph!"

"Tread carefully, Edmund. We handle our own in the Watch. As I said, I will continue this investigation. If this Whitestone Killer has anything to do with these missing slum children, I'm sure I'll get to the bottom of it. You, however, are dismissed."

Edmund bit his tongue and spun to leave the room, but not before kicking Exley one final time. He hadn't originally thought Redrick was complicit in these crimes, but now, he wasn't so sure.

The Watch protects its own.

III.

1051 AP

It had been nearly a year since the body of Wilfred Aglent had been found dead outside his manse near the inner city. In that time, some seven more deaths had been attributed to the White-stone Killer. Try as he might, Captain Redrick had not been able to keep the word from spreading, and soon the entire inner city was in an uproar as more of their kind wound up dead.

The slums, however, didn't give two shits. And neither did Edmund. He had spent the last year in what was generally considered the worst position that the Watch had to offer. After a rather long stint patrolling the walls, he had been reassigned again to the rougher parts of the slums. Though he tried to make the best of it by helping those he considered his people, there wasn't a true upside to the way the City Watch interacted with the less fortunate.

Edmund's own reputation had soured somewhat in the slums after Exley's execution as well. Those who knew that Edmund was responsible for bringing the corrupt guard to justice still respected him, but the majority just thought that all of the Watch was the same as the dead man. He could tell that was the general feeling of those who watched him now as he continued his patrol.

"Good day," he said, nodding to the women across the street who eyed him suspiciously.

They scowled and turned away. He tried to ignore them as he went on his way, but his annoyance at how the people looked at him now had grown.

Perhaps I should think about being a Paladin again. People still trust them, at least.

Ahead, between two buildings that leaned into one another, Edmund saw who he had been looking for: Liara. She had been waiting in their usual meeting place since Edmund's reassignment. Her position in the Watch gave her the freedom to roam that Edmund once had, so she came to him.

"How were your rounds?" she asked with a smirk.

"Shit, as usual. Yours?" Edmund responded.

"Not shit. You know, if you had been smart, you would've just killed Exley and never involved Redrick. Gods be good, if you had been *really* smart, you would've gotten me involved sooner and I'd have done the bastard."

Edmund shook his head. He had heard the same thing from her nearly every day since Exley's death.

"Too late for that now," he said. "Tell me you've found something about the kids?"

"Aye," she said, her smile fading. "Turns out they didn't vanish as soon as Alaric and Exley left them in the cathedral. They were seen being taken away by a member of the clergy."

"What?!" Edmund exclaimed. "Who? How is this possible?"

"I don't know for certain yet, but more than one pious gossip has told me that they have seen unaccompanied children comforted and taken out of sight by a priest. Unfortunately, none could tell me. It's a man, that's all they remembered."

Edmund looked up at Aenna, his mind racing. When he found no comfort from the gods, his gaze fell earthward again.

"I had assumed that they were just using the Grand Cathedral as an exchange…I never considered that one of the clergy was involved. Damn!"

"It's not looking good," Liara said. "I haven't found any sign of the kids beyond that. If one of the priests is—look, they have the easiest access to the catacombs. It wouldn't be hard to hide a body down there."

"Right under the Seraph's nose?" Edmund was aghast. "I know the Lady Ren isn't aware of this, but is Redrick? The captain—"

"We need to approach this differently than you did before," she interrupted. "Look, there's a meeting this afternoon in the Fourth Spire. The Lady has called together all of the inner city Watch to discuss the Whitestone Killer. Come with me and use this time to poke around."

Edmund nodded and followed her back toward the cathedral. The slums would take care of themselves for the next little bit, as they always did.

EDMUND HAD NEVER SEEN SO many members of the City Watch in one place before. They were crammed into the small chapel at the base of the Fourth Spire, usually reserved for the ceremony that initiated groups of recruits into the Paladin Order. The stained glass windows here depicted Lio, the Fallen One. The previous God of Light leered down at him ominously as he and Liara filed into a pew with dozens of others.

Standing at the front of the chapel was the Lady Ren. The Seraph's wings flexed in an annoyed fashion as she watched the last of the guards trickle in. Beside her, Redrick tried to look imposing, but compared to a bearer of Divine Blood he looked weak. Several Paladins lined the back of the room; Edmund recognized some of their faces but didn't know any of their names. When the flow of City Watch stopped, Ren gripped the pulpit and leaned toward them as if she were going to give a sermon.

"Members of the Watch," she began. "You do much for this city, of that there is no doubt. But, as of late, the people of Illux have not been safe, and they look to us for a resolution! I have spoken to Redrick about the murders of prominent members of the inner city by this so-called Whitestone Killer, and I don't like what I've been told."

Behind her, Redrick's face grew scarlet, yet he seemed to shrink away from her all the same. One of the Paladins behind the pair put a reassuring hand on the captain's shoulder to steady him.

"How have these murders continued unchecked for an entire year? How has this killer eluded your capture? This is a failure not only of your captain but the Watch as a whole. I want him found, and I want him found *now!*" She slammed her fist on the pulpit. "This is now the priority for all of you in this room. After two of your number killed an innocent woman last year, the faith in the Watch has been destroyed. Here is your chance to earn it back. I will be sending Paladins to aid in the search. Do not fail me. Do not fail the Light."

The Seraph left through the back of the chapel to the steps that led to her chambers above. For the next few moments, the members of the City Watch sat in the room in silence, waiting for something to happen. When he had finally regained his composure, Redrick took Ren's place at the pulpit and glowered at those gathered below him.

"What in the High God's name are you waiting for?" he thundered. "Find this bastard. Now!"

The guards stood and began filing out of the chapel. Edmund took advantage of the chaos to slip through a side passage that led into the center of the Grand Cathedral. Liara nodded at him and continued on with the others. They both knew what this meeting meant: the slums would see more patrols from the Watch. Homes would be searched, and lives upended. All while a much worse evil was right under their noses.

Inside the central sanctuary, Edmund walked up and down the rows of pews, looking for anyone who seemed out of place. Hundreds were gathered in prayer, as was customary throughout the day. Dozens of priests walked up and down the aisles as well, stopping to converse with members of the congregation or to provide blessings to those who requested them. Upon the central dais, an older man gave a sermon about the sanctity of children.

Edmund shivered and took a seat in one of the middle rows. He bowed his head in mock prayer and began eyeing each clergyman in turn. They varied in age and gender, though all wore the same white-and-gold vestments of the Gods of Light. While the central chamber was nominally for worship of the High God, it was staffed with priests assigned to each of the other three spires and the individual Gods of Light.

How do I narrow it down?

As if by divine providence, Edmund heard harsh whispers to the rear of the row in which he sat. Turning, as many who prayed did, he saw the hulking form of what must have been a Paladin arguing with a priest in an alcove. Edmund stood and briskly walked in that direction, trying to catch them before they separated. He was too slow, and the Paladin turned and stomped out the large doors that led back to the city.

Edmund cursed his luck and eyed the priest. He was an older man, wizened but not yet bent with age. The priest's face was kind, but something about his eyes set Edmund on edge. The alcove he stood in was filled with candles. Small velum labels with names written on them sat in front of each candle. It had been years since he had been here, but Edmund knew this place. This shrine was dedicated to the lost and deceased children of the city. The candles burned for those children whose families would likely not see them again until they all rejoined the High God.

The guard's stomach began to churn. *Of course* this is where he would find him. The very person tending to the candles was the one causing them to be lit in the first place. The priest smiled at Edmund in the way an old man does, and Edmund nodded in return before kneeling in front of the candles.

"Is one of them yours?" the priest asked.

"All of them are, father," Edmund replied. "They are all our children. May their souls find their way to the High God, and their killer find *his* way to justice."

Edmund stood, locking eyes with the priest. The other man took an involuntary step backward, his smile failing. He was the one, and they both knew it.

One of us will get you, old man. You better pray that it's me.

Edmund turned and ran from the sanctuary in an attempt to catch the Paladin who had been arguing with the priest. Outside in the plaza, there were dozens of Paladins walking to and from the barracks that the majority of them called home. He would never be able to find the exact one who had been arguing with the priest.

Realizing that it was a lost cause, he turned to go back into the Grand Cathedral to confront the priest more directly when he very nearly ran into Captain Redrick. The Captain of the City Watch huffed and grumbled to himself, but seemed as if he was going to completely ignore Edmund for the moment. Then his face soured as he recognized him.

"Edmund? What in the High God's name are you doing here? Are your duties done for the day?"

"Sir, I—" Edmund stammered.

"Were you ignoring your orders?" Redrick was quickly growing furious. "This is your last day in the Watch, you insolent—"

"Sir!" Edmund interrupted, an idea taking shape. "I know how to catch him! I know how to catch the Whitestone Killer!"

As NIGHT FELL, the two members of the City Watch crouched outside the home of Raziel Hammerfall, the priest in charge of attending the Shrine of Lost Children. At first, Redrick had been furious that Edmund had refused to drop his investigation into the missing children. But he was desperate to catch the Whitestone Killer, and Edmund's plan was the best idea they had.

The younger man was sure now that the Paladin he had seen arguing with the priest was connected to the murders. This killer had been targeting corruption in the inner city, and who would have better access than a member of the Paladin Order? If Edmund was right, then the Whitestone Killer was closing in on Raziel, just as Edmund was.

"If this doesn't work, you are finished, Edmund," Redrick mused. It wasn't the first time he had said that this evening. "It doesn't make sense to me. Why would Raziel be the one taking the children? He's a respected member of the clergy."

"Who better?" Edmund growled. "Forgive me, sir, but few care about missing children beyond their own parents, and fewer still if they are from the slums. Wilfred used his dealings with the poor to get the children and sell them to Raziel while Alaric and Exley covered it up. While *you* covered it up."

"I—" Redrick began.

"You knew Wilfred was a thief, and you knew Alaric and Exley were corrupt, but you did nothing. Gods help us, this rot falls at your feet as well. I don't care what you do to me when this is over, but I'll see that priest hang."

"And the Whitestone Killer?" Redrick whispered.

"He's your problem," Edmund said.

Then they saw it. A bulky shape lithely jumped from rooftop to rooftop. Edmund was reminded of the stories from the older members of the Watch of chasing the Demon that killed the previous Seraph through the city. This was no Demon, though.

The silhouette landed on top of the priest's house and slipped through an upper window. Redrick and Edmund both drew steel and made for the door. For the first time that evening, Edmund wished that the two of them hadn't been alone.

Gods of Light, watch over us. Let us bring justice tonight.

The guards kicked open the door and burst into the lower level of the priest's home. Overhead, they could hear the muffled cries of pain from the old man already. Feeling their way through the dark, they found the marble stairs and continued to the top of the landing. Behind a large door, they heard more screaming and a gruff, almost inhuman voice.

"What did you do with them?" the voice asked. "Where are they?"

"No! Please!" Raziel cried weakly. "Mercy!"

"There is no mercy in my heart for the likes of you. You have stained the Light. Where are they!?"

Redrick threw open the door and shouted.

"City Watch! Stand down!"

The hallway lit up with blue light, and Edmund was thrown back into the wall.

HE WASN'T sure how long he had been unconscious, but when he opened his eyes, his head throbbed and the home was deathly silent. Edmund slowly forced himself to his feet and looked for some sign of Redrick. He started in the priest's room, and what he found was no surprise. Raziel was dismembered, his body parts scattered around the room like refuse. Written on the wall in blood were the words CHILD MURDERER.

Unlike when he found the body of Wilfred, Edmund felt no pity for what had been done to the man. Ignoring the carnage after a few more moments, Edmund ran back downstairs to see if he could find some sign of his captain. Back on the lower level, he found him. Redrick was blindfolded and tied with his hands behind his back in an ornate chair. A noose was tied around his neck, but for some reason, he hadn't been strung up yet.

"Sit down," a voice from the shadows behind Redrick growled.

Edmund noticed another chair set out in front of the captain. He did as he was asked and sat in the chair. Try as he might, he couldn't make out the face of the shadowed figure behind the captain.

"I thought about killing you both," the voice said. "But something stayed my hand. I know Redrick is corrupt, though I doubt even he would allow a crime of this magnitude to occur. It's you that I'm unsure about. Someone had to care about those children enough to track me here, and that certainly wasn't the captain, here. So tell me, who are you?"

"My name is Edmund," he rasped. "I have been trying to find the missing children since I met with Sebastian's mother, Victoria, before she was murdered."

"Ah, so you are the one who turned in Exley, then? That's good. It seems I might have been right about you. Even so, I can't let you stop me or learn who I am. This city is too corrupt, too full of sin. The rot starts in the inner city and extends out to the walls. The Lady Ren is a good woman, but her vision is clouded by the stresses of ruling. That is why I must do this. Why I must bring *justice*, as I have done today."

Edmund tried not to get distracted by the man's words, no matter how much he agreed with what the voice was saying.

"What of the children?" Edmund asked.

There was silence for a time.

"Quit talking to him!" Redrick shouted.

The rope around his neck pulled taut for a moment, cutting off any further words.

"He told me everything as I pulled him apart. When he was done with them, he buried them in the catacombs among the sacred dead. Start there so that they can truly rest. Can I trust you to do that?"

"Aye," Edmund said.

"Good. Now, as to your captain, he has his own crimes to answer for. But I will leave his fate up to you. Don't expect to see any signs of me again. I'll be much more discreet from now on. If you need a piece of meat to give to the Lady, you've got one right here."

Redrick was yanked upward, where he hung from a beam on the ceiling. Flame sprang to life where the voice had been coming from, but the Whitestone Killer was gone. Edmund watched as Redrick flailed helplessly, gasping for air that was already filling with smoke.

"Edmund!" he gasped. "Please! Cut me down!"

Edmund eyed him for a moment, his hand resting on the pommel of his sword. His sense of duty told him to cut the man down, but his sense of justice told him to let him burn.

"Edmund! Please!"

"Did you know?" Edmund asked, even as the flames spread around the room.

"Edmund!" His cries had grown shrill as he began to strangle.

"Did you know about the children?"

"No! Gods be good, no!"

Edmund cut the rope and Redrick fell to the ground. He slit the man's bonds and pulled him from the flaming house. Both men collapsed, gasping on the street outside as the flames overtook the structure.

"I won't forget this, Edmund," Redrick said, rubbing his throat. "I take care of those who take care of me."

Edmund stared into the flames, unmoving. He wished again that he had become a Paladin, and perhaps he still would. But for now, the Watch would be his tool to help the slums.

"Raziel was the Whitestone Killer," he said. "He was killing to cover his tracks for the murders of the children. We will find their bodies and tell their families. The Lady gets her murderer, and the parents get closure. We never speak of what we really found in that house again."

"Aye, lad. Good plan. And I think a promotion is in order. You will be second only to me from now on."

"I don't want power, Redrick. Little good that it does."

"I don't have a choice but to promote the man who caught the Whitestone Killer."

Edmund sighed and rubbed his temple.

Gods be good. What have I done?

THE BARD'S DEMONS

I.

1051 AP

The strings of the lyre tightened as Tuck adjusted the knobs, preparing the worn instrument for a song. This was Tuck's fourth night here, and by now the few patrons had come to expect the bard's voice. Tuck stretched their arms, rolling their shoulder blades beneath the pale-blue jerkin. Smoke from the fire and pipe-weed made the air thick and sour. What would have been a raucous revelry in another tavern was only a dull murmur here. This place was getting tiresome already, but the extra time to fine-tune this new song was worth it.

Besides, something interesting is bound to happen at the edge of the world.

Tuck had been staying at what was possibly the most useless inn on the Mortal Plane: *The Chasm Tavern*. As its unoriginal name suggested, *The Chasm Tavern* was located in Strega, possibly the most remote village in the wilderness. Strega was not more than a few days ride from the Great Chasm, the treacherous hole in the ground where the God Lio slew his enemy Xyxax over a thousand years before. That was what the priests and bards claimed, anyway.

Strega was built on what was the last fertile ground between the Great Chasm and Illux. Any nearer to that accursed spot meant dust, stones, and sour earth. What lay beyond that, none knew. Gods be good, they said even Demons avoided this place, its evil was so great.

And yet for some reason, this was the spot that Tuck had chosen to sing their heart out, to the one or two bar patrons who weren't welcome in Illux, Seatown, or any other villages for some reason or another. Who else would live here but washouts and cutthroats? Even the Paladins who kept watch over this sorry excuse for a town were edgier than most. Maybe that's why Tuck hoped they would feel right at home? There was no need to fit in here, no way to fit in at all, really, which was something Tuck was bad at doing. And yet, this place was a bore.

The shallow conversations quieted some as the bard plucked at the strings of the u-shaped instrument, still making sure that the tuning was right. Even in a shit-hole, one needed to have standards, and Tuck wouldn't play until everything was ready. Another twist here, a pluck there, and Tuck let out a melodramatic sigh. Finally, when they could put it off no longer, Tuck began to play the lyre and allowed the slow, melodic words to come out of their mouth.

> Through Illux they ran,
> The streets blood-red,
> Where this tale began,
> Cross paths where o'ly dead do tread,
> The Whispers of a Red God.
>
> Illux was saved,
> But the killer did rave,
> The Whispers of a Red God.
>
> The Paladins both brave and chaste,
> Burdened by the death of their own,
> To the Rim they made great haste,
> The Whispers of a Red God

There they were joined by a Grey Monk,
She had been sent from above,
To avenge those whose blood he had drunk,
The one who killed all because of,
The Whispers of a Red God.

THAT WAS ALL they had written so far. It had been over three years since whatever had happened in Rinwaithe in the mountains, but word traveled slowly around the Mortal Plane, especially to somewhere as remote as this. That meant that Tuck was possibly the first bard to memorialize the defeat of the bandit cult, or at least the first to sing about it to the people of Strega.

The story was, that a cult had formed in the Rim, made up of bandits and other unscrupulous types who were worshipping someone or something that they called the Red God. They even had agents in Illux, committing murders that they considered sacrifices to this made-up deity. At least, that is what the woman Alyssa in Rinwaithe had told them. She was the proprietor of the inn there and had seen the cult's defeat first-hand. Or claimed to, anyway. One of the local Paladins there, a man called Gil, refused to talk about his involvement with it, especially to a nosy bard. So Tuck had gotten what they could from Alyssa and made up the rest.

Tuck had been on the trail of this story for a few months before actually ending up in Rinwaithe. The bard had been looking for something exciting to write a song about. Something that no one else had sung before. It seemed that this had been it. Drunks and gossips spoke about it in hushed tones over watered-down ale in the taverns where Tuck sang. Whispers abounded of a bandit blood cult that had taken root in the Rim of Paradise. They had killed the legendary hero Broderick Breaksword, as well as caused a rash of killings in Illux and elsewhere. Only when a group of Paladins and a Balance Monk joined together was the threat ended.

And I missed the whole damn thing.

"Good as the last few nights, umm—" the barman said, walking over.

"Tuck," the bard said curtly.

Tuck placed the lyre back in its case. The case was solid wood, wrapped in black leather with gold filigrees around the edges. If Tuck was being honest, the case was probably nicer than the lyre, which was an old hand-me-down from a washed-up drunk who wanted another ale. The case, though, that had been a gift.

"Aye, Tuck. That's right," the man said. "Forgive me. My memory isn't what it once was. Here, have a drink on the house."

The man sat at the nearest table, setting two cloudy beverages down in front of himself.

"Aren't all of the drinks on the house, so long as I play for your three customers?"

The barkeep seemed to chew on his tongue for a moment before he responded. Tuck felt that too much sweat was glistening on his bald head. "Aye. But this drink is with me. Ain't none of the others been with anyone but yerself. Isn't that right, Tuck?"

The bard sighed, rubbing their forehead with the palms of their hands. Tuck hated talking.

What kind of bard dislikes people?

"I suppose you're right," Tuck said, taking a seat beside the man.

The room had quieted down again, not that it had been loud to begin with, even before Tuck had sung. *The Chasm Tavern* was a small establishment. Tuck thought that it must have only had five real rooms for guests, and the bard doubted that more than three of them were ever filled at one time. Still, the locals congregated here on occasion. Where else could they drink overpriced ale that tasted like Demon-piss?

"Tell me, Tuck," the barman said. "Did you write that one yerself?"

"I did," Tuck said, perking up some. "I have been waiting my whole life for a song that could be my own. Something no other bard or scribe had ever uttered. *Whispers of a Red God* is that song."

"It's not half bad."

"It's only half done. I haven't even gotten to the good parts yet, and the introduction needs some work. I didn't mention the heroic death of Broderick Breaksword, the hero of Seatown. Still, this is good practice. I expect that I'll have it finished before I leave here."

"Leave?" the man asked.

"Well yes," Tuck laughed. "You didn't expect me to stay here forever, did you? No offense, but not much happens out here in Strega. Not that I've seen, anyway."

"You've seen a lot, have you?"

"Enough to know."

"You'd be surprised," the barman said, distantly. "Names Gorman, by the way. I'm sure I told you that, but I'll be damned if I can remember a name without hearing it half a dozen times."

"Yes, Gorman. Nice to, err, formally meet you, I suppose."

Gorman took a hard pull on his ale glass, slamming it down when he was done. Tuck could tell that the man was used to drinking himself into the poorhouse by draining his own stock. He waved at the barmaid, who Tuck thought might have been his daughter, and she brought him another. As she turned away, he slapped her on the backside.

Not his daughter. Gods be good she better not be.

Tuck looked down into their glass, trying to avoid the prying eyes of Gorman as they fell back on the bard.

"Where you from, anyhow? Not from these parts, obviously."

The bard took the biggest drink they could muster, choking down the thick liquid that passed as alcohol in this town before answering.

"I was born in Seatown, just after the rogue Paladin Cecilia attacked the place, actually. Or during, really. Depends on who you ask."

"You don't say?" Gorman said. "Well, that makes you a much younger man than me!" He slapped his hand on the table as he laughed.

"Right," Tuck said, awkwardly.

Surprisingly, the man seemed to be more insightful than he looked. He stopped laughing and gave Tuck another once over.

"Forgive me, you are a young man, ain't you?" the barman asked.

"Actually, I'm not," Tuck said, taking another wretched drink.

"Lots o' ladies keep their hair short like yours I suppose."

"I'm no lady, either. I'm just me. Just Tuck. The bard. Not a man, not a woman."

"But what bits you got?"

"None of your damn business!" Tuck blurted, drawing the eyes of the few patrons.

To his credit, Gorman held up his hands in a placating gesture, his face remaining rather soft. Few barkeeps would have taken such an attitude from anyone, especially not a bard.

"I, ah, meant no offense, Tuck. Just asking questions, ya see."

Keep it together, Tuck. You don't want to get thrown out. Not yet anyway.

"I understand. Look, I don't like talking as it is, and I've been answering the same damn questions my whole life. I'm not gonna bed you, so it doesn't matter what's in my breeches, does it?"

Gorman studied the bottom of his glass for a moment.

"No, I suppose not."

The following silence drug on for an interminable amount of time. Tuck forced down the last bit of ale and begrudgingly motioned the barmaid over for another glass. This one seemed to taste slightly better, though Tuck wasn't sure if that was real or imagined. When Gorman got himself his third ale, Tuck decided it would be less painful to break the silence than to allow it to continue.

"So, uh, Gorman, you said I'd be surprised at what goes on around here. Enlighten me."

The man perked at the signs of a new conversation. He took another swig of ale and sat straighter in his chair, running his hands over where his hair used to be. The sheen of sweat came off and stained the cuff of his old shirt.

"Yeah, things definitely happen round here, from time to time. Ya know. A Demon raid, Paladins come through, people go missin."

"That happens everywhere," Tuck said, exasperated.

"Aye, it does. But not like here my bard friend. Not like here, at all. Ya see, we are in Strega, the closest village to the Great Chasm." Tuck rolled their eyes. "Ya don't need me to tell ya what happened there, I imagine? You've probably sung about it once or twice. Well, they say that the ground near that place is poisoned. The hate from Xyxax done seeped into the earth. It makes people do wicked things, they say. Demons and Accursed steer clear o' the place."

Tuck had heard such stories, but they were rarely anything more than that. Still, the bard's ears perked up. Maybe there was something worth writing about out here after all.

"I'm listening," the bard said.

Gorman leaned in. "Ya don't strike me as the kinda man, err, person, who would miss out on seeing some danger up close? Ya'd like to see the effects of the Great Chasm first-hand, no? Maybe write a song about it?"

"You have no idea. *Whispers of a Red God* is my greatest song, no doubt, but it will always lack that spark, you know? I wasn't really there. I didn't see anything myself. I'm always just singing other people's stories. I want a song from my perspective. I want to see something great and terrible up close."

"I bet ya would..." Gorman said, trailing off. He cast a furtive glance at the rest of the tavern before standing. "It was nice chatting with ya, Tuck. Please, stay with us a few days, at least. I'm sure you'll see something that catches yer interest before ya leave this place."

Tuck watched the man go in abject silence. It felt like Gorman was so close to sharing some juicy secrets about Strega or the Great Chasm, but he just turned out to be another drunken slob who told tall tales.

And this time there wasn't even a tale to tell.

The bard finished the rest of the less-foul tasting ale and walked up the creaky steps to their room on the floor above. Just as Tuck reached the upper landing, the door to the outside opened again. At this hour that was unusual, so Tuck paused to take a look at who it was that was coming in for a late-night drink.

Two Paladins walked into the tavern.

Tuck sized them both up. They didn't look familiar at all. In the few days they had spent there, it was possible that Tuck hadn't met every Paladin in town, but it was unlikely. These Paladins were probably rangers from Illux. They both looked fairly young. One was pale with shoulder-length red hair, while the other was darker-skinned with a tight black beard.

Tuck had already had enough disappointment for one night, so the bard went to their room without giving the new visitors much thought.

It was still dark when the heavy hand clamped over the bard's mouth. Tuck tried to struggle, but the man that the hand belonged to was too strong. Panic began to overtake the bard as the smell of ale and body odor wafted to their nose. It was Gorman. The great oaf could only be here for one reason...

"Hush," the barman whispered. "I'm not here to hurt ya, Tuck. I just can't have ya waking me other guests. I have something to show ya."

Gorman released Tuck from his grasp. The bard backed up to the far side of the bed, allowing their eyes to adjust to the darkness. Gorman was dressed in dark garb that most certainly was not what he had been wearing earlier in the night. He was also armed for some reason.

"What in the High God's name could you have to show me at this time of night?" Tuck asked.

"Aye, it's late," Gorman said, "or early, perhaps. I suspect sunrise isn't too far off. Even so, this is the hour when we depart. I told ya that Strega wasn't as boring as she appeared, and I plan to prove it."

"What do you mean? Where are we departing to?"

"Ya said you wanted to see something terrible up close right? Something worth writing a song about?"

Tuck nodded.

"Well bard, yer in luck."

II.

Gorman led the way out of the village as if they were thieves. The man wore a hooded cloak that turned his wall of flesh into a dark, shapeless mass. He hunched as he walked, like a bear preparing to stand on its hind legs. Tuck felt out of place in the pale-blue jerkin and matching breeches. They had been all the rage in Illux's inner-city the bard had heard. Right about now, that didn't seem to matter for some reason. Perhaps some less-garish attire was in store when this was over.

Strega had grown deathly quiet, adding to Tuck's discomfort. The only sounds were of the occasional dog barking within the village, or the howl of a wolf without. Overhead, the crescent moon hung in the middle of the sky beside Aenna, the window to the Divine Plane. That meant that sunrise was still much farther off than Gorman had let on. Tuck cursed under their breath for leaving their one knife in the tavern.

At least I grabbed my lyre. The High God knows this is the perfect time for someone to rob my room.

On the edge of the village, without casting another glance behind them, Gorman sprinted from the last line of outbuildings toward a small copse of trees in the distance. The large man moved faster than

Tuck thought was possible, leaving the bard standing bewildered behind him. When Tuck regained their senses, they ran after Gorman in an altogether unflattering manner, clutching at the case of the lyre as if it was a small child. Once Tuck reached the tree line, Gorman let out a quiet laugh.

"Not used to running, eh?" The barman said.

"These clothes weren't made for such activities. I was a natural sprinter as a child."

"I never did meet a bard that told the truth," Gorman said, turning.

"Nor I a barkeep," Tuck said, flatly.

Gorman walked deeper into the trees, angling his way southwest, toward what was surely the Great Chasm. Tuck fingered the case of the lyre nervously. This wasn't what they had bargained for. What exactly was the barman playing at? Surely there were bandits ahead, ready to set upon the bard and take all of their money.

Good thing this oaf doesn't pay well.

Soon they were on the other side of the trees, staring out at the barren expanse in the distance. What would have been grassy fields to the east, was dried up and rocky slopes in this direction. Strega truly was built on the edge of the world, and Tuck was now staring off that edge at what lay beyond. The evil of the Great Chasm was so strong that it killed nearly all living things in the area. Tuck swallowed hard. That didn't bode well. There were songs about this kind of thing.

"Gorman, stop," Tuck said.

The large man paused. "Yes?"

"Where in the High God's name are you taking me?"

"To a secret place," the man laughed. "It's indescribable. Ya wanted to see something terrible up close, didn't ya?"

"I believe I said great and terrible, and right about now I'm regretting that choice of words. Look, I'm a storyteller, so I can appreciate a little suspense, but I just met you, so I hope you can understand my hesitation. Following large men out into the wilderness is how one gets raped or killed."

"I'm no bandit, lad," Gorman said, anger filling his voice.

Tuck ignored the "lad" bit and forged on.

"I'm not saying you are. I mean, that's obvious. But I wouldn't say that owning a tavern in the most undesirable village on the Mortal Plane is the least suspicious profession one could have."

"Aye, I suppose yer correct, Tuck. Look, do ya want to see what I have to show ya, or do ya want to hear my life story? We only have time for one. I swear to the gods that ya will come to no harm this night."

But which gods?

"Fine. Lead on."

Tuck waved the man ahead dismissively but internally kicked himself again for leaving that knife. Almost as soon as they stepped onto the dry earth, the sounds of nightbirds and the distant baying of wolves seemed to stop. Even the chill night breeze fell away. This place felt unnatural. It made Tuck's skin crawl.

The barkeep no longer ran or crouched, but instead walked at a brisk pace, picking his way through the uneven terrain with a confident familiarity. Though the man was armed with a short sword, he kept the thing in its scabbard. For some reason, he wasn't afraid of being attacked by the Forces of Darkness out here. Perhaps the saying that even they feared this place was true? Tuck didn't want to be around long enough to find out.

Ahead, dark shapes rose in the night, haphazardly jutting from the earth. Tuck's uneasiness returned in earnest. At first, it wasn't clear what it was that they were walking toward, but soon the thin sliver of moonlight brought the outline of the shapes into sharp relief: they were approaching another cluster of trees, but all of these were dead. The leafless branches reached up skyward, pleading for a reprieve from their terrestrial prison.

When they were finally underneath the dead sentinels, Tuck whistled aloud, drawing a harsh look from Gorman. These trees were ancient by human reckoning. Had they grown and died since this area had become an arid wasteland, or had they died when the rest of the land did a thousand years before? Were they as old as the Great Chasm itself?

"What is this place?" Tuck whispered.

"A place worth singing about, to be sure," Gorman said. "I call it the tree graveyard. Maybe ya can put that in yer song?"

"Maybe," Tuck said, "though I'd surely come up with a better name."

"Well, naming isn't my strong suit no doubt…"

It was while Tuck was examining the closest of the dead trees that they saw it. Standing motionless in the distance, between a pair of trees, was what looked to be a rotten corpse. Tuck had sung enough songs to realize by the way it was standing there that it wasn't actually dead. This was an Accursed, and Tuck had wandered into a trap.

The bard wheeled about, trying to make a break for the open field behind them. The barman grabbed Tuck and squeezed them into his bulk. Up close he stank even worse than Tuck imagined. Though his grip was firm, he didn't seem to be doing anything more aggressive than stopping Tuck from running and screaming into the night.

"I promised ya that ya wouldn't be harmed," the man said.

"How in the High God's name can you promise that?" Tuck spat. "That's an Accursed standing there! If there is one, there is a dozen, and a Demon to boot! Are you mad?"

Gorman grabbed Tuck by the shoulders, holding them an arm's length away from his body. His face had gone a shade redder, and the glisten of sweat still shined on his brow. It looked like his mind had gone to mush as he searched for the words to say next, judging by the glassiness of his eyes. Finally, after chewing on his tongue for what felt like hours, the man spoke.

"Ya are smarter than most bards, Tuck. There is probably just shy o' dozen of them things standing watch in the trees. They keep the graveyard safe from Paladins. But ya don't need to worry, yer with me. And now, ya can't turn back."

"Can't?"

"Ya heard me. Yer in now, my bo—bard. No harm will come to ya, and I expect a good song out of this, but ya have to see it to the end."

"And if I refuse?" Tuck asked, defiance coloring their voice.

The barman motioned at the nearest Accursed. The creature didn't move, but its hollowed-out eye sockets fell upon Tuck, who could feel the malice radiating off of them. If the Accursed could have been said to be looking at anything, it was certainly looking at the bard and not at the barman. Tuck nodded in understanding. Gorman smiled a toothy grin and released the bard, patting them on the shoulder.

"Come on, it's not far now. Wait till ya see the lights."

With an almost spring in his step, Gorman made his way through a surprisingly well-worn path between the trees. He wasn't alarmed in the slightest by the corpse-warrior that stood ominously to their left. As they passed it, Tuck cast one quick glance at the thing, to get the details right for the song of course. It stood stark naked, its body visibly rotten in places, and leaking pus in others. Each arm had been replaced with swords from the elbow down. Above the sewn mouth, its eyes had been forcibly gouged out. The bard nearly retched, pulling absent-mindedly on the rings in each of their ears. This had been a mistake.

As the pair passed the first of the Accursed, another popped into view, shambling out from behind another tree. This one had a primitive-looking crossbow grafted to its right arm, and a hook to load it on the other. The bolts that would be fired from the weapon were sticking randomly from its thighs. Worst of all though, was the smell. It was a stench that Tuck hadn't experienced since their brother had died at home from fever.

What am I doing? I should push him down and run.

As if it could read his thoughts, the Accursed loaded a bolt into its arm before standing still again. Tuck looked away, scrambling over fallen branches to be as close to Gorman as they could stand. The barman only smelled slightly better than the corpses, after all.

The dead trees finally spread out in a small clearing, surrounding what looked like a giant stone that was impaled in the ground. A large cleft in the rock gave way to a cave, from which emanated a faint blue glow. When they got close, Tuck realized that the glow was coming from a spongy lichen that covered the walls of the cave in great patches.

"And what do you call this?" Tuck asked. "The glowing rock?"

"I don't call it anything," Gorman snorted. "It's ya bards that have to name everything. This, this is just a gateway."

Tuck went cold.

"A gateway to what?"

"Ya ever hear of the catacombs beneath Illux?"

"Of course I have! Didn't you pay attention to my song?"

"Right," Gorman replied, flustered. "Well, this is like that. We are about to go underground, to where only the dead live. Kinda like yer song."

"Gorman, please," Tuck said, the defiance leaving their voice. "What's down there? Why are there Accursed up here, and why don't they attack you?"

"We have an agreement," Gorman said. "Look, if I had known ya'd be such a coward about it, I wouldn't have brought ya here. Don't let the others hear ya whining, or they might overrule me and slit yer throat. I like ya, so I don't want that."

Tuck swallowed. "Others?"

"Don't break a string over it. People. *Men.* Not those things." He gestured at the trees.

"Though I wouldn't let them hear ya neither, they aren't into weakness themselves, generally."

The bard nodded dumbly, holding the lyre before them like a shield.

I should have brought my knife.

Gorman smiled again, his teeth looking more canine than Tuck remembered. There were old wives-tales of men that turned into beasts. Gods be good that's all they were. The bard's imagination was simply getting away from them. That's all.

"We won't need no torches down 'ere," Gorman said, matter-of-factly. "The truth of it is, the smoke'll make ya sick in such tight quarters. I bet ya never heard that in a song."

"Can't say that I have," Tuck whispered.

Inside the mouth of the cave, the floor canted steeply down. It was slick and moist, causing Tuck to nearly lose their footing more than once. Though the glowing lichen wasn't pleasant to the touch, it did provide some level of stability as the two worked their way downward. Something about the blue light made Tuck's head hurt. It was like swimming in a pond after dark.

"I wouldn't eat this stuff if I were ya" Gorman muttered.

"Why in the High God's name would I do that?" Tuck asked, annoyed again.

"Some people do, that's all."

Scattered between the slimy lamps were carvings in the rock, chiseled out by a practiced hand. At first, Tuck took them for naturally occurring formations, but soon the bard realized how wrong they had been. These didn't just appear to be intentional, but ritual. The carvings all shared a similar theme. They seemed to represent a horned being in various forms. The most common motif was what looked like the horns of a bull emerging from a spiral. In those instances, the spiral was colored in a brownish-red substance.

I couldn't make this up.

The farther down they went, the more prevalent the carvings became until they covered every part of the cave walls the lichen did not. The red paint dripped down the walls from each spiral like they were wounds on the walls of the cave. The sight of them made Tuck shiver. This was an evil, evil place.

"These markings was here when I found this place, mind ya," Gorman said. He spoke as if he was guiding Tuck on a tour of some ancient chapel. "Not sure what they mean, but they meant something to *him*."

"Him?" Tuck asked.

"The one our agreement is with. Big chap. Ya'll recognize him no doubt." The barman saw the look of dread on Tuck's face. "What? You didn't think that I was negotiating with those mindless things up top did ya?"

Gorman chuckled, the sound reverberating up and down the tunnel. The way he was unfazed made the hairs on Tuck's neck stand up.

"I can't remember which of us found this place first, to tell ya the truth," Gorman went on. "I think it may have been me, but who knows. In any case, we came to an *understanding* pretty quickly. Yer safe, as I've said. Think of yerself as my guest. Besides, I gave him a prime gift earlier this evening. Two of 'em, in fact."

As they got lower, the air became more humid, and the lichen more prevalent. The bard never would have guessed that it would have gotten brighter the deeper into the earth they got. The ground started to level off finally, meaning Tuck didn't have to steady themself on the slime-covered walls any longer. No sooner had that happened, Tuck noticed two distinct sounds: the first was the subtle but constant drip of water, and the second was muffled voices.

The hall terminated in a sudden drop. The lichen didn't seem to grow on the walls of the pit, and the top of a wooden ladder peaked up out of the black. Gorman smiled and motioned at the hole.

"Ya first," he said. "I hope ya understand."

Tuck sighed and lowered themself to the edge of the ladder. The wood was roughly cut, as evident by the slivers that dug into the bard's palms. With one final deep breath, Tuck climbed down rung after rung into the darkness.

Almost instantly, it seemed to swallow them up. The journey felt like it went on forever, the ladder far taller than Tuck would have assumed Gorman could have made and carried down here. More than once the ladder groaned above Tuck, no doubt from the weight of the barman above. After a time, the faint glow of the lichen returned, which signaled that they had reached the bottom. Tuck hopped down and stepped out into a large cavern. Stalagmites and stalactites formed a barrier that Tuck couldn't see clearly beyond, not unlike the jaws of some predatory beast.

"Now this," Gorman wheezed, coming up behind Tuck, "I did name. I calls it the arena, though *he* calls it the Jaws of Xyxax."

Xyxax. Well, that explains the carvings.

Tuck nodded, trying to look interested. That was better than looking afraid, they reasoned. For the bard was afraid, possibly the most afraid that they had been since their brother had gotten sick. Xyxax had been the most vile of all of the Gods of Darkness, and it seemed that his presence could still be felt over a thousand years after his death.

"Gorman," Tuck pleaded, as bravely as they could, "I appreciate you bringing me here, I really do. But I implore you, please for the love of Luna, can we get out of here."

"I wouldn't say that name down here if I was ya," the man said.

Out of the distant shadows, roughly six men of various sizes walked toward them. Tuck quickly recognized most of them as the lichen illuminated their faces. They were regulars at the tavern. In fact, it looked as if every man who had been drinking that very night was here already. Each wore dark clothes, just like Gorman. As they got closer, Tuck noticed one of them had a tattoo on an exposed shoulder that looked eerily similar to the carvings in the tunnel above.

"Hey, Gorman!" One called.

"What's this?" Asked another. "You brought the bard from the tavern? Now, why'd you go and do a thing like that?"

Gorman seemed to grow a bit then, his girth hardening from flab to muscle in the shadows.

"I run this operation, and I don't take kindly to being questioned. He says that he wants more of us, so I've brought more. Besides, what better way to spread the word than a bard?"

"You can't be serious? A bard? Do you want to bring the Paladins down here? You might as well move all of this into the common room of *The Chasm Tavern*."

"No, no, ya've got it all wrong," Gorman explained. "Tuck 'ere will change enough of the details of course. The song won't lead 'em directly to us, but it'll get the idea out there. Why Tuck's already been singing about that cult in the Rim, I figured…"

"So you're a cult?" Tuck blurted.

The men all laughed.

"Not exactly," Gorman said. "We aren't praying to the Gods of Darkness if that's what yer gettin' at. No, me an' the boys come 'ere for entertainment more than anythin'. He gives us that, so long as we provide him with what he wants. The tattoos are just for flavor, really."

Tuck wasn't convinced.

"What does he want?" Tuck asked.

"Same thing we do, really," one of the men said, "a little fun to pass the time."

A scream rang out from beyond the stone barrier.

"Fuck, ya made us miss the first round."

The men turned and ran like a bunch of children around the stalagmites. Gorman had to pull Tuck along. The bard barely noticed. No sooner had the scream greeted their ears had Tuck seen the pile of clothes, barely illuminated by the lichen. Even in the limited light, Tuck could tell that some of the clothing had belonged to children. Bile rose in the bard's throat.

When they rounded the barrier, Tuck saw a smooth clearing on the rock-face, lit by lichen and torches both. Standing in the middle of the circle was the hulking black form of what had to be a Demon. In front of the beast, a woman cowered next to the body of another person who she clung to as if they still lived. The Demon towered over her, its shiny black armor reflecting the orange and blue light. Small spikes covered its armor, and its helm had two large horns, not unlike those in the carvings.

The Demon raised its giant blade and cut the woman in two, showering the gathered men in a red spray. They all cheered, punching and shoving each other like they were watching a tavern brawl. Tuck could smell the blood even from where they stood. The Demon picked up the woman's torso and flung it to the men. All of them, Gorman included, kneeled and stuck their fingers into her body, drawing horns and spirals on each other with her blood.

Tuck turned and vomited the piss-ale onto the ground. The wet sounds of the splattering bile drew the attention of the Demon. It walked over, causing Tuck to cower in the moist puddle they had just made.

Once the creature was standing over the bard, a hollow laugh echoed from within its helm. Tuck saw that the Demon had the same spiral painted on its chest like the markings on a bug carapace.

"This is a bard," Gorman said, his face streaked in gore. "He, uh, they, will spread the word, playing songs of this day in my tavern. I hope ya approve."

The Demon laughed again, turning back to the center of the cavern. Once it was there, Tuck heard a sound that they would never forget to the end of their days. The Demon seemed to speak.

"Bring the Paladins."

The men other than Gorman nodded and ran off to the shadows. When they returned a few moments later they were dragging the bound and seemingly unconscious forms of two Paladins. The same two Paladins that Tuck had seen enter the tavern earlier that night, in fact.

A heavy black chain was fixed to the neck of each Paladin. The men staked the chains to the center of the cavern before quickly retreating to a safe distance. Beside Tuck, Gorman visibly rolled his eyes.

"Wake them, ya louts. He wants a challenge!" The man shouted.

The others grumbled and returned to the Paladins. One pulled his member out and began to piss in their faces while another slapped them. It took a few moments for their eyes to flutter open.

"I told ya it would be unwise to eat the lichen," Gorman said, leaning down to the bard. "This is what happens if ya do. I ground some up and served it to them earlier. If it wasn't for old Drak pissing on them, they'd probably sleep for two days."

The man called Drak went flying through the air as the chain on the darker-skinned Paladin went taut. The Paladin stood and roared.

Then the Demon did the same.

III.

"Trent!" The Paladin yelled. "Wake up, damn you!"

The Demon swung its sword ponderously. The Paladin, groggy as he was, was able to duck the blow with relative ease. He tugged on his chain; the spike groaned but it wouldn't come loose. The Demon kicked him hard in the chest, sending him flying until the chain caught him and slammed him back into the ground.

It's toying with them. Gods...

The red-headed Paladin seemed to stir. When he realized where he was, he pushed himself up just in time for the Demon to send him sprawling with a backhand. Tuck winced. Even if the men hadn't been chained down, they would have had a hard time defeating this beast in their current condition. A blinding flash of blue ripped through the air, smashing into the Demon. Tuck covered their eyes, reflexively scooting back through the puddle of vomit again. Red rose up to meet the blue in an explosion of heat. The smell of sulfur filled the cavern.

"Ain't this a show!" One of the men yelled.

"Open yer eyes, Tuck," Gorman said. "Ya can't write a song about something ya didn't watch, eh?"

Tuck rolled onto all fours, crawling along the ground back to the side of Gorman. Rocks fell from above, peppering the bard on the back of the head. They looked up, just as the Paladins were sent sprawling from another blast of red flame. The Paladins' magic flared to life when they were struck, preventing them from being incinerated.

"Hey, bard," a man said, "you gonna be able to keep your mouth shut about this?"

The man was nearly as large as Gorman, but he had a white scar that traced the left side of his face.

"I thought the reason I was brought here was to *not* keep my mouth shut?" Tuck asked, wryly.

"Gorman, I'll say again that this was a mistake." The man looked Tuck over more than he had before. "What is you anyhow? I don't see any teats, but yer face is soft."

Tuck visibly rolled their eyes. The man snapped a hand down to grab the bard.

"How 'bout we find out."

Gorman was there suddenly, grabbing the man by the arm. The barkeep shoved his companion back toward the circle of fighters. He stumbled backward over the lower half of the dead woman. The other men looked on in silent shock. Just then, the Paladins each pulled on the chain with all of their limited strength and the spike came free. It flew through the air, impaling the man that had been accosting Tuck through the throat. He sputtered and fell to his knees. The other men stood agape for a moment before letting out another raucous cheer.

The barman offered Tuck a hand up and gave the bard a weak smile.

"I gave ya my word," he said.

Tuck nodded in thanks, though their stomach still churned in anticipation. The protection offered by an evil man wasn't much protection at all.

In the arena, the Paladins ran at the Demon, pulling the chain tight between them. It caught the Demon by the legs, knocking it to the ground. They rushed it, the red-headed one kicking its sword away while the other wrapped the chain about its neck. The Demon howled in fury.

"Trent! Blast it!"

Trent? Where have I heard that name before...

Realization whipped through Tuck's mind faster than the flash of blue light that filled the cavern. Trent was the name of one of the Paladins that had destroyed that cult in Rinwaithe. Based on what the woman Alyssa had told Tuck, the other Paladin was likely Devin Lighthammer. The bard was watching firsthand as the subjects of *Whispers of a Red God* were being slaughtered. The High God certainly had a sense of irony. Tuck needed to do something, but what?

The bard's eyes fell to the lyre case on the ground. It wouldn't kill a man, certainly, but it was heavy enough that it could knock him down. And then what? Run back to Strega and ask for help? Even if the village Paladins came, it would be too late for Trent and Devin. And that was assuming that Tuck could get up the ladder without the other men coming after them. That assumed Tuck could get past the Accursed in the trees.

Just then, Tuck heard a wet crunching sound, like someone dropped a rotten piece of fruit off of a food cart. The bard winced and looked back up at the battle. The Demon had shaken the Paladins off. Now they circled it warily, hands glowing faintly blue. The Demon's sword was out of the reach of all of them. If that wasn't where the sound came from...

Again came the wet crunch. Tuck spun and saw something through the Jaws of Xyxax. The bard moved closer. The bodies of two Accursed were broken in a heap at the bottom of the ladder. Moments later, another Accursed dropped from above, landing on its companions. Bones exploded from within the creature's legs, but it still stood, limping toward them. Another fell, the silence between cheers filled with the popping and snapping of bone.

They are coming to help their master. I have to do something.

The men watching the fight started to move in closer. It seemed the battle was slowing, so they wanted to see how it ended up close. The Demon grappled with Devin, the two warriors rolling over each other while the hollow laughter of the beast echoed throughout the chamber. The Accursed limped into the arena, shouldering past the men who normally would have given them a wide berth.

Tuck's eyes fell back toward the lyre case. The bard quickly opened the case behind Gorman, who had seemingly forgotten that they existed for a moment. Trent was punching and kicking the Accursed now, and though they were wounded they still could harm him, as evident by the cuts on his face and neck.

The case creaked open, but Gorman still didn't notice.

No one ever sings about the bards.

Tuck loosened the thickest string, wrapping each end around their hands. Once the makeshift weapon was ready, the bard sprang onto the barman's back, wrapping the lyre string about his neck. Tuck pulled the string as tightly as possible, causing Gorman to sputter and choke. The large man slipped a finger between the string and his throat, causing fresh blood to run down his chest.

A meaty hand reached over Gorman's shoulder and clawed wildly at Tuck. The bard held fast, even as the face of the barman turned scarlet. Tuck began to kick at the backside of the man's knees until he stumbled to the ground. Just at that moment, the string snapped. Gorman sucked in air and howled like a mad dog. Tuck rolled off his back, grabbing the hilt of Gorman's short-sword. The barkeep shoved the bard backward while Tuck pulled the sword free of its scabbard.

"Trent!"

Tuck had no time to look up and check the progress of the Paladins. All they could think about was what a mistake trying to be a hero had been. A bloody fist knocked the bard backward into a stalagmite. Tuck glanced up, noticing the ceiling over the arena was covered in even more stalactites than elsewhere. Each thunderous blow from the battle below brought another small shower of rocks and debris falling from those spear-like stones. Another punch robbed Tuck of any further visual observations.

"I gave ya my word, lad!" The man shouted, red foam at the corners of his mouth. "Ya asked for this! Ya wanted to see a real adventure up close! I trusted ya!"

Tuck wasn't good with a blade, and getting one's head pummeled by a half-dead barkeep didn't help one focus their thoughts.

"I'm sorry," the bard muttered, weakly. "You've been a good host."

Gorman stopped his assault momentarily, confused. Tuck blinked away the tears from their swollen eyes and swung the sword at the red line on the barman's throat. The line got wider and a gout of red covered the bard's blue jerkin. Tuck cursed. Gorman fell.

"But your ale tastes like goat piss!" Tuck shouted. "And I hate talking to people! And you kill travelers! You kill children! And I'm not a lad!"

The eyes of the barkeep looked up at Tuck, glassy and hollow. His dark clothes were stained even darker from a giant blotch below his neck.

"You were polite for a murdering monster though," Tuck whispered.

Devin cried out in pain. Tuck looked back up, returned to the moment. The Demon had broken his arm and looked like it was preparing to finish him with a blow from one of its gauntleted fists. Trent was no longer surrounded by only Accursed, but the audience as well. It seemed that the men wanted to get their entertainment firsthand.

Tightly gripping the sword, the bard sprinted ahead to the edge of the arena, trying to come up with an idea of what to possibly do to save the Paladins. A stray stone fell from above, hitting Tuck on the shoulder. The blow stung, causing Tuck to look upward. Once again they noticed just how sharp all of the stalactites were.

"Trent!" they yelled. "The ceiling! Bring it down! It's your only chance!"

The Paladin looked from the bard to the top of the cavern. Blue light erupted from his fists, slamming into the ceiling like a hammer blow. At the same moment, Devin broke free of the Demon, throwing the brute into the crowd of enemies attacking Trent. His left arm hung limp at his side.

Then the stalactites came raining down.

Just like the songs.

. . .

Tuck had no idea what time it was when they sat down in the empty common room of *The Chasm Tavern*. Trent and Devin were both covered in dirt and gore but otherwise seemed to be alright. Even though Xyxax had a hold on that place, it seemed that the Gods of Light had been watching out for their champions that night. The Strega Paladins healed them upon their return to the town before quickly following instructions from Trent and Devin to destroy the entrance to the Jaws of Xyxax.

Trent and Tuck sat at a table in the corner while Devin rooted around behind the bar, looking for something to drink.

"I can't believe that you'd drink anything from this place after what happened last night," Trent said, amused.

"It all tastes like piss anyhow," Tuck muttered.

"He likes it that way," Trent whispered.

"I heard that!" Devin said, returning with a roll in his mouth and a full goblet of the questionable liquid.

Tuck sized both men up. The Paladins weren't quite like how the bard had imagined them, but they were close. Devin had a great axe strapped to his back, the one that had belonged to Broderick Breaksword, Tuck imagined, while Trent carried a sword and shield. Their weapons had been hidden outside the cave mouth—no doubt the men had been afraid to store them with the belongings of the rest of their victims until the warriors were well and truly dead.

"The food should be safe," Tuck said, as Devin finished the bread and heartily drank from the goblet. "Gorman, the barman who drugged you, told me that it was the glowing lichen from the cave that did it. I guess he mixed it in with whatever you ate or drank last night, but it's not in all of the stuff."

"You know," Devin said, "that brings up a good point. What in the High God's name do you have to do with this anyway, and how do you know so much?"

"I'm a bard," Tuck replied. "That's my job."

Trent snorted. "Short and sweet. I thought bards liked telling stories?"

"I like writing and performing songs. I don't like talking."

"Then sing it," Devin said, his voice losing some friendliness.

Tuck felt at their back for the lyre case. It wasn't there of course. The instrument had been smashed when the roof of the cave crushed nearly everything else in the arena. What a waste.

"Sadly, I don't have my lyre anymore. I suppose I can tell you…"

Tuck sucked in a deep breath and snatched the half-full goblet from the Paladin, draining it in one gulp.

"I came here to see if I could see something interesting for myself. I've been writing a song about the two of you destroying that cult in the Rim actually, but I felt like it was missing something. Some first-hand experience."

"You're writing a song about us?" Trent asked.

"Of course they are!" Devin said, laughing.

"*Whispers of a Red God*, I call it. Anyway, it doesn't matter. I performed here for a few nights. Realizing that I might have come to the most boring place on the Mortal Plane, I decided to leave. That is, until the barkeep, Gorman, promised to show me something interesting. He took me down to that cave, and then shortly thereafter you two were drug in. That was far more than I bargained for, so I killed him."

"Ah," Devin said. "I'm sure it would have been better if you'd sang it."

"The Light is in your debt, Tuck," Trent said, ignoring his friend.

"Well?" Tuck asked. "Now it's your turn. If I saved your asses, the least you could do is give me enough details to flesh the song out. Why are you here? It wasn't just happenstance that two of the most famous Paladins of the current generation ended up in Strega."

Devin motioned for Trent to tell it.

"You're sharp, aren't you? Well, people have been vanishing off and on from Strega for months. Not enough to cause general alarm, but enough to get noticed. The local Paladins are a little inept, and they were concerned that they were too close to the people of the village to investigate anyone. So they sent word to Illux, and the Lady Ren tasked us with the job—"

"Being her favorites and all," Devin interjected.

"Nothing more to it than that, really," Trent continued. "We figured that either bandits had made camp out here, or that Demons hiding near the Great Chasm were picking travelers off who were leaving Strega in the middle of the night. Not everything is some grand mystery."

"But this was," Devin laughed again.

"What do you think was going on down there? They killed a couple of people before dragging you out, and I saw a pile of clothes. I think Gorman must have been drugging strangers or people he didn't like before taking them down there. Were they a cult, like what you found in the Rim? That's what I thought, but they said that they weren't."

Trent studied the worn surface of the table before responding.

"No, they were nothing like what we found in the Rim. I don't think these men saw any religious significance in what they were doing. It was just bloodsport to them. Bandits fight to the death for entertainment all of the time. I wouldn't be surprised if most of them had been bandits at one point or another. As for the Demon…it's not like it takes much for them to find reasons for wanton destruction, but that place…It's proximity to the Great Chasm, and all of those symbols? I think it was making offerings to dead Xyxax.

"Some places are just evil. I don't know if that cave made the Demon try to start this little operation, or maybe it influenced those men. In any case, no one will ever stumble across it again."

Silence overtook the room. Devin returned to the bar and made himself another drink. He came back and drained his cup again before anyone else spoke.

"In my experience, men don't need the Gods of Darkness to be cruel and wicked. They are perfectly capable of doing that on their own," Tuck said. "Those carvings were old, though. I think they were older than the Demon. Gorman claimed that he found the cave first, and the carvings were already there. You think it's possible someone else worshipped Xyxax there before?"

"I wouldn't doubt it," Trent said.

"That's enough of this talk," Devin bellowed. "I want to get out of this shit-stain of a town and back to Illux. Bard, you wanna come with us? I promise to give you the material for a thousand songs before you come to an untimely end."

Tuck thought it over for a few moments. Then the door opened and the barmaid walked in. She looked surprised to see the Paladins and the bard sitting in their alone.

"What'll happen to this place?" Tuck asked.

"It'll probably get sold off. Or the local Paladins will just give it to someone," Trent mused.

"Could you get them to give it to me?" Tuck asked.

"What?" Devin spat some ale onto the table.

"Tired of adventure after one time?" Trent asked.

The barmaid walked to the back of the bar and started cleaning up the mess from Devin. She tried to pretend that she wasn't listening, but Tuck knew that wasn't the case.

"It's not that, I just think I need some time to work on the material that I have," Tuck said. "I like the idea of becoming the first bard to own their own inn. Travelers get to listen to my singing each night. It'll keep the costs down."

Trent nodded.

"We can make that happen."

"Besides," Tuck said, smiling, "owning a tavern at the edge of the world must get pretty interesting."

THE LAST GIFT OF
KANE DARKSEND

THE LAST GIFT OF
KANE DARKSEND

1053 AP

"Will my son come back to me safely?" the feeble woman asked.

Frederick clinked her coins in his pocket. Any answer would suffice, but he felt generous today, so he would give her some good news. He would have moved on to another part of the slums or out of Illux altogether by the time the boy was found or she had given up. The man straightened before answering her in his most enigmatic tone, straightening the ruffles in his flowing purple robes as he did so.

"Yes, good woman, he will be found unharmed. And soon, I should think. Go forth and fear for him no more."

"Thank you, Frederick!" she exclaimed. "Thank you! I knew he was alright!"

The woman stood and hugged the man before leaving his tent with a noticeable spring in her step. Once he would have felt guilt for lying about something as serious as a missing child, but that was long ago. Frederick walked out to the front of the tent and closed the entrance flap. He hung a sign outside that read: NO MORE PROPHECIES TODAY. Not that it mattered. That poor woman had been his only visitor in a few days. It seemed that either he had drained this part of the slums of all of its coin, or his reputation as a charlatan had caught up to him.

Tomorrow is time to move on, I think.

Once again, he considered moving to another part of Illux but decided against it. Frederick was getting too well-known. It was possible that word would make it to either the City Watch or the Paladins that a man was faking the Gift for some easy coin. That would certainly end with him in irons. No, he figured it was time to make the journey to Seatown or one of the distant villages like Marna and work his way back. By the time he reached Illux again in a few months or a year, it would be safe for him to start up again.

Frederick went back into his tent and sat on the large purple cushion that he used during his prophesying. His gold-laden pouch landed on the wooden stool that he used as a table. He had been performing this particular con for the last few years, to great success. In these trying times, people looked for omens and signs of good things to come. That was what had given him the idea of pretending that he had the High God's Gift.

Throughout history, there had been multiple people of note with the Gift; souls with a connection to the High God that gave them the gift of prophecy in their dreams and waking moments. Springjack, a noted member of Daniel Nightbreaker's retinue, was one such, and Arran, the deceased friend of the current Seraph, was rumored to have had it as well. Who was to say that Frederick of the slums did not? Besides Frederick himself, of course.

He counted the gold pieces in silence, wondering if he should charge more or less in the villages. It wasn't as if the people of the slums had any wealth to speak of, but he wasn't sure what the economic climate of Seatown or the other settlements was. Truth be told, he hadn't even been outside the walls of the city.

Suddenly, the curtain of his tent was thrown open and a small woman in a white cloak rushed inside. Her hair was black and tied with a blue ribbon, but it was the sparkling green of her eyes that caught his attention. She didn't look dirty and downtrodden like a citizen of the slums. No, this was an inner city girl, and potentially a big payday. Still, he didn't like being bothered when the flap was closed.

"Can't you read?" he snapped.

"Shh!" she hissed as she held her finger to her lips.

The sounds of the slums outside continued unabated, though it seemed that Frederick's new guest was listening intently for something. When she was satisfied, she turned back to look at the perturbed man.

"I am in need of your help," she said.

"Most are."

"You don't understand. I'm in danger, and you're supposed to help me."

"Danger? You must have me confused for someone else. I'm not a fighter. I have the Gift, my dear, and I help those in need with prophecy."

The woman stiffened and covered Frederick's mouth. He grumbled in protest, but she simply clamped down harder. The moments drug on like this with neither making a sound. Then the side of the tent was torn open by the point of a sharp blade.

"Run!" the woman shouted, pulling Frederick behind her.

He couldn't see who or what was chasing them, or even grab his coin purse. A cold sweat blanketed him as the pair darted through the muddy streets of the slums, winding their way toward the northern gate. Exasperated, he finally slipped her grasp and stopped running.

"What in the High God's name is going on?" he panted. "Who are you?"

"My name is Teresa Darksend, and we are being hunted by a Balance Monk. There is no time for idle chatter, we must go!"

Frederick shook his head as if to make the information flee his mind.

"A Balance Monk? In Illux? Gods be good, woman, are you mad?"

"No, I'm not mad. But unlike you, I actually have the Gift."

He looked at her dumbstruck for a moment.

How?

Teresa slapped him across the face to get his attention. When he looked at her again she was pointing at the skyline behind them. Following her finger, Frederick saw a hooded figure running on the rooftops. They did not wear the grey robe of a Balance Monk, but a cloak as black as the armor of any Demon. In the figure's hand was a polearm, glinting in the afternoon sun. He swallowed hard. It was obvious at that moment that the weapon was a modified version of the staves the Balance Monks were said to use—no doubt to hide the assassin's identity.

"You were right!" he shouted and he started moving again. "We should be running!"

The pair continued ahead, constantly looking over their shoulders at the dark figure bounding after them. Ahead, the northern gate loomed. It was closed, as the gates always were since the death of Jerrok. Beside it sat the gatehouse which was manned by members of the City Watch.

Teresa angled in that direction, shoving through the door just as it opened. The surprised guard was knocked onto her back as the pair ran past her and up the stairs. Frederick gasped but didn't dare to stop following this madwoman, lest he be caught by the Balance Monk. Still, charging into a gatehouse, like this was likely suicide. And yet, somehow she moved as if she knew this place intimately.

Behind them, the guard shouted in alarm, but neither Teresa nor Frederick slowed. After several flights of stairs, they stood on the very top of the wall, overlooking the city behind them and the wilderness beyond. Members of the City Watch ran up the steps behind them and converged from both the left and right sides of the wall.

"What do we do now?" Frederick cried.

"Jump!"

Teresa grabbed him by the arm and pulled him from the wall to what would surely be their deaths below. Frederick didn't see the ground rise up to meet them—he blacked out before they had fallen more than a few feet.

· · ·

WHEN FREDERICK OPENED HIS EYES, the shouting of the City Watch was distant and barely audible. His back and legs screamed at him in pain, but nothing seemed to be broken. The world around him was still dark and smelled faintly of manure. He struggled for a few moments before Teresa pulled him free of the pile of hay in which they had landed.

Frederick stared at her in disbelief.

"This isn't possible," he muttered, staring at the house-sized pile of hay that had saved his life. "A fall from that height should have killed us no matter what we landed on…"

"Aye," Teresa said with a smile, "it should have, but as I told you, I have the Gift. I saw our escape in a vision and I knew that we would survive. A few days ago, and this pile wouldn't even have been here. The hay got a blight on the way from one of the villages, and a caravan dumped it here before being let into the city."

Frederick quickly brushed himself off and tried not to retch. Nothing the woman said made him feel any better.

"We've bought ourselves some time," Teresa said, "but not much. We have to move. Our destination is still days away."

"Where are you taking me?" he asked.

"The last gift from my father to me."

"Who was your father?"

"The Paladin Kane Darksend."

THOUGH HE HAD PROTESTED the entire journey, Frederick had been too afraid to leave her side. Teresa had warned him that if he did, not only would the Balance Monk find and kill him, but he would doom the entire Mortal Plane with his cowardice. That scared him into staying.

They made a small camp with no fire in a copse of trees to the north of the city. There wasn't much to eat besides mushrooms and berries, but he had grown tired of complaining. When the only light left was the faint illumination of the moon and Aenna, Frederick finally broke his silence.

"You need to tell me what we are doing out here. Why did you come to me, of all people? How did you know that my Gift was a farce?"

Teresa sighed and rolled back over to look at him. The dark shadows of the night pooled around the curves of her body, making him forget his question momentarily.

"I told you, I have the Gift. Ever since I was a child, I have dreamed of things that were to come. When my father disappeared nearly twenty years ago, my mother made me swear to keep it a secret. She didn't want undue attention to fall on our family. My oldest brother became a Paladin when he was of age, and I considered doing the same, but in my dreams, I was never a Paladin. Yet, I knew that I was meant to do something important.

"Then a few weeks ago I began to see my father in my dreams. I know now that he is truly dead, killed in single combat with the Herald. I also saw that I would journey to the place where he was killed and take possession of a great power that will be a boon to our people in the years to come. These dreams also showed me you, as my protector."

Frederick laughed. "I told you once before, I'm no warrior. I'm a charlatan, and a damn good one at that, though you wouldn't be able to tell as I had to leave my money behind when you brought an assassin to my door!"

She must be daft. There is no rational explanation for this. Even the great heroes of myth that had the Gift were most likely liars and cheats like me.

Teresa sat up and leaned in, her green eyes nearly black in the darkness.

"I know what I saw," she said. "I have heard that some with the Gift see their visions as riddles and metaphors, with nothing to be gleaned from a surface reading. Mine, however, are as clear as you are now. I even know who hunts us and why."

"And who, pray tell, is that?"

"A former Balance Monk named Cinder. She left the Grey Temple just a few weeks ago, when I started having visions of my father. Few have left the Balance Monks over the years, and none for the reason this woman did. She, too, has the Gift, and she has seen that what we will do will upset the Balance of the world. In response, she left to kill me and by extension, you, without even the leave of the Grey God."

"Why wouldn't she just tell Ravim what she had seen, then?" Frederick asked. "Why make herself an apostate? I've heard that they don't take kindly to those who renounce the grey."

"Her visions tell her that doom will come to the Balance Monks if she reveals the truth to them," Teresa said ominously.

"You learned all of that from your vision?"

"No. I asked her that very question before she tried to kill me in my bedroom this morning. Now, goodnight."

She laid back down and was asleep before Frederick could even think of another question to ask her. He sighed and rubbed his temples. This would be the best time for him to sneak off. If this Cinder woman was close to finding them, perhaps she would stop hunting him after she found and did away with Teresa. Perhaps all of this was the raving of a madwoman, and the assassin after her was just an unnaturally strong slum tough? He sighed and laid his head down on the firm ground. He would have to consider those options again tomorrow. For now, he would stay with her.

THE NEXT FEW days transpired with little dialogue between the pair. His doubts about the validity of her tale began to fade when she told him that they would find the remains of a caravan over the next hill and, to his surprise, they did.

The smoldering remains of the wagons and the slaughtered horses appeared to be a few days old. If it had been the work of bandits, there would have likely been human bodies scattered around the wreckage, but their lack implied that this was the work of Demons. If the rumors were to be believed, these poor souls had been dragged off and turned into Accursed.

Still, they found some unspoiled food and were able to eat better than they had since fleeing Illux. Then Teresa really surprised him.

"Underneath the black horse, you'll find your sword," she said between bites.

"My-my sword?" he stammered. "What need do I have for a sword?"

"To kill Cinder with when she finds us."

I shouldn't have asked.

Frederick walked over to the dead animal, holding down bile as he was hit with its stench. He saw the pommel of the blade sticking out from under the saddle and pulled it free. It wasn't a fancy weapon— nothing from the villages was, but it was still sharp. He sighed as he carried it back to her.

"I don't even know how to use this," he lamented.

"The High God will guide your hand."

"I hope you're right."

THEY FOUND the remains of the battlefield the next day. Though much had decayed or been looted in the previous two decades, there were still signs of conflict here: rusted blades and armor along with bleached white bones dotted the rocky plain and outcroppings around them. Frederick grimaced as he thought of all of the Paladins and soldiers killed here fighting Demons and Accursed. Teresa had told him that this battle had been the last time that the Herald had been seen by mortal eyes.

"Up there," she said, pointing. "That is where we will find my father."

She was indicating a cleft in the rocks above that looked almost like a skull. He shuddered at the calm way that she talked about the corpse of her father, though he supposed dreaming about it had taken some of the sting out of its discovery. Not for the first time since they had begun traveling together, he wondered what it was like to have love or adoration for your parents. His own mother had sold his body to older men after his father had been killed in a robbery.

That old bitch got what was coming to her, at least.

As they began the ascent up the defiles that led to the cave opening, he remembered with some glee the look on his mother's face when one of the men she had taken money from strangled the life from her rather than rape the boy. The man's name was Patton, and he taught Frederick the ways of the street. They had run many a scam together before the man had contracted gout and died in agony sometime later. There was no justice in the world, it seemed.

When they reached the top of the pathway, Teresa stopped at the mouth of the cave and looked back at the landscape behind them. Her green eyes glistened in the light with a skein of tears.

"She is close," Teresa said. "Be prepared."

Frederick gripped the sword tighter and nodded. He was sure that if this Cinder truly was a Balance Monk, he would be dead in short order. Even so, he found himself reassured by Teresa's faith in him. Something about her gave him a strength that he had previously lacked.

The young woman turned and walked into the darkness of the cave. He wished that they had brought a light source of some kind, but she walked through the inky black without so much as stumbling—something that could not be said for Frederick.

Suddenly, Frederick gasped as the shallow chamber in front of him became visible from a faint blue light. Small glowing fungi dotted the floor and walls of the cavern, seemingly originating from within the armor of the skeleton propped against the far wall. Beside the corpse that was undoubtedly Kane Darksend himself was a small spring of water that bubbled up from a crack in the earth. Sticking out of the center of the spring was a remarkably white lance.

The Lance of Retribution.

Frederick gasped in spite of himself. Teresa had mentioned that her father had last been seen carrying the lance that had once felled the mad Seraph Arkos by then-Paladin Arendt, then two Heralds, including the one preceding the current one. Even though he didn't consider himself a pious man, Frederick knew that this weapon was holy.

Teresa was kneeling beside the body of her father, her head bowed in prayer. Frederick didn't want to interrupt her, so he leaned closer to the lance, studying its surface. To his surprise, the weapon was unblemished, even after spending nearly twenty years exposed to the waters of this cave.

"She's here," Teresa whispered, fear filling her voice. "Quickly, drink from the spring."

"What?" he asked dumbly.

A blindingly sharp pain tore through his back as he was thrown from his feet. Frederick slammed into the corpse of Kane Darksend, causing the skeleton to collapse into a pile of bones and armor. Teresa spun and ducked under the next swing of the polearm, though a lightning-fast kick likewise sent her sprawling. She cried out as her head hit the wall of the cave with a resounding thunk.

"Stop resisting me," Cinder pleaded. "You threaten the Balance of the world by what you do. I have seen it. The gods are in peril. If you drink from this spring, the Mortal Plane that we know will come to an end."

"Why would the High God send her visions that she should ignore?" Frederick asked to his own astonishment. "Surely we were meant to come here, as were you. Perhaps we are to work together?"

"I wish it was so," Cinder replied, "but I have seen the misery that is coming. In less than a year, the Grey Temple will burn and all who call it home will be dead unless I act now and destroy everything in this cave."

Teresa stood, though her footing was shaky. Even in the faint light, Frederick could see the blood that ran down her face. She scowled at the Balance Monk with a fury he had not seen in her before. Her continued strength made him almost forget the burning pain across his back.

"You will not defile the resting place of my father. I was brought here for a reason, and I will not fail his memory."

The Balance Monk sprang at her, sweeping the polearm in what should have been a fatal blow had Frederick not parried it with his sword. He shouted, his cry echoing throughout the cave like thunder. The Balance Monk was surprised and was given pause by the man's fury.

"The spring!" Teresa shouted. "It's our only chance!"

Not thinking beyond the moment, Frederick dove away from the women, face-first into the waters of the spring. It was icy cold and shocked his senses as it filled his mouth. The pain in his back disappeared, replaced by an even more uncomfortable sensation. He howled; his muscles rippled and tore free from his robes and his bones cracked and grew stronger and longer. Small curls of smoke and steam rose off him, dancing in the faint light until they reached the roof of the cave. He didn't notice that Cinder swung her polearm at him, nor that Teresa shoved her at the last moment, causing her weapon to miss. All that he did notice was the pain and the power.

Just as suddenly as it had begun, it was over. Frederick kneeled in the center of the spring, a giant of a man, his torn clothing floating in the water beside him. Teresa fell from a stroke of the polearm, clutching at the wound in her stomach. The weapon came crashing down at him next, but he found that he was now fast enough to catch it. The haft shattered in his grip, sending shards of wood in all directions.

"No!" the Balance Monk shouted.

Frederick felt something within him surge to life, a warmth like a flame overtaking his right arm. As he raised his hand, the cave was filled with the blinding blue light of the fire that exploded from him. The magic hit the Balance Monk in the chest sending her careening backward into the darkness. The power continued to flow through him, an intoxicating rush that threatened to overtake his self-control. He bathed the area where Cinder had landed with the blue flame until there was nothing left of her but a smoldering pile of ash. Then he remembered that Teresa had been hurt and the power faded, returning the cave to its previous dim light.

"Teresa," he whispered as he rushed to her side. He cradled her head in his arms. "What do I do? What did your vision show you?"

She smiled faintly at him.

"I didn't see past us finding the spring. That probably means I'm fated to die here with my father. Do not worry, we found the power that I dreamed about. You are the first of a new breed of Paladin, Frederick. You must guard this spring until others come to serve the

Light. We cannot share it with the rest of the Mortal Plane too soon…"

Her voice trailed off as the light began to fade from her green eyes. Frederick found himself crying for the first time since he was a boy.

What good is being a Paladin if I can't even save my only friend?

An idea struck him. He tried to channel the same power that had destroyed Cinder, but this time he willed the warmth not to come out of his body as a destructive torrent, but as a healing salve. His hands began to glow the same faint blue as before, but this time no flames erupted from him—instead, the glow began to envelop Teresa, and he could see the wound on her stomach start to close.

In a few moments, her ragged breathing returned to normal, and her eyes regained their usual luster. She placed a hand on his cheek as she sat up.

"You really are a Paladin," she said.

"Fuck," was the only response he could think of.

WHAT TO READ NEXT

To find out what happens next to the Mortal Plane, read *Wrath of the Fallen* and the rest of the Broken Pact Trilogy!

ABOUT THE AUTHOR

Kris Jerome was born in the middle of a snowstorm in Pendleton, Oregon, several decades ago. Since then he moved the great distance across the state to study at Willamette University. He obtained a BFA in Digital Communication Arts in June of 2016 from Oregon State University. Kris enjoys reading books and comics while sipping wine and craft beer. He currently lives in Albany, Oregon with his wife, seven children and two cats.

darktidingspress.com
darktidingspress@gmail.com

www.ingramcontent.com/pod-product-compliance
Lightning Source LLC
Chambersburg PA
CBHW061800190726

48289CB00007B/2011